The Widow Jane Parker

Also by Judy McGonagill

The Widow Jane Parker

The River Rider

The Twelve Mile School

The Widow Jane Parker

HEARTS OF TEXAS

BOOK ONE

JUDY MCGONAGILL

RISE UP PUBLICATIONS

Book design by eBook Prep
www.ebookprep.com

November 2022
ISBN: 978-1-64457-309-9

Rise UP Publications
644 Shrewsbury Commons Ave
Ste 249
Shrewsbury PA 17361
United States of America

www.riseUPpublications.com
Phone: 866-846-5123

Acknowledgments

Heartfelt thanks to my son, Brian, for your constant encouragement and technology support.

This book is dedicated to my beloved husband, George, and our two sons, Brian and David.

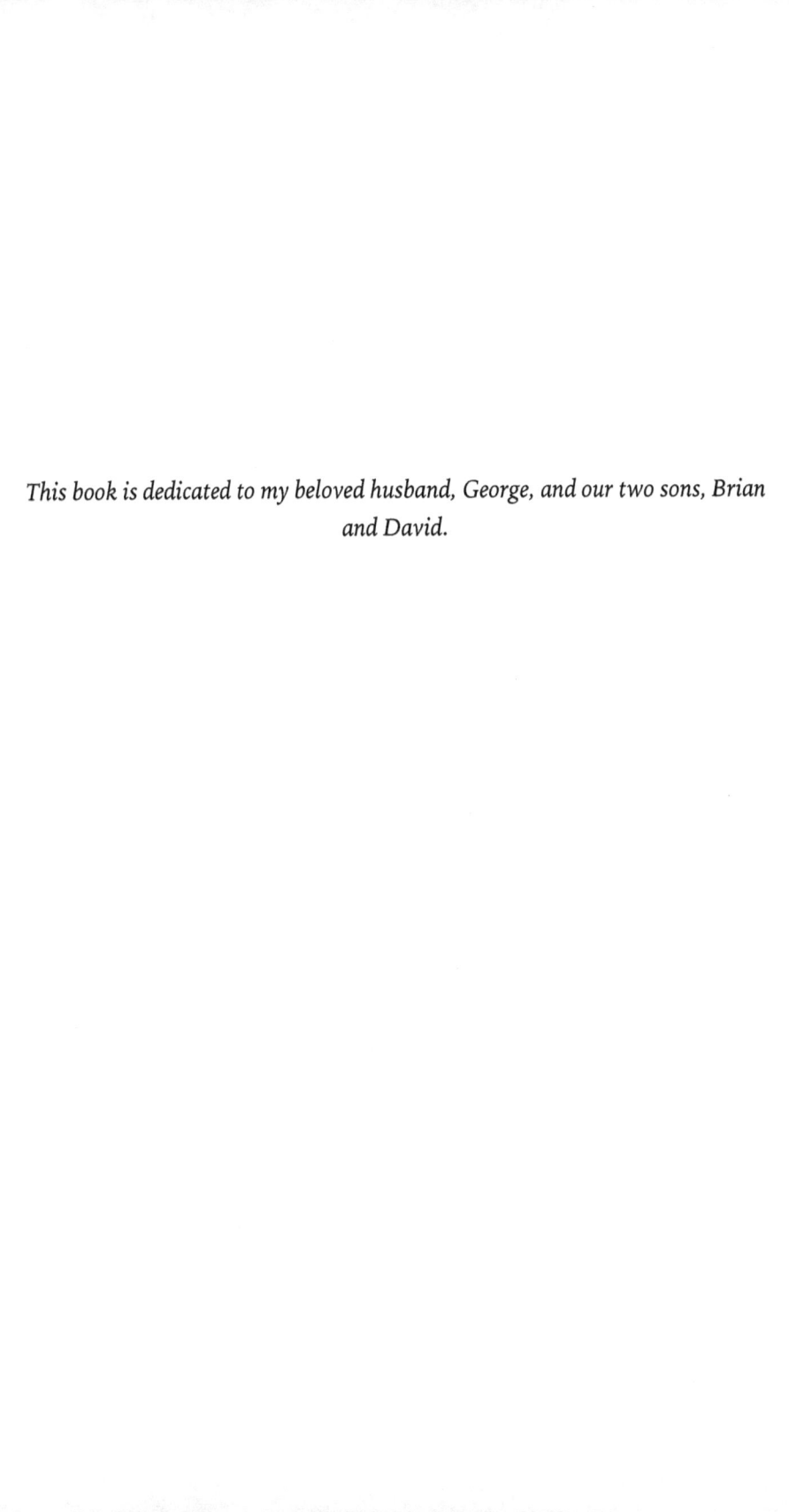

Chapter One

1897

I was only seven, but I still remember what happened.

Janc Parker rolled over in the sweat-soaked bed and reached for the damp cloth that lay on the table by her bed. She rubbed the damp cloth over her face and arms. It was sultry hot, not a breath of night air stirred. She lay looking through the open door at the shadows of an almost moonless night. Far in the west she saw a brief flash of lightning. Oh, dear Lord, please let it rain, she prayed silently. It had been an unusually dry spring and still dry in late June. The crops suffered in the fields, the cattle and other animals would soon be drinking from stagnant puddles instead of flowing streams. Rain, rain, she thought, oh how we need rain.

Jane sat up, lifted her long auburn hair, and wiped the back of her neck with the almost dry cloth. It gave a brief moment of faint coolness. She was tempted to wipe Ruby's face and arms but didn't want to wake the sleeping child that shared her bed. Ruby would just fret and whine about the heat. Let her sleep, Jane told herself.

She almost unconsciously turned her gaze toward the open door as she heard the faintest creak of a board. Then silence followed. Jane thought about getting up and going out to sit on the porch. It might be cooler outside. She didn't want to disturb her sleeping children by moving around too much. Seven-year-old Ruby, ten-year-old Sam and fourteen-year-old Opal was all she had left. Samuel, her husband of eleven years and four-year-old Pearl had passed last winter when the flu hit hard in their community.

There came another creak of a board, slightly louder this time. Jane wondered if some animal had ventured onto the porch in search of food or water. Even at night most animals didn't usually come this close to people unless they were starving. It was as if they could smell them, or sense them, and kept their distance. Jane gently wiped her face with the cloth again.

Suddenly the dim light of the door was filled with a shadowy figure of a man. Jane's heart seemed to stop. The shadow stepped quietly into the room and quickly moved behind the open door. Jane may have thought she imagined it had she not heard the slight squeak of the door when it moved. Jane stared at the now empty doorway and could barely see the door was ajar. What if she hadn't been awake to see the man sneak into her home? she wondered. He could have attacked her and the children while they slept. She shivered at the grim thought. Very slowly, she lifted the loaded gun she kept by her bedside and aimed it toward the door. At that very moment, she saw another shadowy figure cross the yard in front of the door. She held her breath. How many shadows were there? Why were they here in the middle of the night? Jane wondered, but she partly knew the answer. They were up to no good, that was for sure.

Then the stench reached her. The smell of soured sweat, stale tobacco, and whiskey wafted across the room, and Jane almost gagged. Instead, she steadied herself and spoke.

"Mister," she said in as calm a voice as she could muster, "how many more are there outside?"

No answer came.

"I'm just asking one more time, and if you don't answer I plan to shoot," she said in a matter-of-fact tone.

A brief silence, then, "Just one, Ma'am," come a solemn reply.

"You better be telling the truth."

"Mama," came Sam's sleepy voice from the far bed, "who you talking to?"

"There's a man standing behind the front door and he says one more is outside," she replied in a quiet voice hoping to not wake Ruby. "Wake Opal and tell her to get over here with me and Ruby," Jane half whispered to Sam.

"What they want?" Sam asked, as he yawned and attempted to rub the sleep from his eyes.

"Nothing good I'm certain," Jane replied matter-of-factly.

Sam moved to his sister's bedside and gently shook her. "Wake up, Opal. Opal, wake up," Sam said in a hushed tone so he wouldn't wake Ruby.

"Quit!" came Opal's irritable reply.

"Opal, there's trouble. A man is behind the door and one outside. Mama said for you to come to her bed and don't wake Ruby."

"What do they want?" Opal asked in a more civil tone.

"Mama said they're up to no good."

Jane could hear the rustling of Opal moving to her bed and the give of the springs as Opal sat next to the still sleeping Ruby.

"Mama, what are we going to do?" Opal asked with a slight quiver in her voice.

Jane didn't know and didn't want to answer Opal's question. Instead, she addressed the man behind the door.

"Mister, what are you and that other one up to? Tell the truth,I have this gun pointed at your black heart," she told the stranger.

"Well, Ma'am, we was, we was, just passin' by and thought we would, uh, uh."

Jane raised her voice slightly and emphasized, "I said the truth, now say it."

"Well, I ain't quite sure what Luc—," he hesitated, realizing he had almost used his partner's name. "I mean my friend just told me to come on in and stand behind this door and he would let me know what to do then. Yes, Ma'am, that's what he told me."

Jane pondered what the man said. "Do you always do as you are told?"

"Well, uh, I uh, no, Ma'am, not always. Just if it seems suitin' at the time," he offered in way of an explanation of his actions.

Jane didn't answer immediately but took time to think about what he had said.

Then she questioned, "Just what do you suppose your friend intends to do now that you are standing behind my door with a loaded gun pointed at you and he is outside where he could just take off and leave you here in this predicament?"

"I don't rightly know, Ma'am," he admitted.

The room fell silent as Jane pondered what to do next. She needed to get help but wasn't sure exactly what to do. The only thing she could think of was to send Sam to fetch Mr. Armstrong and some of his men.

She took care of Mrs. Armstrong and the house and did most of the cooking for the farm and ranch hands. The Armstrongs were good people and had let her and the children live on here after Samuel and little Pearl had died last year. Lord only knows what would have become of her and the children if Mrs. Armstrong hadn't taken sick and needed help about that time.

It was about a quarter of a mile to the Armstrongs if Sam cut across the pasture. He would have to cut through a few trees by the dry creek but other than that he would be in the open and could see anyone following him. She wished they still had their faithful old cocker spaniel, Boots. He was a good watchdog and would go everywhere with Sam. Boots would have been a comfort to Sam, but the poor old dog had died last month. But there was the man outside. How could she be sure he wouldn't hurt Sam?

She picked up the cloth and wiped her face again. Her hand shook slightly as she tried to decide what to do.

"Ma'am, it's gettin' mighty hot behind this door," the man complained. "Do you think I could just step out for a breath of air?" he asked.

"Huh! I reckon not. You was mighty keen on getting behind that door so you just stay put!"

"Yes, Ma'am," he sounded a bit dejected, "but what if I faint?" He whined and let out a loud breath.

"If I see that door move you are a dead man, so just faint, and you won't have to be worrying whether you're hot or not," Jane replied with no sympathy.

Jane made up her mind about what to do. She could see the lightning growing brighter and knew the storm was coming their way. She couldn't delay any longer or Sam and Mr. Armstrong's men would also have to battle the storm.

"Tell your friend to step to the edge of the porch in front of the door so I can see him," she instructed.

"HEY, HEY, can you hear me?" he yelled.

"Yeah!" the man replied from not too far away.

Ruby stirred but Opal quickly began to pat her again in hopes she wouldn't wake and start crying.

Jane suspected the man outside already had heard what she told the man behind the door.

"The lady said for you to come to the edge of the porch in front of the door so she can see you," he repeated exactly as Jane had said.

She heard the crunch of his steps on the dry dirt. His shadowy figure appeared in front of the door just as she had ordered.

Jane didn't hesitate. "I'm sending my boy to fetch the neighbor and his men, and you better not try to stop him. If you touch a hair on his head this one behind my door is a dead man, and you will likely join his sorry soul before long. You understand me?" she questioned in a commanding voice.

"Yes, Ma'am," came a deep, gravelly voice in reply from the shadow in front of the door.

"Now step back away from the door," Jane ordered.

"Yes, Ma'am," he replied and disappeared from her view.

Ruby stirred in the bed and let out a slight moan. Their voices had disturbed her sleep. Jane could hear Opal gently patting Ruby to lull her back to a sound sleep.

"Sam, get your dad's gun - it's already loaded - then come here."

Jane could hear Sam moving about in the dark, but he didn't need a light to know where she kept his dad's gun. She had let Sam use the gun to go hunting a number of times, and he had become a decent shot. He brought home a variety of game for her or Opal to cook, and it helped in feeding the family. Sam came and stood quietly beside his mother, waiting for her to tell him what she wanted him to do next.

"Sam, I know you are a brave boy. I know I have to ask you often to do a man's job, and this is another time I'm asking you to do a man's job. Take the quickest way to Mr. Armstrong's, you know what I mean," she paused.

"Yes, Mama," Sam answered.

"Tell Mr. Armstrong to bring some of his men, that we need help," Jane told Sam, trying to remain calm.

"Listen to me, Sam, if that man tries to harm you in any way don't hesitate one second to shoot him right in the heart. If he gets a hold of you, you won't have a chance; he's bigger and stronger, so don't give him that chance, you shoot!" It broke her heart to tell her ten-year-old son to shoot a man, but it might save his life and theirs.

"I understand," Sam replied with assurance. Sam leaned over and lightly kissed his mother's cheek, then stood straight and walked toward the open door.

"My boy is coming out! You stay back and let him pass!" Jane almost yelled.

Jane silently sent up a fervent prayer for Sam's safety. Sam was more man than child.

Another streak of lightning lit the sky, and before long a low roll of thunder followed.

"Yes, Ma'am," the low-pitched voice replied.

"Now, so I know where you are, you keep talking!" Jane ordered. "I don't normally talk much," he replied.

"If you don't want your friend to get a hole blown right through his heart you best do as I say," Jane told the man in a stern voice.

"Yes'um, I reckon I can find somethin' to talk about for a while. I don't much cotton to women tellin' me what to do but right now you seem to have the upper hand. You know, it would save a lot of trouble if you would just let my friend come on outside and we could be on our way and no harm done. What do you think of that idea?"

"I don't think much of it," Jane answered without hesitation.

"Well, it ain't like we have done anything to you and your young'uns. I let the boy pass just like you said, so it looks like you could return the kindness by letting my friend and me just mosey on down the road before your neighbor gets here causin' all sorts of trouble," he argued.

"Mister," Jane replied in a stern voice, "you and your friend are the ones that have caused this trouble by you sending him into my house in the middle of the night in the first place. If you weren't up to trouble yourself, you would never have stopped here in the first place. So, don't be suggesting I just let him walk out of here as though nothing happened," Jane answered indignantly.

Silence prevailed.

"You best still be outside my porch because I know just how long it will take my boy to fetch the neighbor," Jane addressed the man outside.

"I'm here."

"Just go on talking about something besides me letting your friend go," Jane emphasized again.

"Well, I was just thinking I might just go on down the road and meet up with my friend later when this has all blowed over. Like I said, we ain't really done nothin' to you or your young'uns, so I don't know what you expect your neighbor will do to either of us."

"Well, if you are so innocent why not stick around and see what my neighbor does to the two of you?"

The man outside gave a low chuckle. "Well now, Ma'am, sometimes men get all kinds of notions about what another man was thinkin' or intendin' and might not take time to look at the facts. If I leave, that will give them more time to think about the fact that we really caused you no harm."

"You caused harm alright just by being on my property in the middle of the night. You caused harm by scaring me and my children. You caused harm by sending your friend into my house thinking I was asleep. Yes, you have caused harm. You caused harm by making me send my boy out in the night with a storm coming and wondering if I would see him safe again!" Jane could feel her voice begin to shake with exasperation.

"I'm leavin'," the man said with a sneer. "You come join me down the road where we talked about goin' when this is over my friend."

"You just gonna leave me here to face them men by myself?" the man behind the door questioned in a panicky voice.

"You'll be all right, they ain't gonna do nothin', you haven't done nothin' except stand behind the door. Just stay calm and tell them you know you made a mistake and promise it won't happen again," the outside man answered trying to sound as though he really believed there was nothing to fear.

"That's easy for you to say," the man behind the door complained.

"I'll see you on down the road. You know where. So long, Ma'am. Now you tell them men that we didn't lay a finger on any of you folks, and everything will be all right," the outside man told Jane.

Jane heard the sound of his steps fading into the distance. She couldn't resist the impulse to jab at the man behind the door. "My, but you keep brave company."

There was no reply.

Jane sat with the gun still pointed toward the door. They should be coming soon, she thought. Sam was such a brave boy, so much like his dad. Samuel had been so steadfast and reliable. She knew Sam would do anything she asked of him. She wondered if he was terribly afraid having to leave the house to go fetch Mr. Armstrong. Somehow, she imagined he wasn't as frightened as she was afraid for him.

The old mantle clock that sat on a shelf near the dining table continued its slow tick, tick, tick. Time seemed to stand still.

The clock struck two times. Sam and the men should be coming soon. Another streak of lightning lit the dark sky and the thunder rolled and rolled. A slight breeze drifted through the open door carrying the smell of rain.

Ruby stirred again. She let out a little whimper and turned over. Opal gently patted her younger sister.

SAM HELD THE GUN IN A READY POSITION AS HE WALKED AT a steady pace toward the Armstrongs'. He was relieved when his eyes fully adjusted to the darkness and he could still hear the man talking to his Mama. He walked a bit further and suddenly realized he could no longer hear the man's low-pitched voice. He glanced around to be sure the man wasn't following him. To his relief he saw no shadowy figures.

Sam felt fairly certain his mother could keep them safe until he returned with help. He knew she was a brave woman.

When he came to the stand of trees along the dry creek he stopped and listened for any indication the man might have beat him here. He only heard the usual night sounds. Sam scanned the trees but saw nothing to make him hesitate in going onward. He walked slowly to avoid falling as he went down the rocky embankment. Just as his foot stepped on the rocks covering the creek bottom a shadowy figure swept past him almost making him lose his balance. He jerked to regain his balance and could make out the form of a deer fleeing up the other embankment. The sudden movement had frightened Sam. He breathed out a sigh of relief when he saw it was only a deer. Sam knew falling with a loaded gun could lead to disaster. He cautiously scanned the trees ahead but saw nothing else to alarm him.

JANE HEARD THE DISTANT BARKING OF DOGS AND THEN THE pounding of horses' hooves on the dry dirt. Soon they were riding into the yard.

A familiar voice filled the silence. "Mrs. Parker, this is Jim Armstrong, are you and the children okay?"

"Yes, sir, I have my gun on this one behind my door and the other one took off. I'll have Opal light the lamp," Jane replied.

At her mother's words, Opal moved to the dining table and lit the kerosene lamp.

Jim Armstrong and Jake Rolls stepped into the house. Jake pointed his pistol toward the slightly ajar door as Jim pulled the door away from the man.

"Step on outside and no shenanigans," Jim Armstrong almost growled.

The disheveled man did as he was told. His clothes were filthy; his hair looked as though it hadn't been washed or combed in a month, and his face was covered with several months' growth of whiskers. It would have been hard to decide which was worse, his nauseous smell or his scruffy appearance.

Sam stepped into the room just as Jane quickly moved behind the dressing curtain and pulled her dress on over her nightgown. She wanted to hug him, hold him close, and savor his safe return. Jane knew Sam wouldn't like it if anyone saw her. They might think he was being treated like a baby.

Jane could hear the men's voices as she dressed.

"Just what in tarnation did you and that other fellow think you were doing coming in here in the middle of the night scaring this fine lady and her children?" Jim Armstrong asked seething with anger.

"Well, uh, my friend told me to—," the man started to answer.

"I don't give a tinker's damn what your so-called friend told you to do, you tell me just what you two were up to," Jim insisted.

"Well, you know, we was just thinking of having a little fun with the ladies. Nothin' too bad mind you," the man hastened to add.

That brought several sneers and muttered curses from the men.

A voice Jane didn't recognize asked, "Where did the other one go? And you better tell me straight," he said with contempt.

"Well, we was gonna meet up at Hico, but I ain't so sure that's where he headed."

Jane lingered where she could hear but stayed out of sight of the men.

"Seth, I think you better stay here just in case that other fellow decides to come back, and we'll take this one with us to track his friend," Jim addressed the man she didn't recognize.

Jane felt a little uneasy at having another stranger in her house even if he was Jim Armstrong's son. She had heard the Armstrongs mention him numerous times.

"I can go or stay," the man answered.

"You've probably had enough riding for one day. I would feel better with you here to protect Mrs. Parker and the children," Jim answered.

Jane heard boot steps on the porch.

"Mrs. Parker, I want my son, Seth, to stay with you and the children while we track the other fellow and turn them in to the sheriff." Jim turned and motioned the man forward. "This is my son, Seth. He just rode in from the Army today. Seth, this is Jane Parker. She is the lady I told you about that takes care of your mother and cooks for us and the hands."

Seth tipped his hat to Jane. "Mrs. Parker, I'll camp here on the porch and keep an eye out in case the other one decides to come back."

Jane thought Seth strongly favored his father. They were both slender built but muscular, about six feet tall, light brown hair, and had the same smoky blue eyes.

Jane saw the lightning flashing, and the thunder rolled louder. The cool breeze from the approaching rain filtered into the stuffy house. Maybe the stench would soon be gone, Jane thought.

"Mr. Armstrong, I'm afraid you and the men are going to get caught in this storm. Maybe you should wait until it passes over before you go," she suggested with a worried look.

"Don't worry, we'll be all right. It looks to be moving pretty fast and won't last long. If it gets too bad, we'll find shelter somewhere," Jim reassured her.

"Thank you for coming to help us."

"I'm just glad we got here before anything bad happened," Jim answered.

Jim turned, mounted his horse, and the men departed in silence.

Jane watched Seth lead his horse toward the barn. He was a striking man for sure, she thought.

Jane gathered up several quilts and a pillow. She watched the approaching storm and knew Seth would get soaked on the porch. She spread the quilts inside the front door. To her surprise, it didn't bother her to have this stranger under her roof after all since she had met him.

Jane felt as though she knew him from hearing his mother talk about him and reading excerpts from his letters describing army life out west. He seemed to enjoy that life in spite of the danger, which he managed to adequately gloss over.

Seth stepped onto the porch and saw the pallet laid out inside the front door. He glanced at Jane as she looked up at the sound of his footsteps. He found Jane Parker to be an attractive woman and wondered if the men had come for her or her and the older girl who was a young beauty. They must have been watching the place to know there was no man around to interfere with their intent. Whatever their motive, he was glad she had the courage to send Sam for help and hold them off until they arrived. Seth smiled to himself; Jane Parker, with her unwavering nerve and pistol, must have come as quite a surprise to the two outlaws.

"No need in getting soaked on the porch," Jane said and turned away as he entered the house. "Thank you, Ma'am. Try to get some rest, it has been a long night for you and the children," Seth replied.

"Do you need anything else?" Jane asked, as she sat on the side of the bed.

"No, Ma'am, everything is fine," Seth answered. He stretched out on the pallet and laid his loaded gun on the floor next to the pillow.

Jane blew out the lamp and lay listening to the sound of the first drops of rain falling gently on the roof and parched earth. She was certain sleep would not come easily.

JIM ARMSTRONG, HIS TWO MEN, AND THE STRANGER RODE several miles before taking shelter at the abandoned Draper place. The storm moved on in about a half-hour, and they continued their search for the other man.

They found the man that had stayed outside in Hico at the local saloon. The man was identified as Lewis Boston, better known as Lucky. He had been indulging in several vices and gave no resistance when the sheriff from Hico arrested him as he slouched over the bar in the Silver Spur Saloon.

The man with Armstrong said his name was Jackson Polk.

After both men were arrested, the sheriff turned them over to Armstrong and his men to be escorted back to Clairette. The two men gave no trouble on the ride back and the party arrived near daybreak. When Sheriff Tully tried to put the men in jail, Lewis Boston decided to make a run for it. Apparently, Lucky had sobered up enough on the ride back to Clairette to realize once he was locked up it would likely be a very long time before he would be free. Running was his last mistake. Sheriff Tully and Jim Armstrong got off simultaneous shots that both hit the target. He fell dead in the street. Jackson Polk walked meekly to the jail cell.

SHERIFF TULLY SHUFFLED THROUGH A STACK OF WANTED posters. The first one he found was on Lewis Boston, Lucky, for robbery in Sherman. Next, he found one on Jackson Polk for the same robbery. There were posters on each man for robbery in Dekatur. Then the sheriff found posters on the pair that had broken into Jane Parker's home, and that made the hair on the back of his neck bristle. Robbery and Rape in Fort Worth.

Chapter Two

For two more nights Seth Armstrong slept on Jane's front porch. She assured him that, with one man dead and the other in jail, she and the children would be fine. He did not listen.

As Jane and the girls walked along the dusty road toward her house, she could hear the distant sound of hammering and could see Seth and Sam on the front porch. She was curious to see what they were hammering.

"Mrs. Parker, Mrs. Parker," she heard the sound of Sheriff Tully's voice from a distance behind her and turned to see him riding his horse toward her. She stopped to let him catch up with her and the girls.

"Mrs. Parker, I need a private word with you," Sheriff Tully said, as he rode along beside her and the girls and dismounted. Sheriff Tully was not a large man, standing about five feet ten inches tall, with a medium build, but his facial expression and the demanding quality of his voice commanded respect.

"Opal, you and Ruby run on ahead and see what your brother and Mr. Seth are up to," Jane told the girls.

They skipped on, kicking up the loose dirt as they went, anxious to see what was happening at their house.

Jane turned her attention to the sheriff when the girls were out of earshot.

"What is it?" she asked.

"As you probably already know one of those scallywags decided to run the other night and was brought down for his actions," the sheriff said with no trace of regret in his voice. He did not add that his and Jim Armstrong's shots had hit him in the back and back of the head when he refused to stop. She did not need to know the gory details of the event that led to Lewis Boston's finish.

Jane nodded, indicating she already knew of his demise.

"His name was Lewis, Lucky, Boston from up around Sherman and had a long record of questionable behavior and downright law breaking. I guess you might say Lucky ran out of luck. Now the other fellow is not much better but did have the good sense to take his medicine. His name is Jackson Polk, also from the Sherman area. They may be cousins, but I don't know for sure. Anyway, Judge Daniels will probably want to talk with you about what exactly took place at your house when he comes to town next week."

Jane nodded her consent.

"I expect Jackson Polk will get a number of years for this episode and previous unlawful deeds he and Lucky inflicted on innocent folks," Sheriff Tully continued.

"Good," Jane replied. "I am grateful for Mr. Armstrong and his men and you for taking care of them so quickly," Jane said sincerely.

"Just glad no harm came to you and them children," Sheriff Tully replied in a serious tone, especially thinking of the last wanted posters he had found. "Never understood why some men turn into scoundrels and can't seem to see the error of their ways. We sure don't need the likes of them around here," the sheriff said. He shook his head to indicate his lack of understanding such men.

Jane nodded in agreement. "Thank you again, Sheriff. I'll be to town on Thursday."

WHEN JANE NEARED THE HOUSE, SHE COULD PLAINLY SEE A patchwork of window frames that held new fly screen where there had been none before. Sam and Seth were hanging a similar frame on the front door. The frames had a long board down the middle and three cross boards spaced evenly up the frame. She smiled slightly at the appearance but quickly understood the purpose of such peculiar looking door and window frames.

Seth turned as he heard her approach the porch.

"What do you think?" he asked, as he nodded toward the frames.

"I think it's a very fine," she paused, "creation," she added.

"Well, I must admit it's not the prettiest house decoration, but it will provide a measure of safety for you and the children. The new screen will keep out flies and mosquitoes. Anyone trying to come in will have to make a hell of a racket." Seth seemed to catch himself and realize the word he had just used. "Beg your pardon, Ma'am, I am more accustomed, to talking to soldiers than ladies, I'm afraid," Seth apologized.

"No harm done," Jane assured him. "I have heard that word on a number of occasions and the children aren't near enough to hear."

Seth smiled at her response. Jane Parker was a wise woman as well as brave. He admired both qualities and didn't mind her looks either. The two nights he spent sleeping on her porch had afforded him an occasional glimpse of Jane with her rich auburn hair undone and shining in the lamplight as she brushed it. He could make out the swell of her full breasts and curving hips under the cotton nightgown she donned just before bedtime. She was still an attractive woman and would probably be downright pretty if she had time and the desire to fix up a bit. Her eyes reminded him of a blue gray winter sky. Her mouth was supple when she smiled, a mouth that would bring great pleasure to kiss. Seth calculated in his head that Jane was probably about his age, thirty-three. Seth quickly brought his thoughts into check, as he had no business pining after Jane Parker. He was too accustomed to army life and feared he would make a poor family man.

"I truly appreciate all you've done for us these past few days. I know the children and I will rest much better with the," she nodded toward the new frames, "protection you have provided. Do let me pay you for the materials, and I can cook you a fine meal of your choosing for all of your hard work," she suggested.

"No pay, these were discarded boards I found at the farm, and the screen didn't cost much. The fine meal I will accept," Seth replied with a smile. "I know you are an excellent cook from the meals I've already enjoyed at Pa and Mom's house."

Jane felt a slight blush on her cheeks at his praise of her cooking. "What is your favorite meal?"

"Well," Seth pondered, "if Sam could catch a nice mess of fish to fry up crispy with some mashed potatoes and some kind of greens that would be mighty pleasing."

Jane smiled, "I'm sure Sam will be happy for the chance to go fishing. Do you eat desserts?"

"Yes, Ma'am," Seth emphasized the *yes*. "I am mighty fond of chocolate pie with a heap of golden meringue on top," he smiled and gave a slight smack of his lips.

Jane laughed at his response.

"I'll send Sam fishing Saturday morning and send word as to his luck."

"I just might join him to be sure we have fish Saturday night. Where does he fish?"

"At the big bend in the creek about a half-mile east of here."

Saturday morning Sam had just finished eating a hardy breakfast when Seth rode into the yard. Sam rushed out to meet him and before long they were on their way to the creek.

Jane set three large washtubs on the crude table outside the kitchen door. The girls filled the first washtub with hot sudsy water and two tubs with rinse water. Jane and Opal took turns washing or doing the final rinse and wringing the clothes out so they would dry faster. Ruby did the first rinse, as she was still too young to thoroughly wash or wring out the clothes. She often had to be prodded to rinse the clothes instead of just playing in the water. By mid-morning the clotheslines were sagging with the week's laundry.

The girls dusted their meager pieces of furniture, swept, and mopped the wood floors. The house was one large L-shaped room. In the front there were three beds, a wardrobe holding their few good clothes, and two trunks that held their everyday clothes and household linens. A rock fireplace sat across the southwest corner of the room to give heat to the big room and kitchen. Jane's treadle sewing machine stood near one of the front windows to take advantage of the light when she sewed. The small part of the L was the kitchen. The wood cook stove and a few cabinets lined the back wall. Jane was grateful she had her mother's old round oak dining table with its claw feet and five of its six cane-bottom chairs that remained intact. It wasn't much of a house, but Jane was grateful to have a roof over their heads.

Jane made a large pitcher of sweet tea with a hint of fresh peppermint that grew near the kitchen door. She put it in the window cooler and made sure to keep the surrounding cloth wet so the tea would be cool for supper.

She hummed as she baked two chocolate meringue pies, one for supper and one to send home with Seth.

SETH PUSHED HIS CHAIR SLIGHTLY AWAY FROM THE TABLE and declared, "I think you can tell by the pile of fish bones on my plate that I thoroughly enjoyed that superb meal, Jane."

"I'm glad it was to your liking," Jane smiled.

"Yes, Ma'am, it sure was, and that chocolate pie is the best by far that I have ever tasted," Seth said giving Jane an appreciative smile.

Once again Jane felt a slight blush reach her cheeks at Seth's generous praise for her cooking. At times it seemed years instead of seven months since Samuel had passed. Seth brought back the pleasure of having a man at her table.

Sam gave his fingers a noisy lick and joined in the praise. "Ma is for sure a goood cook!"

Everyone laughed.

The evening had passed pleasantly.

"Could I refill your tea while Opal and I clean the kitchen?"

"Yes, thank you," Seth replied as he handed her his empty glass.

"Tell us some stories about being in the army," Sam suggested.

"Well, the ladies might not be too interested in army stories."

"Yeah, they would," Sam assured him before anyone could say otherwise.

"I like army stories," Ruby put in bobbing her head making her red curls bounce up and down.

"Yes, do tell us about life in the military," Jane joined in.

Seth entertained his captive audience with several stories of seemingly exciting adventures while Opal and Jane finished the dishes. Jane noted that he carefully omitted any danger or particular hardships he may have endured. However, those stories were not what the children needed to hear just yet.

Seth departed near sundown, as he knew Jane and the children would be up early to do chores before Sunday church.

Jane stood on the front porch watching Seth ride away. She thought what a pleasant man he seemed to be and very nice-looking to boot. It was rare for a man like him to still be single and he would be a prize catch for some lucky woman.

ON WEDNESDAY, SHERIFF TULLY RODE OUT TO REMIND JANE that Judge Daniels would arrive late that afternoon and would want to speak with her, Jim Armstrong, and Jake Rolls on Thursday morning before the trial.

Jane left the girls to care for Mrs. Armstrong, and Sam helped around the ranch after finishing his chores at home.

Bea Armstrong had never regained her strength after her bout with pneumonia, and now it appeared arthritis was taking over her frail body. The girls loved "Miss Bea," as they called her. Mr. Jim called her his "Honey Bea." She would read stories with Ruby and patiently teach Opal how to embroider and crochet. Bea assured Jane she and the girls would be fine until they returned from town.

Jane and the two men journeyed together to Clairette. Jane dreaded having to face the man she had held at gunpoint behind her door. Just the thought of seeing him again gave her an uneasy feeling although she knew she and her children were no longer in any danger from him.

They entered the sheriff's office and were introduced to Judge Daniels, a man in his mid-fifties with graying hair and a handlebar mustache. He wore a dark gray suit and a gun strapped on his hip.

Judge Daniels told the sheriff to bring six upstanding, sober men to serve as jurors during the proceedings, and more people could come if they so desired. In less than half an hour the six men were present, and the small office was brimming with local men and a few women. Numerous spectators stood outside near the open windows and door to hear more about what had happened to Mrs. Parker and her children.

The local gossip mill had been running full tilt during the past days with all kinds of rumors circulating through the community. One such tale even had Jane killing one of the men before Jim Armstrong could get to her house. Another rumor had the sheriff and Jim Armstrong in a running gun battle with the outlaws on the way back from Hico.

"Bring the prisoner out here," the judge ordered and nodded his head toward a chair near the desk where he sat.

The man that entered looked a bit better than the last time Jane had seen him. His long hair was combed back away from his face and his several months' growth of whiskers had been removed and he was now clean-shaven. Just those two things were a great improvement, but Jane believed he still wore the same wrinkled, dirty clothes.

Jane and the two men all identified Jackson Polk as the man that had entered her house uninvited in the middle of the night.

Judge Daniels questioned each witness to establish what had taken place at Jane's house on the night of June 12, 1897.

From time to time there were murmurs and random outbursts from the onlookers. The tone became ugly when Jane told about having to send her son, Sam, just a boy, for help with a man outside her door that might harm him.

The judge kept the proceedings moving with limited interference. He did not hesitate to pound the desk with his big fist to restore order to the proceedings.

After about twenty-five minutes the judge turned to Jackson Polk and said, "This is your opportunity to tell your side of this story, so you better make it good, and truthful."

Polk looked around the room but didn't appear to think the odds were in his favor when he took in the angry faces staring at him.

"Well now, you see here, Judge, me and Lucky didn't really do these fine folks no harm, so I don't know what all the fuss is about," he tried to sound puzzled about the charges against him.

"Just tell me this, Mr. Polk, why were you and Lucky there in the middle of the night? That is hardly the time for a social call, especially on folks you don't even know."

"Well, you see, earlier that day we was ridin' past and saw the pretty little blond gal out in the garden, the one that looks to be about sixteen or maybe older. Well, naturally we admired such a beauty, but we was quite a ways off so we weren't real sure she was as pretty as we thought, so we just thought we'd uh, uh, go back by and have a closer look."

"In the middle of the night?" Judge Daniels asked in an incredulous manner.

Polk looked around the room again in an attempt to gage the listeners' reactions to his story. "Well, we 'tweren't quite sure about the time since we had been in town drinkin', just a bit mind you," Polk offered as some defense.

"So, you expect us to believe that you and Lucky were just making a social call to see if the young lady, who is only fourteen, was really as pretty as you thought." Judge Daniels reprimanded Polk.

"Sure," Polk answered as though he thought the judge would believe his poppycock story.

Judge Daniels banged his fist so hard on the desk that almost everyone in the room jumped.

"Sheriff Tully, show the prisoner those wanted posters you found," Judge Daniels instructed.

Sheriff Tully picked up the wanted posters and walked over to where Polk sat. He held up the first two posters of Polk and Boston for robbery in Sherman.

Polk shook his head in the negative as though denying the accusations.

The sheriff held up the next two posters for robbery in Dekatur.

Polk continued to shake his head.

Then Sheriff Tully held up the last two wanted posters. He raised them up so everyone in the room and those peering through the windows and door could read, "Wanted for Robbery and Rape in Fort Worth."

Bedlam broke out in the small office and street.

Polk tried to stand. "You ain't got no proof of that!" he shouted, as the sheriff shoved him back into his chair.

Judge Daniels banged his fist on the table again and shouted above the furor, "ORDER! ORDER!"

The crowd gradually quieted.

"I don't want to hear another damn word from you!" he roared at the prisoner. "Beg your pardon, ladies, for my language," he apologized.

"Gentlemen of the jury, how say you on the guilt or innocence of this prisoner for unlawfully entering Mrs. Parker's house and posing a threat to her and her children? Answer 'Guilty' or 'Not Guilty,'" the judge instructed.

Each man answered "Guilty," loud enough for all within earshot to hear.

"Now, I sentence Jackson Polk to one year in prison for the crime committed in this county. Sheriff Tully, send a telegram to Sheriff Martin up in Fort Worth to let him know you will be escorting this prisoner to his custody to stand trial for crimes committed in Fort Worth. Court's Adjourned!" Judge Daniels declared with a final bang of his fist on the desk.

The onlookers erupted into talk about the situation and several ladies rushed forward to comfort Jane.

"Deputize me and Rutherford to escort Polk to Fort Worth and you won't have to worry about any more trials!" one of the hands from the White Rock Ranch yelled.

"Let's don't have no more talk like that," Sheriff Tully shot back.

The crowd began to disperse, but Jane could still hear murmurs of discontent with Judge Daniels' ruling.

JANE WAS GLAD WHEN THEY LEFT THE TURMOIL IN TOWN. The sooner Sheriff Tully took Jackson Polk to Fort Worth the better, she thought, as they left Clairette.

Her insides seemed to still be quivering from when she saw the last wanted posters from Fort Worth. The words "Robbery and Rape" seemed forever stuck in her mind. She would tell Opal about the men and ask Mr. Armstrong or Seth to talk to Sam. Seth might be the best choice, she thought. Mr. Armstrong might be embarrassed to speak of such matters to a boy of ten.

Chapter Three

Jane knew that in a few weeks the uproar over Jackson Polk's trial would die down. The gossips would soon have a new target to flap their tongues about besides what happened at the Parker place, and that would suit her just fine.

The summer heat persisted with only occasional brief showers that hardly settled the dust and left the air oppressive and steamy in their wake.

The new screen on the windows and doors did keep the house almost free of flies and mosquitoes. Sleep came more easily except on the nights when the air didn't stir. The heat seemed to settle in and did not relinquish its hold until just before sunup.

The girls accompanied Jane to the Armstrongs' daily, while Sam often stayed home to tend to the garden, chickens, and milk the cow. He would draw buckets of water from the cistern and tote them to the garden in an attempt to save the plants from withering in the relentless heat.

Most Saturdays, Sam would meet Billy Johnson at the creek to fish and while away an afternoon with a friend. Billy lived on the next farm and was a grade ahead of Sam in school. He came from a big happy-go-lucky family. All nine of the children had reddish brown hair with a smattering of freckles on their cheerful faces like their pa.

Most Saturdays Sam brought a good mess of fish home for supper and Seth would be invited to share another evening meal, which he rarely turned down.

On one such Saturday afternoon Sam and Billy became bored with fishing when neither got a bite for an hour or more. They shucked off their clothes and jumped in the cool stream shaded by a big cottonwood tree. Neither boy was embarrassed about swimming in the raw as that was a common practice among boys and men. They felt fairly certain the only person that might happen by the creek would just be one of the nearby cowboys or farm hands. After splashing around for an hour or more the boys started out of the water when they heard the unmistakable, dreaded sound of rattling in the underbrush near the creek bank.

Billy jumped back in the stream and shouted at Sam, "Rattlesnake!"

Sam froze and listened intently for the repeated sound. The distinct rattle sounded again about fifteen feet from where Sam stood near the edge of the creek. Sam slowly moved a little farther down the stream.

"What you doing?" Billy whispered as though he thought the snake might hear him.

"Come on," Sam motioned. "We're gonna catch us a rattlesnake."

"You're crazy!" Billy told Sam, shaking his head and wading a little farther away from the creek bank.

Sam paused and turned to Billy. "We're gonna find a forked stick and I'll sharpen the points with my pocketknife. I'll sneak up on the snake and hold his head down and you cut off its rattlers with your knife." Sam grinned as though he had just thought up the greatest game.

Billy shook his head, "Nah, I don't want no rattlers."

"Come on, big baby, it'll be fun to show them rattlers to Hank and Orin when we go back to school. Everybody knows Hank and Orin are daredevils thinking up all sorts of mischief. I bet they never thought of getting rattlesnake rattlers. Won't they be j-e-a-l-o-u-s," Sam laughed and slapped his knee.

At that sound the rattlesnake buzzed again a little nearer Sam thought. "Come on, Billy, we ain't gonna get bit or nothing," Sam assured his friend.

Billy stayed where he was for a few seconds but decided he didn't want Sam telling Hank and Orin he was a scaredy-cat big baby. Everybody knew how brave Sam was for helpin' his ma hold off those outlaws that came to their place. Yep, Sam was probably the bravest boy in the county, in ten counties. Billy sure didn't want Sam thinking he was a big baby.

"Oh, okay," Billy reluctantly agreed, with some misgivings.

Slowly the two boys waded out of the creek giving wide berth to the snake until they could find a forked stick and retrieve Billy's pocketknife.

It didn't take long for Sam to find what he deemed the perfect snake catcher. Billy had his knife ready to cut the rattlers off as soon as Sam gave the word.

The two boys gingerly approached the brush where they had last heard the snake.

Billy swallowed hard, "We gonna tromp through them bushes to find that dang snake?" he asked, a little worried.

"'Naw!" Sam answered with a grin. "Look there," Sam said, as he pointed to a small clearing near the creek.

The snake had been most accommodating. While the boys were getting dressed the snake had obliged by crawling out of the brush into the clearing and stretched out to sun itself.

"Get ready, as soon as I give the word you cut them rattlers off and get way back cause when I let it go it's gonna be madder than," Sam hesitated just for an instant then said it, the word that would get his mouth washed out with soap if his ma ever heard him say it, but Ma wasn't here, "madder than Hell!"

Billy swallowed hard. "Ready," he nodded to Sam, although he could feel his hands quivering.

Sam started his approach, taking one slow deliberate step after another.

Billy watched almost afraid to breathe, for fear he would alert the snake as to what was about to happen.

Sam continued his slow approach with nerves of steel. Suddenly, Sam sprang with the forked stick pinning the snake's head just as he had planned.

"Now!" Sam shouted to Billy.

Billy forced himself to grab the snake's tail. He grasped the rattlers tight in his fist and, with one fast slash of his knife, cut the rattlers off, jumped back, and ran several yards.

Sam yanked the stick out of the dirt and sprang back out of the snake's striking distance.

"Ya-hoo!" Sam shouted as he ran to Billy for a look at the prized rattlers.

Billy thrust the rattlers into Sam's hand. "You keep 'em; iffin' I take 'em home with me, one of my brothers is sure to find 'em and I'll get a licking from my pa."

"Sure," Sam agreed eagerly. "I've got a treasure box I'll put 'em in, and nobody bothers my treasure box."

On the way home Sam admired the rattlers and thought with a smile about how jealous Orin and Hank would be when they saw what he and Billy had done. Maybe before school starts, we can get a few more, he mused, and laughed out loud at the thought of showing off several rattlers. He and Billy would be the envy of every boy in school. Yes, siree!

Chapter Four

One Saturday evening in late August Seth joined the family for dinner. After another delicious meal, with chocolate meringue pie for dessert, Seth and Jane moved to the porch to sit and visit for a spell. The evening was pleasant as there had been showers for the past couple of days, and it looked like more rain clouds building in the south.

Jane took a deep breath and slowly let it out. “Everything smells so fresh after the rain.”

Seth looked at Jane and smiled.

“What are you smiling about?” she asked.

“Oh, I was just thinking how pleasant it is to come spend an evening enjoying your fine cooking and visiting with you and the children.”

“Well, I’m glad you feel welcome in our home, and the children look forward to hearing your soldier stories.”

“And you?” he gave her a questioning look.

“Oh yes, I enjoy the stories too. I know though that it isn’t quite as glamorous and fun as you make it sound.”

Seth gave a short laugh, "That's for dang sure. Well, the kids don't need to hear the other part of the stories just yet," he answered.

No, it wouldn't do for the children or Jane to hear about the treks they often took through the rough, rugged Texas country where they wore blisters on their feet, their skin baked in the hot relentless sun, and at times they went far too long with no water. Occasionally a soldier's body just couldn't take the unrelenting conditions any longer. He would fall from his horse and gasp his last breath thinking hell couldn't be much worse.

"No, but you might let Sam know it isn't quite as fun as you make it sound, just in case he gets ideas about joining up when he's old enough," Jane suggested, with a worried look.

"Ah, Jane, don't worry, by the time Sam's old enough he will have thought of any number of exciting things he would like to be and probably won't pursue any of them. When I was his age, I was going to be a lion tamer in the circus, and then I wanted to be a trapper in the northwest. The one my pa was really excited about was the riverboat gambler," Seth laughed and shook his head.

"That was quite a variety I must say," Jane laughed.

Seth looked pensive, then heaved a sigh. "I'm still not sure what I want to be when I grow up," he said, with a slight chuckle. "I have about reached the conclusion that I am not cut out to be a farmer or rancher. I haven't said anything to the folks yet, but I am thinking of joining up again."

"Oh?" Jane gave him a questioning look.

Seth gazed off into the distance. "I can do farm work or ranch work, but it just isn't something I really look forward to like Pa does," he sighed. "Pa seems to have it in his blood, I don't," he said, with a bit of regret in his voice.

Jane felt a stab of disappointment to think Seth might be leaving soon. She wasn't sure why she felt that way except she did enjoy his company, and she treasured his friendship. She also knew he was a good influence on Sam. A boy his age needs a good man's guidance, she thought.

"Yes, I'm sure your folks will hate to see you leave but I believe they would want you to do what is best for you."

"Well, I haven't completely made up my mind so don't say anything."

"It's not my place to say anything," Jane replied.

"I know you wouldn't, I don't know why I even said that," Seth smiled, reached for her hand, and gave it a little squeeze. "I do know that if I go, I will certainly miss you and the children." Seth was beginning to wonder if he wasn't becoming too attached to Jane and her children. He certainly felt an attraction to her but wasn't at all sure if the feeling was mutual. Perhaps it was too soon for her to think along those lines since her husband had been deceased for less than a year.

"We'll miss you too," Jane murmured.

Seth looked at Jane for a long moment, taking in her pleasing expression, before releasing her hand. "What about you, Jane? What do you dream of doing if you had the chance?"

Jane paused before she answered to think about Seth's question. What would she like to do? she wondered. She had never had the luxury of thinking of her own desires since she married so young. All she had ever wanted to be was a good wife and mother. She had been a good wife to both of her husbands, and she did her best to be a good mother. Mothering seemed to have become harder since Samuel passed. Perhaps because she was trying to fill both pairs of shoes, mother and father.

"Well," she gave a short laugh. "I think I would like several acres of good land to raise a really huge garden and sell the produce. I get great satisfaction digging in the dirt, planting those tiny seeds, and watching them grow. You know, I'd be real content doing just that. I can be tired or worried, but let me go to gardening and it's like everything suddenly seems all right," she mused. "How is that for dreaming?" she asked, as she looked at Seth to gauge his reaction.

Seth gave her a serious look. "I think that is a great idea."

"Yeah, well, great ideas take money and that I do not have!" Jane said, with a small shake of her head.

"Hmm, have you ever thought of asking for a loan from the bank to get started?"

Jane threw back her head and laughed. "Seth, what banker would lend a widow with three kids to support enough money for that kind of business?"

"You might be surprised," Seth said seriously.

"Oh, Seth, I mainly just want to keep a roof over our heads and feed my children. That's about all I can hope for."

Deep down Seth knew she was probably right. It was hard enough for men to get loans for new businesses, much less a woman. A sad fact, he thought, especially for a woman like Jane, who could probably make a go of it.

A FEW DAYS LATER SETH PULLED THE TEAM INTO THE YARD just as Jane stepped out of the barn carrying a pail of milk.

He held up a letter. "Got this while I was in town," he said, as he handed her the letter.

"Got time for a cup of coffee and piece of pie?" Jane asked, as she took the letter.

"Yes, Ma'am," Seth grinned and climbed down from the wagon.

Jane noticed Seth had a fresh haircut and looked especially nice, rather quite handsome. She wondered again how such a not only good-looking but good man had escaped getting married by now. She supposed he just hadn't found the right woman that would be willing to live the life of an army man's wife. She was sure there were a number of women that wouldn't mind moving from here to no telling where, especially for a man like Seth.

As they walked toward the house Seth commented, "Where are the kids? It seems unusually quiet around here."

"It's the Johnson twins' birthday and they have gone to have cake."

"Why didn't you go too?"

"They could stay longer if I did the chores here," Jane replied. "They don't get to do a lot of fun things, so it seemed better for me to stay home."

They sat at the kitchen table enjoying the fresh apple pie and coffee.

"Go ahead and open your letter," Seth suggested.

"Oh, I can wait," Jane said, but she kept eyeing the letter.

"Go on," Seth encouraged.

Jane opened the letter and quickly scanned the one page. It was from her cousin, Opal, for whom her daughter was named.

"Oh, no," Jane sighed, and tears welled up in her eyes.

"What is it?" Seth asked with concern when he saw Jane's reaction.

She choked back tears. "Uncle John passed two weeks ago. He had been ailing a few days and died in his sleep."

"Is this the uncle that helped raise you?"

Jane nodded as the tears rolled down her cheeks.

Seth moved his chair next to hers and put his arms around her in comfort. "I'm sorry, Jane," he soothed. Seth continued to hold her as he felt her quiver and knew she was still crying. Then he kissed her gently on the forehead much as a parent would do to comfort a child. However, he realized that he had no desire to kiss her as a parent but as a man. He would like very much to kiss her on the lips. He paused and thought better of it at this time or perhaps at any time. If he joined up again, he would be leaving soon. Seth knew it wouldn't be fair to Jane to court her and then leave.

Jane sat up straight in her chair out of his embrace and gave her eyes a final wipe with her apron.

"Uncle John and Aunt Mary were so good to me. We lived about five miles from town and their farm was just on the edge of town. I spent about as much time at their house as I did at home. During the winter I stayed with them, so I didn't have so far to walk to school and back home. The rest of the year their three girls and I would beg for me to stay to go to Church or parties in town, or any other excuse we could think up," Jane said with a smile, remembering the happy times. "Uncle John and Aunt Mary always seemed happy for me to stay. When Mama and Pa would make me come home after a day or two, I would start begging to go back to their house."

"Did they just have the three girls?" Seth asked.

"Oh, no, they had three older sons and one boy younger than the girls. One of the older boys got killed in a mining explosion and another died of typhoid fever all in the same year. That was a sad time for the family, but we made it through," she said, with a distant look into the past reflected in her eyes.

"Where did your aunt and uncle live?"

"Uncle John and Aunt Mary always lived in Mississippi. The two older girls and the older boy still live there. The youngest girl and her family live in Louisiana, and the youngest boy has gone out west somewhere. I don't think they hear from him often. I miss getting to see their family. Pa and Mama decided to come to Texas when I was twelve. It nearly broke my heart to leave my three girl cousins and Aunt Mary and Uncle John. The girls and I begged Mama to let me stay with them, but she and Pa wouldn't hear of it."

Seth smiled. "I can understand them not wanting to leave their daughter behind even if it would have been with relatives. It's a long way from Mississippi to Texas. Who knows, you may never have seen them again," he gave a slight shrug of his broad shoulders.

"You're right. I can understand that now. I made new friends and the Gains family lived on the next ranch. From the time I met Peter, I think I started falling in love with him," she laughed. "At twelve, of course, it was a crush but by fourteen it was love. We married just after I turned fifteen," Jane's eyes sparkled and her face almost glowed at the memory. "We were married almost two years, and I was seven months pregnant with Opal, when he drowned in the flooded Trinity River trying to save some of our cattle. His death almost killed me too," she said, and the sad memory was reflected in her gaze. "I took to my bed and prayed to die, but God knew the baby I carried needed her mother. I'm ashamed to say I took no pleasure in her birth, and my ma had to force me to nurse her and care for her," Jane sighed from the weight of telling the story, but she needed to talk. She needed to talk about the past and let go of the sad memories, cherish the good memories; and, somehow, she knew Seth was a willing listener.

"Opal is so much like her father. Peter was a handsome man with blond hair and sparkling blue eyes, the color of an April sky. They have the same smile and laughter."

"How did you meet Samuel?" Seth asked. He sensed Jane needed to keep talking to relieve the built-up pain she had suffered. Perhaps then she could remember the good times in her life.

Jane smiled again. "I met Samuel at a church social when Opal was about eighteen months old, but I didn't notice him at first. Samuel said he noticed me the first night we met but knew I was still grieving over the loss of my first husband. He was a patient man and waited for me to finally become aware of him and his attraction to me. At first, I was surprised by my feelings toward Samuel. I felt certain when Peter died, I could never love another man, but I found love again," she paused, "just in a different package."

Jane turned to look at Seth. "I count my blessings every day. I loved and was loved by two good men. No, they were exceptional men. I gave birth to four children and still have three to comfort me," she said, with obvious pride and gratitude.

"I didn't know you had another child," Seth remarked.

"Yes, Pearl was four when she passed away. Last winter the flu hit our community really hard. Samuel and Pearl both came down with it and there was nothing the doctor could do to save them. Samuel passed one cold November night and little Pearl died about daybreak the next morning," Jane said as tears filled her eyes again.

Seth reached out and took her hands in his. He held them gently in a gesture of comfort.

Jane breathed a deep sigh. "It was a hard time, but I knew I had to keep going. I couldn't take to my bed and feel sorry for myself this time, as my children had to have a roof over their heads, food to eat, and now it was up to me to provide for them."

Jane looked at Seth again and smiled slightly. "Your parents have been a Godsend to us. They've been wonderful to me and the children. I don't know what would have happened to us if it hadn't been for them."

Seth returned her smile. "I know they are grateful to have your help too, and they adore your children."

"Did you ever think of going back to your family?" Seth asked gently, as he continued to hold Jane's hands.

"After I was engaged to Samuel, Mama and Pa decided to go back to Mississippi. It was hard for me to see them go, but they left shortly after we were married. It was certainly hard for me to stay in Texas, but I loved Samuel and knew I belonged here with him. Mama took sick on the trip back to Mississippi and passed away about four days after they got back to Uncle John's house. Then Pa kind of went crazy and took off out West."

"Do you ever think of going back to Mississippi to be near your cousins?"

"It has crossed my mind at times, but I doubt I will ever actually go back. It wouldn't be like before," she said with a wistful expression.

"Do you keep in touch with your family?"

"I hear from my sister once in a while. She was already married with two babies when we came to Texas. I hear from my three girl cousins fairly often. The boys have drifted off and I don't hear from them or Pa. The last I heard of Pa, he was way out west somewhere, but it's been years since I've heard about him."

Seth gently squeezed Jane's hands and lifted them to his lips for a gentle kiss.

"Thank you for listening. I've needed to talk about these things for a long while," Jane said softly, as he rose to leave.

Seth gave her a warm, understanding smile. "Yes, I know," was all he said as he walked to the door.

Chapter Five

School started in mid-September. The second day of school Mr. Johnson came to bring the children home from school, which puzzled Jane as his farm was closer to town, and they could have easily walked the rest of the way home. Then Mr. Johnson told her about Sam and Billy's day at school.

"Did you bring 'em?" Billy whispered to Sam as they entered the schoolhouse.

"Got 'em in my lunch pail. We'll show 'em to the boys at recess. I can't wait to see the looks on Hank's and Orin's faces when they see those rattlers." Sam was almost bursting with hilarity.

"Me neither," Billy agreed with a short laugh.

Sam could hardly concentrate on what Professor Hicks, a tall, thin man in his late thirties, was saying. It seemed like the morning drug on and on until recess time. Finally, the professor told the class to put away their books and line up to go outside in an orderly manner.

Sam stepped out of line to fetch his lunch pail.

"Back in line, Sam Parker," Professor Hicks scolded.

"I just need something out of my pail, sir," Sam answered. He quickly retrieved the rattlers and slipped them into his pants pocket.

When Sam got to the door Professor Hicks pulled him aside. "Now, Sam, when I give you a directive, I expect you to follow it. If you need to do otherwise you raise your hand and ask permission first," Professor Hicks emphasized the first.

"Yes, sir," Sam agreed.

Sam breathed a sigh of relief when the professor didn't demand to see what he had gotten from his lunch pail. He ran to the playground where Billy, Hank, Orin, and several other boys waited.

"Now, just what you got that's so all-fired great?" Orin asked with a cocky smirk.

"I'll show you what I've got," Sam replied and tossed one of the rattlers at Orin.

Orin jumped back as it landed by his foot. "Oh shit, where did you get that?" he asked in awe.

"Same place I got these," Sam replied and tossed another rattler at Hank and the third at one of the other boys.

They erupted into questions laced with all of the curse words they knew.

"Keep it down," Billy cautioned. "We don't want the professor coming over here to see what all the commotion's about."

"Tell 'em, Billy, how we came about gettin' these fine rattlers," Sam almost crowed.

Billy and Sam gave a play-by-play description of how Sam would pin the snake's head with the forked stick and Billy would cut off the rattlers. They omitted that just as Sam jerked the forked stick to release the third snake it instantly struck and missed Sam's leg by a hair. That was when they decided three rattlers would be enough to impress all of the boys.

"'Geez," Orin breathed. "Can I have one?"

"No, go get your own!" Sam challenged.

"Man, oh man," Hank put in, "that's just—just—incredible. Weren't you afraid you'd get bit?"

"Naw!" Sam and Billy both boasted.

"Huh! We could get all the rattlers we could find if we wanted to, but, you know, after a while it gets dull just catching rattlesnakes," Sam bragged.

Billy could see the adoration on the boys' faces as they looked at Sam. They all already knew how brave Sam was when the outlaws had come to his house, and this just proved beyond a doubt that Sam Parker was the bravest of them all. Billy felt honored to be standing by Sam as his best friend and companion snake hunter basking in their esteem.

During lunch Sam and Billy plotted to further lift themselves even higher in the other boys' opinions.

SHORTLY BEFORE THE DISMISSAL BELL RANG SAM RAISED his hand, with a pained expression on his face, and begged to be excused to use the outhouse. Permission was granted.

Sam discreetly worked his way around to where Professor Hicks kept his horse and buggy stationed. Sam hitched the horse to the buggy, as the boys often did for the professor. He quickly retrieved the string from his pocket and tied it to the three rattlers and then tied them loosely under the buggy seat. He gave it a little jiggle to be sure they would rattle when the professor took off in the buggy. They rattled!

Sam met Billy out front just as school was dismissed.

"All is ready," he whispered so only Billy could hear. The two boys shared a secret grin.

Opal called as she and Ruby left the school, "Come on, Sam, chores are waiting."

"We'll catch up in a minute," Sam called back.

Billy and Sam slowly walked along, anxiously anticipating Professor Hicks' departure. They didn't have to wait long before the professor came out with an armful of papers and locked the door.

The professor strolled to his buggy and placed the papers on the seat. He untied the horse and climbed into the buggy. He gave the reins a gentle shake to get the horse moving. The horse lurched a bit on the uneven ground for his first few steps and the inevitable happened, the rattlers rattled just as Sam and Billy planned. The professor let out a yell and tried to vault out of the buggy. The yell startled the horse, and he took off at a gallop. Professor Hicks' trouser leg caught on the buggy frame, and he hit the ground, shoulder first, with a loud thud and a moan of excruciating pain. The frightened horse continued to gallop and drag Professor Hicks over the gravel road banging his head and upper body as he went, and with each bounce came another gut-wrenching moan.

Sam and Billy watched frozen with horror. How could such a supposedly funny trick go so wrong so quick? they wondered, as they watched the misadventure unfolding before them.

They watched poor Professor Hicks' bouncing body whiz past as they stood rooted to the ground. Not knowing what to do, Sam and Billy looked at one another with their mouths hanging open, huge unbelieving eyes, and terror showing on each boy's face.

A few yards ahead, several of the older boys had turned to see what had happened when they heard the professor's loud groan and all those that followed. Jimmy and Tommy White sprang into action as the galloping horse reached them. Jimmy leaped across the road, and he and Tommy grabbed the horse's head forcing it down to gain control of the runaway animal. Both boys drug their feet while shouting, "Whoa, Whoa!"

The horse obeyed and came to a halt within a few yards.

Several boys ran to the buggy and released the professor's pant leg. Another ran to fetch Doctor Adams.

The truth about what had frightened Professor Hicks and his horse soon came to light. The sheriff and several other townspeople had arrived on the scene to help Doc Adams get the professor to his office.

Sheriff Tully sent one of Billy's older brothers to get his pa. He told Billy and Sam to wait for him at his office.

JANE LISTENED INTENTLY AS BILLY'S PA TOLD HER ABOUT the two boys' shameful behavior. She looked at Sam and wondered what had come over the boy to make him act so irresponsibly. Then Mr. Johnson cleared up the matter for her.

"You know, Mrs. Parker, my boy has really looked up to Sam since that incident last summer with them outlaws. Billy's been thinking Sam is about the bravest boy around. It seems this rattlesnake venture gave Sam something else to brag about, and naturally Billy wanted to be a part of it too. I don't know how you feel about it, but I think these two boys need to be kept apart for a while to think about what they've done. Besides hurting the professor, there are three rattlesnakes crawling around with no rattlers to warn anyone they're about to strike. I believe these boys best stay away from the creek," Mr. Johnson suggested, in a somber tone.

"I agree, Mr. Johnson. I was so proud of Sam when he went for help but, now, I don't know what to think," Jane said, with a catch in her voice and a look that conveyed her disappointment in Sam's behavior.

"I reckon we best be going. Don't fret too much, Mrs. Parker; it'll all sort itself out soon enough," Mr. Johnson advised as he drove his wagon out of the yard.

Jane turned and looked at Sam for a long moment. She felt the anger build within her for what Sam had done. She felt she had failed in his upbringing for him to do such a despicable, irresponsible thing.

Sam ducked his head, not knowing what to say on his own behalf. He could plainly see the disappointment and anger reflected on his mother's face. There didn't seem to be anything he could say to defend his actions. He hadn't meant to hurt Professor Hicks, it just all went wrong, but Ma probably wouldn't think that was any excuse for what he had done, he reasoned.

Jane let out a long sigh. "Go to the barn," she said, as she turned toward the house.

Jane opened the trunk and dug to the bottom until she could feel the razor strop that had belonged to Samuel. She pulled it from beneath the clothing and grasped it firmly in her hand. Jane knew she had to punish Sam for what he had done. Oh, how she missed Samuel at times like this. He had rarely laid a hand on any of the children. They minded him with little question. Now especially, since Samuel had died, Sam had to know he had to mind her as well.

Jane slowly walked past Opal and Ruby, who were sitting quietly on the porch. She entered the barn and paused for her eyes to adjust to the shadows. Sam stood near the horse stall.

"Turn around and hold on to the stall door," she almost whispered. "I don't like this, Sam, but I have to do it."

She watched Sam slowly turn and grasp the top rail. He had not lifted his head or tried to speak on his own behalf.

Jane drew back the strop and delivered the first lick, the second, the third, and the fourth. The stinging blows seemed to echo through the old barn.

Sam cried out in pain and jumped with each blow. He did not beg his ma to stop but took the punishment more like a man than a boy.

As Jane drew the strap back for another lick a hand firmly seized her wrist. Before she could turn around, she heard his low voice.

"Jane," Seth almost whispered her name. He firmly grasped her wrist to prevent her from lashing Sam again.

Jane looked around with anger showing in her eyes, but she did not speak.

Seth continued to hold her wrist as he gently lowered it to her side. He could feel her trembling and wanted to put his arms around her in comfort, to reassure her she had done enough in punishing Sam. He wanted to hold her and—, what else? he asked himself.

Sam turned at the sound of Seth's voice and their eyes met.

Seth saw the hurt in Sam's eyes and sensed his plea for mercy, although, he had not uttered a word.

Seth spoke quietly. "Go on to the house, Sam," he said gently.

Sam hesitated only a second, gave his ma a quick look, and bolted through the barn door.

When Sam had gone Jane turned to Seth. "You had no right to step between me and Sam," she said softly as tears filled her eyes. Seth could hear the ache in her voice and understood her anxiety.

"I know, Jane, but I didn't want to let you do something you would regret."

Jane shot him a puzzled look. "I had to punish Sam for what he done. Do you know what he and Billy Johnson did?"

"Yes, I heard about it while I was in town."

"Do you also know there are three rattlesnakes crawling around with no rattlers to warn they are going to strike?" Jane asked near tears.

Seth could plainly see the heartfelt look of concern on her face and hear the genuine fear reflected in her voice. "Yes, I heard about that too, but you've punished Sam enough. He knows what he did was wrong. I learned the hard way in dealing with men that beating them into the ground is not always the right answer," Seth said as he let out a long breath. "Jane, if you beat Sam into submission, he will grow to hate you and may really rebel. When I first got a command, I thought that was the way to have the men respect me and follow my orders, but it wasn't. I soon learned that to gain their respect I needed to dole out fair, swift punishment, and then move on. You have done that, Jane. Please don't punish him more, it won't do him any good," Seth explained.

Jane sank onto the milking stool that stood nearby. She looked at the razor strop still clutched in her hand. She lifted her face to look at Seth. "It's a terrible thing to have to whip a child," she said, as more tears welled up in her eyes.

Seth knelt beside her and embraced her. They didn't have to speak. She just needed to be held for a time.

THE NEXT MORNING AS JANE AND THE GIRLS STARTED toward the Armstrongs', Jane noticed Sam limping toward the garden.

"Go on," she told the girls, "I need to tell Sam something."

Jane walked toward Sam and motioned him to come to her.

"Sam, are you hurt?" she asked.

Sam wanted to tell her no, but he knew she would know he was telling a lie and then he would be in more trouble.

"I'm just a little sore," he answered.

"Let me see, Sam."

Sam turned and lowered his pants just enough for Jane to see his backside.

Jane felt sick, a sickness like she had never felt before, when she saw the angry red whelps across his buttocks and lower back. Then the tears were stinging her eyes.

"Oh, Sam," she breathed. "I never meant to, to, mark you like this," she said, finding it hard to speak.

Sam did not turn but quietly replied, "I deserved it, Ma; I ain't mad at you. You gave me what I deserved."

"No, Sam, you didn't deserve this. I only meant to spank you, not mark you like I've done. I'm so sorry," Jane whispered and gave him a tender hug.

Then Jane gently laid her hand on Sam's shoulder and gave it an affectionate squeeze. Neither spoke.

She walked back to the house and found the razor strop lying on top of the trunk where she had flung it the day before. She rolled it up and crammed it into her apron pocket. She would give it to Seth and thank him for stopping her when he did, she decided, as she walked toward the Armstrongs'.

Chapter Six

About mid-morning that day, as Jane worked in the kitchen, she looked out the window and saw Seth alone by the corral. She walked to the corral and called his name, as he was about to mount up.

Seth turned at the sound of Jane's voice and saw the troubled look on her normally pleasant face.

He took a few steps toward her. "What is it, Jane?" he asked concerned.

Jane reached into her apron pocket and withdrew the razor strop. She handed it to him before she spoke.

"Thank you for stopping me when you did," she said without hesitation. "I marked Sam bad with this thing. Put it in the bunkhouse, and let it be used for what it was intended," she said, with anger aimed at herself as reflected in her voice.

Seth pulled her gently to him and enfolded her in his arms. "Oh, Jane, I know you didn't intend to hurt Sam, and I expect he knows that too. I'm glad I got there when I did," he uttered and gave her a gentle hug. Then he gently lifted her chin with one finger and looked into her anguished blue eyes for a long moment. He sensed her pain as he looked at the tears welling up in her eyes and her lips begin to tremble. "You carry quite a burden, Jane, and you can't always say, or always do, the exact right thing." Then he gently brushed her quivering lips with a soft kiss.

Seth momentarily lifted his head, and then he lowered it again and kissed her the way a man kisses a woman. He relished the warmth he felt from Jane's lips and the way her body seemed to mold to his.

When Seth kissed her for the second time, after a few moments, Jane wasn't sure if she was quivering from confessing what she had done to Sam or from the rekindling of long suppressed desires she felt within herself, and she sensed those desires mounting in Seth. She savored the warmth of his strong arm holding her snug to his muscular body and breathed in the faint smell of his bath soap. He was an appealing man, but Jane had a feeling this needed to stop.

Jane quickly pulled away and stepped back from Seth. She felt her cheeks heating with a blush. She searched for the right words, as she didn't want to hurt Seth in any way. He had been so good to her and for her these past months. She put her hands to her rosy cheeks and said with a small laugh, "Oh my, here we are actin' like two young people carrying on in broad daylight."

Seth just looked at her and then understood that he had probably acted too hastily. "Jane, I'm sorry, I had no call to kiss you like that. I know it hasn't been all that long since your husband passed, and I—I just should have never done that."

Jane ducked her head, too embarrassed to look Seth in the eyes, "No, it hasn't been all that long, and I don't want you to get the wrong idea about the kind of woman I am."

Seth gently laid his hand on her shoulder, "Jane, I know what kind of woman you are. I was the one wrong, not you. I hope you can forgive my impulsive behavior," he pleaded.

Jane hesitated a few seconds then answered, "Yes, yes, I can do that," she answered softly.

Seth turned, mounted, and rode out of the yard.

Jane looked after him for several minutes. He is a fine man, she thought. Maybe in time I could learn to love him, but if he goes back to the army, I just don't know. She turned and walked briskly back to the house.

JIM ARMSTRONG STOOD IN THE SHADOWS OF THE WORK shed to give Seth time to ride out and Jane time to return to the house before he left his obscure place in the shed.

He was a bit taken aback when he started outside and saw Seth and Jane in an affectionate embrace. He knew Seth had spent several evenings enjoying Jane's fine cooking at her house. Jim supposed Seth enjoyed her company as well, but somehow it had never occurred to him that Seth or Jane, for that matter, had developed feelings for one another other than friendship.

Jim decided he would mention what he saw to Bea in strictest confidence and see what she knew or thought about the situation.

Chapter Seven

About noon the man driving a sleek black two-seated buggy pulled by a matching team of horses drove into Clairette. He stopped on the edge of town and asked directions. He then continued on the main road into the bustling business district and soon spotted the sign that read "Sheriff's Office."

Sheriff Tully glanced up just as the handsome buggy came to a stop in front of his office. He keenly observed the well-dressed gentleman in a finely tailored gray business suit. As the man stepped down from the buggy, the sheriff observed his unusual height. The man was most impressive with his striking good looks, slightly graying hair, and no less than six foot three or four inches in height.

That must be him, the sheriff thought as he stood and walked to the door to meet the stranger.

"Good day to you, sir," Sheriff Tully greeted as he opened the door.

"Good day to you also," the man returned in a deep baritone voice. He extended his hand to the sheriff and gave a hardy handshake. "I am Brent Towns from Fort Worth."

Sheriff Tully smiled, stood aside, and motioned the man inside. "I figured that might be who you were."

"Have a seat," the sheriff invited. He pulled a sturdy wooden chair near his desk for Brent Towns.

When the two men were seated, each with a stout cup of coffee brewed earlier in the day, the sheriff looked directly at his visitor. "I need you to explain to me just why you want to meet Mrs. Parker and her boy. I ain't putting up with anybody coming here to upset her after what she and her family's been through," the sheriff said, in his no nonsense manner.

"I assure you, Sheriff, that I have no desire to upset Mrs. Parker or her son. In some way I hope to do just the opposite. I will tell you the entire story, and then you will understand why I have come to find Mrs. Parker. However, I must insist on your strictest confidence in this matter. I do not even want Mrs. Parker to know the entire matter, and once you have heard me out, I am sure you will understand the reason I am asking you for your confidentiality," Brent emphasized. He looked Sheriff Tully in the face to help him judge if he could trust this man. In what Brent saw he found no reason for doubt.

"I'm listening," Sheriff Tully responded.

From time-to-time Towns would stand and pace the small office while telling his story. Once he walked to the front window and stared out at the busy street. He did not speak for several minutes, and when he continued the sheriff could hear the agony in his voice. Sheriff Tully remained seated, watching, and listening, sizing him up before he would consent to take him to meet Jane Parker.

After about an hour of listening to Mr. Towns, the sheriff leaned back in his chair and looked at Mr. Towns for a long moment. "That's a damn shame to have happen to anybody," Sheriff Tully commented as he shook his head and rubbed his day's growth of whiskers with his right hand. "I'll go with you tomorrow morning out to the Armstrong place to meet Mrs. Parker. It will probably be better to talk with her while the youngsters are in school."

Brent Towns nodded in agreement.

"I'll let you do the talking but do spare Mrs. Parker the gory details you have told me. She doesn't need to know that and dwell on what might have happened at her house."

"I totally agree."

The sheriff stood and stretched his legs, "Why don't you go on over to the hotel and rest up from your trip? We'll leave about eight o'clock in the morning."

THE NEXT MORNING AT PRECISELY EIGHT O'CLOCK, SEVERAL businessmen and other citizens saw Sheriff Tully riding out of town followed close behind by a well-dressed stranger in a fine-looking buggy drawn by matching horses. This scene spurred the curiosity of all who witnessed it except Fred Hollis, the local baker. The only thing that interested Fred Hollis was who walked through the door of his bakery to spend part of their hard-earned money.

Jim Armstrong looked out of the barn when he heard his two dogs barking to see Sheriff Tully riding into the yard followed by a man driving a sleek-looking buggy. He naturally wondered what could be bringing the sheriff and this stranger out to his place.

"Morning, Sheriff," Jim called from across the yard.

"Morning, Jim," Sheriff Tully called back as he dismounted.

The two dogs were still barking at the man in the buggy, who had not moved from his secure place out of reach of their bared teeth.

"He's okay, call them dang dogs off," the sheriff hollered at Jim above the melee.

Jim gave a shrill whistle and the dogs immediately turned and ran to him. "Let me put them in the barn," Jim called, as he and the dogs retreated to the barn.

When Jim returned the sheriff introduced him to Brent Towns and briefly told Jim why Towns wanted to meet Jane.

Soon the three men, Jane, and Bea were seated around the big round dining table. Bea and Jane served coffee and freshly baked cinnamon rolls. Brent noticed this coffee was a large improvement over what the sheriff had served the previous day.

Sheriff Tully removed his hat and ran his fingers through his graying hair. Tully had been sheriff in Clairette for more than fifteen years. In those first years he had worn his badge with pride and backed it up without hesitation. Many folks gave him credit for taming Clairette. He had watched it grow from a wild cow town to a pleasant farming community with relatively few disturbances in recent years. The sheriff cleared his throat as he looked at each person seated around the table. "Mr. Towns is from Fort Worth and has some information about Jackson Polk he would like to tell us," he said, as he nodded toward Towns.

Brent Towns nodded his head slightly to the group who were collectively focused on him.

"I am not sure where to begin, but I think the end may be the best place to start," he said. He closely observed the three faces trained on him. "In late August Jackson Polk stood trial for the crimes he committed in Fort Worth of which you are somewhat aware. He was given life in prison."

The others at the table seemed to all breathe a collective sigh of relief.

"Oh, thank the good Lord for that," Bea said aloud, as she squeezed Jane's hand. "No more worrying about him coming back here to cause any more trouble."

"That is good news," Jane agreed. It was plain for all to see that was truly a load off of her mind.

"I felt you would want to know what had finally become of Polk," Towns commented.

Brent paused, and then continued, "I am also here on behalf of the young woman who was unfortunately violated by those two men. Her family has strived to protect her from as much public knowledge of the incident as possible and have asked me to represent them in this matter." Towns looked directly at Jane as he continued. "The young lady's family wishes to express their eternal gratitude to you folks for aiding in catching those two despicable outlaws. They wish to bestow a reward of five hundred dollars to be divided among those involved in the arrest of those two men."

Jane, Bea, and Jim looked at Brent Towns with their mouths gaping in astonishment.

Jane had never heard of such a thing as being rewarded by a family for helping catch a criminal. She thought only the bank or railroad did those kinds of things.

Jim was the first to collect his thoughts and find his voice. "Mr. Towns, that is a mighty generous gesture you are speaking of, but I could not accept their money."

"Why not, Mr. Armstrong?" Towns questioned, a bit puzzled.

"I just—I was only helping my neighbor and would do so for any neighbor that needed my help. I don't expect to be paid for being a good neighbor and law-abiding citizen."

"But, Mr. Armstrong, you and your hired hands could have been in great danger getting Jackson Polk out of Mrs. Parker's house and then tracking down Lewis Boston. Luckily they were too drunk to cause as much trouble as they might have had they been sober."

Jim remained silent for a few minutes as though thinking over what Mr. Towns had said. "You could well be right, Mr. Towns. I would like for the five hundred dollars to be split between Jane and the two men that helped me that night. I have been quite blessed material wise," Jim said, as he looked around his comfortable home. "Jane and my hired men could sure use some extra cash," he said appreciatively.

"That will be fine, sir, they are most deserving," Towns acknowledged with a nod of his head.

Jim turned to Jane before she could speak. "Jane, you and your fine family could certainly use that money so don't you hesitate to accept it. Those children have many needs, and I know what we pay you is barely enough to get by on," he said, almost in a fatherly manner.

Jane ducked her head, as though a bit embarrassed about accepting the money, but then looked up at those around her. "Yes, I surely could use that money for my family, but I never expected to be paid for doing what I done. I was just trying to protect my family," she added with modesty.

Brent Towns looked at Jane with great benevolence in his heart. He knew she must have been having a difficult time supporting herself and her children. The sheriff had told him about her circumstances.

He would be willing to do far more for her and her family, but he had the uneasy feeling she would totally refuse any reward if he offered too much. Instead, he beseeched her in another manner. "Mrs. Parker, it isn't pay, it is a gift of gratitude for what you and your young son did to help catch those two contemptible men. I would also like to extend a small reward to your son."

"Oh, no, what you have offered is more than enough," Jane protested.

"The reward I have for your son is not money, but a gift, and I would hate to have to keep it as I would truly look silly riding a bicycle around Fort Worth," he said with a smile.

"Oh, my," Jane breathed. "Oh my, Sam will be so—so excited, so happy. He has dreamed of having a bicycle. That is very generous but way too much," she tried to insist, but everyone could tell she really wanted Sam to have the bicycle.

Mr. Towns gently laid his hand on Jane's hand and implored her with his look and tone, "Mrs. Parker, I have not had the pleasure of meeting your son, but I am sure he is a fine young lad and must be brave to boot."

Jane instantly thought of the rattlesnake episode but said aloud, "Oh yes, sometimes he is too brave for his own good, but you're right, he is a fine lad. I know he will take good care of the bicycle. Thank you."

Mr. Towns started to stand but Bea interrupted his movement when she looked directly at him and asked, "Would you tell us a little more about what those two men did in Fort Worth?"

Brent Towns glanced at Sheriff Tully who gave a slight nod of his head.

"Yes, Ma'am, I can tell you briefly what took place in Fort Worth. A young couple that had only married about six months previously was in the process of building a fine new home on the outskirts of the city. Most of the work was complete, and, of course, they were anxious to move into their lovely house. Along the back on the upper floor was some work that had not been completed thus leaving the house vulnerable to easy entry. Apparently, Boston and Polk had been watching the house and saw where they could get in undetected. One night, around two in the morning, they used a ladder to gain entry to the back of the house. Since it was a large home, their presence was not known until they burst into the young couple's bedroom and easily overpowered them as they slept."

Jane let out an "Oh!" and placed her hand over her face as though trying to block out the ugly images that were sure to come when she heard what Brent said.

All eyes turned toward Jane.

Mr. Towns looked at the sheriff for guidance.

Sheriff Tully cleared his throat, "Maybe that is all we need to hear."

Jane shook her head. "No, I want to hear the rest of what Mr. Towns has to say. I know it was lucky I was awake and could get the drop on them before they could attack us. Please go on," Jane insisted.

"Yes, please go on," Bea added.

Jim remained silent but had slipped his arm protectively around his wife.

Sheriff Tully nodded again for Brent Towns to continue his account of the attack.

Brent continued on silently hoping he would not lose his own composure. "The two men tied up the man and demanded to know where he kept any money, which he told them. Then they rifled through jewelry boxes, stuffing their pockets with the couple's finest jewelry. The couple didn't care what they took just so they would leave. But then," Brent paused, cleared his throat, and wiped his brow with his handkerchief, "the two men had been eyeing the young lady as they rifled through their things. It seems Lewis Boston decided he wanted to have his way with her and when her husband tried to bribe him to leave it just seemed to spur him on to, to, attack her." Brent Towns paused again when he felt his voice choke and took a few deep breaths.

Jane sensed his difficulty in telling this part of the events.

"Sir," Jane's soft voice conveyed her sympathy for his discomfort, "if it is too painful for you to speak of these matters, please do not go on."

Towns gave Jane an appreciative look. "I would like to finish," he said simply. "It seems Jackson Polk, under Boston's directions, dealt the young man several harsh blows and further prevented him from protecting his wife. Polk says that only Lewis Boston attacked her, and the couple confirmed his story. Nonetheless, it was a terrible ordeal for the young couple. The lady has been under the care of the finest doctors and the couple recently relocated in the event the story gets around Fort Worth."

"My, oh my," Bea whispered as she shook her head and leaned closer to Jim's comforting embrace.

Jane wiped a tear from her cheek and ducked her head in an attempt to hide her emotions from those seated around the table. She inwardly shuddered at the thought of what might have happened to her family. What if they had attacked Opal or even little Ruby? What if Sam had been killed going for help? Could she have had the courage to go on living? So many horrible thoughts swam through her brain that her head soon began to pound. Even after hearing Mr. Towns' story it was hard to believe such scum roamed the country ready to pounce on any innocent person that caught their attention.

Finally, Sheriff Tully broke the silence that seemed to engulf those present. "Mr. Towns and I best be getting back to town," he said, as he rose from the table.

"One last bit of business, please, before we go," Brent Towns said, as he remained seated.

"Mr. Armstrong, could you spare Mrs. Parker and the two men that are to receive the reward for a few hours tomorrow?"

Jim gave an affirmative nod of his head.

"Perhaps they could meet me at the bank about noon and I will have their money ready."

"That will be fine with me," Jane agreed.

"Good, then I'll see you and the others tomorrow." Towns nodded to Jane as he rose and followed Sheriff Tully out.

As Brent Towns drove the buggy behind the sheriff back to Clairette he thought about the details of the unfortunate episode that he did not share with the others and even some he had not told the sheriff. It would have served no useful purpose.

He did not say the young woman's husband had begged the two men to leave with money, jewels, and anything else of monetary value they desired just leave and not touch his wife in any way. He implored them to leave as his wife was expecting a child, and their presence was upsetting her. He groveled, he begged for mercy for his wife's safety, not his own.

It seemed the more he begged the more Lewis Boston took pleasure in tormenting the young husband. Early on Jackson Polk had also tried to get Boston to be satisfied with the spoils they had found and leave before the situation became truly ugly. Boston railed at Polk to just shut up and follow his orders. Polk soon surrendered to Boston's demands.

The young husband was forced to watch, listen, and perhaps endure as much pain and humiliation as his young wife, for he was unable to save her from this horrific assault.

The final parting act of barbarous disregard for the woman he had violently ravaged was when Lewis Boston turned to her broken husband and snarled, "Pregnant, ha, ha!" Then he doubled his fist and brutally slammed it into her stomach. The devastated couple could hear Boston laughing, and laughing, and laughing, as he and Polk retreated down the long dark hallway.

The trial had been held behind closed doors to protect the young couple. The woman and her husband had not appeared in court as further precaution against their identity being discovered.

The story was told that, while the young couple was dining with her family, their lovely new home burned to the ground. As a result of the shock the poor dear lady suffered a miscarriage. The few people that saw her after that were not surprised to see her looking so gaunt and appearing so jittery.

The young couple supposedly decided it would be in their best interest to move to a new location. They needed a place for a fresh start with no reminders of the sadness that had occurred in their lives from the loss of their child and home. It was a plausible story that no one seemed to question.

Brent Towns wondered why such utterly unnecessary atrocities occurred. Why them, he often wondered? He prayed daily that his youngest daughter and her husband could weather this horrific storm. He prayed for them to be strong. He prayed for their love to grow even deeper for one another. He knew in his heart that what had happened, though the fault of neither, could so easily destroy what had started out so good, so loving, so, so, so—he wiped a tear from the corner of his eye with the back of his hand. For the first time since his beloved wife's passing, he thanked God she was not there to witness what had happened to their precious daughter. Then, through much practice, he forced himself to think of other matters.

JANE COULD NOT KEEP HERSELF FROM SMILING AS SHE LEFT the bank. She now had one hundred and sixty-six dollars in the bank. She had never had any money except what it took to live on from month to month. Jane felt rich although she knew in reality she was not. It was such a comforting feeling, but she knew she would have to use the money very sparingly.

During both marriages they had hardly scraped by, and there were several times when they wondered where their next meal would come from. Luckily Peter and Samuel were both good hunters and fishermen. Often, whatever they could manage to kill or catch provided their next meal and, if they were lucky, more than one meal. Now it was wholly up to her to be the provider, and many nights she lay awake thinking about that almost overwhelming responsibility. Sam was quickly becoming more help. He was becoming a hunter and fisherman like his father and the game he brought home certainly helped provide for their family.

"Mrs. Parker," she heard Brent Towns calling her name. She turned and saw him coming out of the bank behind the other two men that had received the reward money. He quickly caught up with Jane.

"Would you consider joining me for lunch at the hotel?" he asked, with a flicker of a kind smile.

Jane had planned to return to the ranch as soon as the business at the bank was completed, but she felt it would be rude to refuse after what he had just done for her. "I would be pleased to have lunch with you, Mr. Towns," she returned with a smile.

LATE MORNING SETH RODE IN AND SAID HE HAD TO GO TO town to do some business. This came as a surprise to Jim as Seth had not mentioned anything earlier about going into town.

Seth arrived in town near noon. He looked around to see if he could find Jane. He had it in his mind to take her to lunch and spend some time with her away from the ranch. He spotted her about halfway down the block near the bank, but he quickly realized she was walking with Brent Towns toward the restaurant in the hotel. He thought about inviting himself to join them but then thought better of that idea. He had to admit to himself that he felt a pang of jealousy at the thought of her sharing lunch with Brent Towns.

Seth turned and sauntered down the street toward the general store where he looked around for a short time. He decided he might as well have some lunch and get back to the ranch. After all, it was none of his business if Jane had lunch with Brent Towns or the mayor, for that matter. After the intimate kiss they had shared recently he couldn't help feeling a bit jealous and didn't like that feeling. He reminded himself that he needed to control his feelings better. Besides, it was likely he would return to the army before long, so he needed to stop thinking about Jane so much.

Seth sat alone in a small café and ate a dry steak.

As he walked slowly toward the livery, he noticed the hotel was just ahead. He forgot all about his recent lecture to himself. Seth pushed the door open that led to the lobby. Cautiously he peered around some large plant into the dining room. He quickly located Jane and Towns seated near the front windows. She was smiling, as he seemed to be telling her an amusing story. Then she laughed and Towns laughed with her. Seth took several steps in their direction but, before he could make a complete fool of himself, turned on his heel and headed out the door. Seth walked briskly toward the livery stable.

All the way back to the ranch Seth cautioned himself about getting too involved with Jane.

Chapter Eight

On Friday of the third week of October, Jim and Seth joined Bea and Jane at lunch instead of eating with the men.

"Jane, Seth and I are planning a trip out west in a few days and wondered if you and the children could stay with Bea until we return. Our neighbor has been talking about free land being offered in Jones County and we want to check it out," Jim said.

"Free land?" Jane repeated, thinking about what she could do with some free land but doubted they would give land to a woman.

"I hope to buy more land to build a ranch on. Bea and I hope you and the children will move west with us if this works out."

Jane was taken aback by this news.

"Mr. Armstrong, you don't have to be taking me and the children with you. I'm sure I can find some kind of work here."

Jim leaned back in his chair and smiled. "Oh yes, I do, Jane, or Bea won't go one step west with me," he said, as he gave his wife a knowing look.

"That's right, I've already told him that if Jane and those children aren't part of this big plan then just count me out," Bea said, with a smug look.

"You might as well plan on moving if Pa finds good land out west," Seth confirmed. "Pa and Mom won't have it any other way."

Jane hesitated briefly, "Well, I don't suppose there's anything to hold me here. If I could get some land near a town, then maybe I could raise a big garden and sell vegetables to the town folks," Jane said, with a wistful smile.

Seth remembered their conversation not long ago about their dreams for their lives.

Then she looked at Jim and Seth with concern. "What about school? There'll have to be a school wherever I go."

"We'll see about the school too," Seth assured her. "Now don't be worrying, we'll find out all kinds of things and tell you two ladies all about it when we get back."

Jane still wasn't quite satisfied. "How far is it to Jones County?"

Seth rubbed his face with his hand as he thought about her question. "Oh, I expect it's about a hundred 'n twenty miles or maybe a little more."

"Oh, no!" Jane exclaimed in horror. "Aren't there still wild Indians roaming around out there?" she asked. She had a look of alarm on her face.

Seth was surprised at Jane's question but smiled and shook his head. "No, no, the wild Indians have been gone a long time from that area. What made you think there were still wild Indians in Texas?"

Jane looked relieved but still concerned. "Well, I don't know, but I sure don't want to take any chances. What about outlaws?"

"I couldn't say for sure, but it is probably about like here. I expect they have marshals and other lawmen out in that area to keep the peace," Seth tried to sound reassuring.

Jane thought for a minute and then answered. "I guess there can be outlaws anywhere, we sure had some here."

A hundred and twenty miles sounded like an awfully long ways to move. No telling how long it would take, and they wouldn't ever get to come back to see their friends here, she reflected, as she pondered the trip.

Jane had one more question but was a bit reluctant to ask for fear Jim would think she was being out of place. Finally, she steeled herself and asked, "What will you do with this place, if I might ask?"

"Of course, you can ask," Jim told her warmly. "Frank Sorenson has been trying to buy this place for three years and will pay me a fair price. If I can get some free land and then use part of the money I get for this place to buy more land, well, that will work out real well. Here there isn't enough affordable land to expand the ranch. From what I hear there is not only the free land but also plenty of cheaper land out West. If we get there ahead of the railroad, then we can buy land real reasonable. Once the railroad comes then the people come, and land prices will go up just like here."

Jim cleared his throat and looked at Bea. "Bea and I have one more request," he said, as he looked back at Jane.

"What is it?" Jane asked, as she looked first at Jim and then at Bea.

"Well, we've come to feel that you and the children are almost a part of our family. We would like for you to call us Jim and Bea and let the children call us Aunt Bea and Uncle Jim, if that would be all right with you?"

Jim and Bea were both closely watching Jane to gauge her reaction to their request.

Jane smiled, "I too feel like you have become a part of my family since Samuel and Pearl passed, and you have been so kind to us. I'll be glad to call you by your given names, and I know the children will be happy to call you Aunt and Uncle," Jane answered, as she gave Bea and then Jim a brief hug. It will give the children a sense of family and perhaps more security, she thought, grateful that Bea and Jim had accepted them as part of their family. It was certainly a comforting feeling for Jane.

Seth smiled at the three and said, "You can call me Your Handsome Lordship."

They all laughed.

MONDAY MORNING JIM AND SETH LEFT AT SUNUP HEADED west. They each led a packhorse loaded with camping gear and food staples for the trip. They would hunt for small game and fish along the way.

Erath County was the transition between the east Texas timberland and the prairie land. They passed through the flatlands of the river bottoms that were filled with elm, cottonwood, river birch, ash, and several varieties of oak trees. They would seek the best place to ford the river or creek by one riding each direction until one of them found a suitable crossing. The signal would be one gunshot. They would join up again and continue their westward journey. The rest of the county was covered by low flat-topped hills. Between the hills were lower areas of flat grassland conducive to grazing small herds of cattle or sheep. The men worked their way between the hills looking for the best route for the wagons and cattle. Seth drew a crude map as they went along to mark their path and the best river crossings. They kept as straight a westerly direction as possible as they knew if they veered too far north into Palo Pinto or Stephens County, it would make travel too rugged for the wagon and cattle. The hills were steep and covered by thick woods and undergrowth.

They would stop and talk to farmers and people in the scarce settlements about the best route to follow.

Late in the evening of the second day they reached the railroad that crossed from southeast to northwest through Eastland County. About mid-afternoon the wind had shifted from the southeast to the north with an increasing chill toward sunset.

Jim pulled his coat closed and buttoned it against the increasingly cold wind. "I think we better look for some shelter for tonight," he told Seth as he shivered.

"I see some buildings up ahead; might be we can bunk in their barn," Seth answered, as he pointed in the direction they were headed.

As they rode into the yard of a dilapidated farmhouse a sinewy man stepped out onto the front porch with a rifle resting across his arm.

After proper introductions Jim and Seth were welcomed into the man's home for a fine meal his wife had prepared and then bedded down in the barn for the night.

They rode on early the next morning headed toward Albany.

EVERYTHING AROUND THE RANCH AND IN THE HOUSE continued to run smoothly. On Thursday a thunderstorm was building in the north, so one of the hands took the wagon to town to pick up the children at school and get a few supplies and the mail.

By the time they returned, the wind had picked up from the North and the temperature was dropping. Ruby huddled near the cook stove to warm herself. "Do we have to go to school tomorrow if it's still cold and raining?" she asked her mother, hoping the answer would be no.

"Not if it is too bad, but we'll just have to wait and see what happens between now and then," Jane replied. "You better get your homework, just in case you do go tomorrow," Jane reminded her.

Ruby sat at the table humming while she worked her math problems. Occasionally she would ask Jane for some help but could do most of her homework by herself.

Sam came in the door rubbing his cold hands together. "Oh yeah, I almost forgot, here's a letter for you, Ma, and one for Aunt Bea."

Jane took her letter and told Sam to go find Bea and give her the letter. Jane sat down at the kitchen table with her letter. She noticed it was from her cousin, Opal. When she opened the letter a piece of paper fell out on the table. Jane picked it up and looked at it in disbelief. She quickly read the letter. When she finished, she rose and went to find Bea.

Bea had just finished reading her own letter when Jane came and sat beside her. "Listen to this, Bea," Jane said, as she unfolded the letter.

Dear Cousin Jane,
I know this will come as a shock to you. Before Papa passed, he told me to sell everything he owned and divide the money between us three girls, Bo, and you. I think Papa would be surprised to know what his land, house, and stock were worth. He always thought of you as one of us too. I did as he asked, and this is your part. I know you can use some extra money, and Papa and Mama would be happy to know they are helping you and your children. I don't know where to write to Bo so will keep his part in the bank until I hear from him again.
I love and miss you.
Opal

Jane handed the bank draft to Bea.

Bea looked at it with shock. "One hundred and thirty-two dollars! Jane, that's wonderful, just wonderful! Now you really have a nest egg," Bea almost shouted as she gave Jane a hug.

"I just don't know what to think," Jane answered, with a look of awe on her face. "A month ago, I didn't have two nickels to rub together and now I have, let's see, I have almost three hundred dollars. I can hardly believe I have some money. I really have some money." In her elation, Jane didn't know whether to laugh or cry or do both.

JIM AND SETH CONTINUED THEIR NORTHWESTWARD movement, following the railroad that would eventually lead them to Albany. The railroad kept a fairly straight northwesterly path between the low-lying hills. They determined there was enough cleared land to herd the cattle, and it would be much easier traveling for the wagons.

Late on the fourth evening they reached the small but raucous town of Albany that had been established in 1874. The county seat was moved from Fort Griffin to Albany. In 1881 the Texas Central Railroad had extended as far west as Albany. It had become an important shipping point for cattle and other goods headed east and building materials and other needed supplies and equipment headed west.

Jim was right, once the railroad expanded farther west, the prices of land would skyrocket so now was the time to get settled.

Jim and Seth found a room at a small, but clean, boarding house. They walked down the main street looking in the shop windows and eventually found a café that advertised the best steaks west of Fort Worth. They enjoyed a leisurely meal and talked to several of the locals about the free land they had heard about in Jones County. What they had heard was confirmed by several of the men. Eighty acres was to be given to new settlers, along with the right to homestead and purchase other land. They were advised to follow the old trail west to the Clear Fork of the Brazos River and to look for Lieb's Crossing. They were warned to keep on the right-hand fork of the trail when it split, or they would find themselves bogged down in the shifting sand of the big shinnery just east of the river. The shinnery was full of scrubby brush, mostly shin oak and cat claw.

They followed the advice they had received and found Lieb's Crossing toward the end of the fifth day. They made camp on the bank of the Clear Fork of the Brazos River and watched its slow-moving waters ripple over its rocky bottom. The crossing was shallow, and the bottom was covered with a nice layer of small rocks and a few clearly visible larger rocks. The riverbanks were lined with thick clumps of elm, cottonwood, and pecan trees. From here it wouldn't be a full day's ride to the small settlement where they could look at the abundance of grassland.

After supper the two men sat by their campfire, each enjoying a cup of coffee. Seth rolled a cigarette and offered it to Jim. Then he rolled one for himself. Neither man smoked much but relaxing by the campfire seemed like a good time to enjoy a smoke.

The katydids were singing in the trees. At times their crescendo was almost deafening. Jim looked up at a stately old elm tree growing near the edge of the water. "Man, I'll bet that old tree could tell some tales about this part of the country," he mused.

Seth glanced at the tree that seemed to stand out on its own. "Yeah, I expect it could. Probably lots of Indian hunting parties camped here before and after hunting buffalo. The women most likely gathered the pecans and the children caught a few fish."

"Now the buffalo and elk are about gone," Jim said, with a sigh of regret. "Things keep changing, and changing, but I guess that's what you call progress."

"Yes, and things will change even more when the railroad comes on west," Seth commented.

"Just listen to them coyotes baying in the distance," Jim said. "Thirty years ago, I would've been wondering if it was really coyotes yelping or if it was Indians lurking around in the dark getting ready to attack us," Jim continued.

Seth chuckled, "Yeah, and thirty years ago there wouldn't have been just two of you sitting by a blazing campfire making a good target, just in case it was Indians."

"That's for damn sure," Jim answered and chuckled.

They stretched out in their bedrolls but neither seemed ready to fall asleep. Each man was lost in his own thoughts about the past and the changes to come.

THEY AWOKE EARLY AND MADE COFFEE OVER A SMALL campfire that felt good in warding off the morning chill. After breakfast they rode past a small settlement on the west side of the Clear Fork.

The land became almost flat and was covered in grass and clumps of scrubby mesquite trees. Travel was much easier, and it seemed you could see for miles and miles in any direction.

Early afternoon they reached the small community on the eastern edge of the vast Swenson Ranch. This was their destination. They found the land office and were shown a map of the available land. Most of the unclaimed land was to the south and southwest. Not being tired and anxious to see the land they rode to the south for over an hour and then to the west. When they arrived back in town, they found a suitable place to camp for the night. They talked about the land they had seen and decided if Jim could homestead one hundred and sixty acres, get eighty acres of free land, and buy another thousand acres, that would be enough land to start a good paying ranch. They also decided that Jim would sell Jane ten acres of his land that was just on the south edge of the community. It had a good spring for water. On the other property there was a flowing creek and several small springs that were probably seasonal. When the deal was complete, they were ready to head home with all the news about their future home.

Chapter Nine

Late on the following Saturday evening, Jim and Seth returned from their trip. They all gathered around the dining table after supper for the two men to tell the ladies, ranch hands, and children about what they had found out west.

The group listened intently as the men described their trip. "The farther west you go, the flatter the land becomes," Seth told them. "There are fewer trees except along the creeks, but other than that it is mostly scrub mesquites. The grass is a bit thinner but plenty good for grazing. It'll just take a few more acres for the cattle than it does around here but there is plenty of good land."

"We talked to ranchers and farmers along the way to figure out the best route to take and to have plenty of water for the cattle," Jim put in. "We will travel west between the hills and about halfway across Eastland County we'll meet the railroad. We'll trail it northwest to Albany in Shackelford County. From there we travel west to Lieb's Crossing on the Clear Fork of the Brazos River. The rest of the trip is on almost flat land. It will probably take us about nine days if all goes well."

"Where is Albany?" Bea asked.

"It's about eighteen or twenty miles this side of the Clear Fork of the Brazos River. That is as far as the railroad goes for now. We were told there is a big rancher by the name of Swenson in Jones County that is pushing for the railroad to come to his ranch so he can ship cattle from there instead of having to drive them to Albany," Jim said, with a slight shake of his head. "Yeah, Swenson has thousands and thousands of acres, we're told."

"Thousands!" Sam repeated.

Jim nodded, "Yeah, thousands. From the Clear Fork it is about another twenty miles to the property we looked at and bought," Jim said with a big smile. He looked at Bea, "it's gonna make a fine ranch, Honey Bea."

"I have no doubts you made the right decision," Bea said, as she returned Jim's smile.

Jim looked at Bea and Jane who were seated next to each other at the big table. "I was able to homestead one hundred and sixty acres, got eighty acres free, and put a down payment on another thousand acres to go with it. Forty cents an acre is what land is going for now and when the railroad comes it will double in price in no time. There is a good creek running through it and several small springs. I expect it will support four or five cows per acre. This land starts about a half mile south of a small settlement," he smiled. Jim saw the growing expressions of excitement on their faces.

"Jane, Seth and I have talked it over and decided I will sell you ten acres of land for your garden. A good flowing spring will separate our properties," Jim said. A big grin lit his face when he saw Jane's delighted expression.

"Ten acres! I don't need ten acres to raise a garden," Jane said in astonishment.

"We also thought you might want to consider planting some fruit trees on part of your land. With ten acres you'll have space to expand your business as it grows," Seth told her and smiled at her expression of sheer happiness.

"I never thought about that, but it is a good idea," Jane admitted.

Jane and Bea looked at each other with expressions of almost disbelief. Then they hugged with tears of joy rolling down their cheeks.

"That's wonderful, just, just wonderful," was all Jane could manage to say.

"When do we move?" Ruby asked with enthusiasm. Her eyes sparkled, and she giggled with glee.

"Oh, not until winter has passed," Seth answered.

Ruby, Opal, and Sam all gave a united, "Oooh!" of disappointment.

"Why do we have to wait till after winter?" Ruby persisted.

"Well, when we first get there, we'll need good grass for the cattle. We'll also have to live in tents until we can build houses," Jim explained.

Ruby jumped up and down giggling more. "Oh goodie, we get to live in a tent," she squealed with delight.

Jim saw the expression on Opal's face was just the opposite of Ruby's.

Opal turned to her Mother with a horrified look, "Mama, do we have to live in a tent?" she asked almost in tears.

"Well, where else would we live?"

"Couldn't we find a place in the settlement?" Opal pleaded.

Seth shook his head, "Afraid not, there didn't seem to be anything for rent. We didn't even see a rooming house, so we camped out."

Opal's tears began to flow, and her voice quivered slightly, "We'll be like those kids that came to school a while back. They lived in a tent and they were dirty and stunk!"

"Opal, that is not a very nice thing to say," Jane scolded her daughter.

"It's true, Mama," Sam came to her defense. "They smelled so bad we had to leave the windows open even when it was cold outside."

"We won't be like that just because we live in a tent," Jane assured them. "We'll live just like we do now, only with different outside walls."

"Mama's right, Opal, we don't have to be like those folks," Sam tried to appease his sister. "You'll see, it won't be so bad."

Sleep eluded Jane. She thought about the many changes that would occur in their lives by moving to Jones County and starting her own business. While it was exciting, it was also frightening to leave the security of what she knew. She thought about Opal's reaction to living in a tent for a while. She felt sorry that Opal felt it degrading. At least Ruby was excited about it and Sam didn't seem to mind either. After hearing the old mantel clock strike midnight, Jane finally fell asleep.

SETH SAT ON THE SIDE OF HIS BED SMOKING ANOTHER cigarette. As tired as he was from the trip, he should have fallen asleep hours ago but here he sat in the dark thinking about going back to the army, Jane starting a new business, poor Opal's reaction to living in a tent, and on and on. He also pondered whether to speak to Jane now about another alternative to the move to Jones County, or perhaps it would be better to wait until he came back in March to help with the move.

Chapter Ten

The morning Seth rode north toward Fort Worth to reenlist in the army, the wind had shifted during the night and was bearing down with a vengeance. Occasional rain showers added to the misery of the gloomy November day.

Seth had hoped for a few minutes alone with Jane before he left but it was not to be. His parents and several hands as well as Jane came out in the cold wind to see him off. He had merely nodded his good-byes to everyone and said he would write as soon as he was settled. He did take a quick look at Jane as he had longed for just a moment of privacy to touch her cheek or give her hand a gentle squeeze. There were things he wanted to say but had not decided exactly what they were or when would be the best time to say anything about his growing feelings for her.

As he rode, with his hat brim pulled down to avoid the wind as much as possible, his thoughts were still consumed with Jane. Was he falling in love with her, he wondered? She definitely affected him in the way a woman affects a man. As for love he wasn't sure what all was involved in love. Desire, yes. The longing for her company more than any other woman's company, yes. Seeking her affection and giving her affection in return, yes. Was there more? He wasn't sure. He rode on pondering the wherefores of love but not finding any clear-cut answers.

JANE WATCHED AS SETH RODE AWAY WITH HIS HAT PULLED low in an attempt to shield himself from the blustering north wind. Just before he rode off Jane was aware of his eyes on her and wondered about the strange look. She would miss Seth in many ways. She so enjoyed his easy company. He was a good man, good with the children, especially Sam. Sam seemed to respect what Seth said and was fascinated with his life in the army. Seth had pointed out more than once that army life wasn't always so glamorous. Jane had to admit, if only in her own mind, that at times she had found herself attracted to Seth, attracted like a woman to a man. She thought about the kiss they had shared one morning by the corral and felt a blush creep to her cheeks at the sensation the memory created in the pit of her stomach. Better to keep such thoughts at bay, she chided herself as she returned to her chores.

The dark, dreary days of November seemed to drag by. Then the day came when Samuel had passed one year previous and little Pearl the next day. Both days were cold and rainy. Jane's spirit plummeted almost to despair. She realized the children were also thinking of the events of the previous year and were suffering perhaps as much as she. Jane forced herself to smile occasionally, to praise their slightest accomplishment, and prayed fervently for strength.

The last day of November dawned clear and by mid-afternoon the temperature had warmed to make it pleasant to be outside. Jane took the wagon to town and stopped at the small cemetery beside the white plank church with its tall steeple reaching toward the clear sky. She knelt by Samuel's and Pearl's graves and thought about the past year.

She gently moved her hand over their rough headstones and wished she could touch each one of them once again.

Jane wondered what Samuel would think about her working and supporting their family. When she thought about it, she had always been dependent on a man to care for her and later for her and the children. First her father and uncle had taken care of her. Jane had gone from her father's home to Peter's, and, when he had died, she had returned to her father's home. Then Jane had married Samuel and he had cared for her and the children. Jane had never given much thought as to how she would manage in the event something happened to Samuel. Then it had happened, and she had been thrust into the position as head of her household just as the men had been in the past.

When Samuel passed there was no longer her father's or uncle's home to return to for refuge.

Jane thought about other widows that had remarried shortly after the death of their husband. Most women needed a man to support her and her children. Widowers needed a mother for their children and someone to run their household. The marriages were probably seldom based on love, but they seemed to work for the most part. Jane was glad those circumstances were not thrust upon her after either husband's passing.

She reminisced about the last year the six of them spent in the small house. She regretted that she and Samuel did not have more privacy for the times they desired to be intimate. Once in a while he would surprise her and come home for lunch or grab a few minutes during the day for them to be together. It always pleased Jane when she would see Samuel riding into the yard, and she knew how their time together would be spent. It was a pleasant memory she cherished.

A slight smile formed on her lips as she thought about the money that had come to her during this past year. Both instances had certainly been an unforeseen blessing. It was gratifying to know at last she had some security for her family.

It continued to puzzle Jane to think how one person's misfortune turned into fortunate circumstances for someone else. She often thought about the awful events that had taken place in Fort Worth that had such devastating effects on a young couple and how that tragedy brought her a sense of security for her family. Of course, she realized the events at her house could have so quickly turned tragic as well. Then the passing of her beloved aunt and uncle had added to her security. Jane was thankful for the money but became downhearted when she dwelled on the circumstances that had brought it to her.

She wondered what Samuel would think about her impending move to west Texas to start her own business. She didn't think he would have doubted her ability but would probably have thought she needed some male guidance and perhaps she did. It was for certain Jim Armstrong had been her savior in many ways, and she felt certain he would continue to guide her if she needed help. She also knew that Seth was supportive of her desire to have her own business, although he would be far away now.

Jane left the cemetery feeling as though a shadow had been lifted from her soul. She took comfort in knowing she had provided for her family and felt certain she could continue to take care of them.

She made her way to the bank and took out just enough money to buy material to make each of the children a new winter coat, a velvet jacket for Opal to wear to church, a flannel shirt for Sam and she would have enough scraps to make Ruby a new rag doll for Christmas. Jane looked fleetingly at a pretty doll in the store and longed to get it for Ruby. However, she knew she could not afford to squander one cent of the money or spoil her children. She hid the package under some supplies and picked the girls up at school. Sam surprised her by putting his bicycle in the wagon and riding home with her and the girls.

Most of December was cold and overcast with a few fair-weather days. On Christmas Eve Jane always baked a plain white cake with a fluffy white icing. The icing was made with beaten egg whites; a hot syrup was prepared and poured over the stiff egg whites that required much whipping until the icing was shiny and stood in peaks. The cake was left on the dining table and Santa Claus would decorate it with hard candy. It was a special treat the children always looked forward to every Christmas.

By mid-afternoon Jane had such a severe headache that she finally decided to lie down, thinking her head would feel better after a short nap. By the time she awoke it was dark and Opal had prepared supper. Jane still felt so sick she declined anything to eat. She called Opal to her bedside.

"Do you think you can bake the Christmas cake?" she asked hardly above a whisper.

"Yes, Mama, just rest," Opal replied sweetly. Then she leaned even closer and whispered, "Tell me where to find the candy, and I will wait until Sam and Ruby are asleep and I'll decorate it too."

Jane squeezed her daughter's hand in gratitude and told her about the hiding place for the candy and that the packages from Santa were in the barn. She knew Opal knew the truth about Santa Clause, but she wasn't sure if Sam had figured it out or not, and she was certain Ruby still believed in the jolly old elf.

Opal was growing up so fast. In a few years she would marry and have her own family. That fact shocked Jane in a way. Where had the years gone so quickly? she wondered. She knew Opal would make a good wife and mother, but she hoped Opal would wait until she finished her schooling before she got too serious about any young man.

Much to her relief Jane woke on Christmas morning feeling much better. The children were delighted with their new coats and their other meager gifts. Ruby proudly showed off her new rag doll. Each one, including Jane, had a piece of the delicious Christmas cake along with their breakfast.

They shared Christmas lunch with Jim, Bea, and some of the ranch hands. After lunch the hands returned to the bunkhouse to rest and play cards.

"Come on, everyone," Bea called from the living room. "Let's open these pretty packages," she said with a happy smile.

Ruby was first to open her gift. "Oh, thank you for the pretty hair bows. I'll wear a new one to school for five days, a whole week!" Ruby exclaimed with delight.

"Yes, thank you," Opal said, obviously pleased with her hair bows too.

As Sam started to open his gift he remarked, "I sure hope I don't get a bunch of pretty hair bows." Everyone laughed. His face lit up when he found a new spinning top, obviously store bought, with painted stripes in several colors.

The adults exchanged small gifts amid laughter and more talk about the move out west. Jane could tell that Bea and Jim were growing fonder of her and the children. She felt peaceful knowing they were all like family. The only thing that would have made it better was if Seth had been there to share in the festivities.

Jim, Bea, and Jane had each received one letter from Seth telling about his reenlistment in the army. Seth had secured permission to return in mid-March to help with the move west. He would remain in Fort Worth until then and then be reassigned. He didn't know yet where he would be sent. Jane's letter was merely signed, "Affectionately, Seth." Jane pondered over the way Seth had signed his letter. Was he sending her a hint that he cared more for her than just their friendship? Or perhaps it meant nothing, she decided.

The grip of winter remained and on the tenth of January it started snowing about noon and snowed all night. They awoke to an unusual sight, a truly white world. Jane put on her overshoes, took Ruby's ruler, and walked to the middle of the road. When she stuck the ruler in the snow it measured ten and one-half inches deep.

After lunch Opal went out and gathered a large pan of snow. Jane quickly added eggs, sugar, and vanilla. They sat by a blazing fireplace and enjoyed the rare treat of snow ice cream.

"Yummy, this snow ice cream is sooo good. I wish it would snow every day so we could eat snow ice cream," Ruby said as she smacked her lips.

"It's good, but I sure don't want it to snow every day," Sam replied.

"Why not," Ruby asked, surprised at what Sam said.

"I can't ride my bike to school through this stuff, and I don't think you'd really want to trudge to school and back through it every day either," Sam answered.

Ruby thought that over. "Yeah, you're right, I wouldn't like that, even to have snow ice crem."

A few days later a second letter arrived from Seth. It was newsy about the new people he was meeting, several parties and dances he had attended, and he even went to a play at a new theater in Fort Worth. It all sounded very exciting. This letter was signed, "Affectionately Yours, Seth."

Jane could imagine Seth in his dress uniform, whirling the ladies dressed in their fine ball gowns around the dance floor in some lovely ballroom. He was probably sought after by all of the unmarried young women. She felt certain he was the most handsome officer at the ball. Jane smiled as she thought about the vast difference his position in the army provided compared to attending simple barn dances if he had remained at the ranch.

In February the third letter arrived from Seth. He had received orders to report to Fort Clark after his leave in March. He went on to say that Fort Clark was about one hundred and thirty miles west of San Antonio and about thirty miles from the Rio Grande River and Mexico.

Jane's heart sank. He would be so far away they might not see him for years. She figured he would be involved in chasing Mexican banditos as well as American outlaws that would go hide out in Mexico. The thought of the danger he would be in made her feel queasy and worried for his safety.

Occasionally she got to read a newspaper from Fort Worth or Dallas and had read about the constant trouble along the Mexico border. Jane did not like the sound of this assignment, but she also knew Seth was probably excited about the adventure ahead.

Toward the end of February winter began to abate. Then it was March and the urgency of the move was upon them. Jane went through each piece of household furniture, linens, and clothing deciding what would be taken and what would be left behind. She finally decided she needed the dining table and its five chairs, her sewing machine, and the two trunks. She would only carry the mattress off of her bed for her and the girls to use. Sam would use a bedroll and probably want to bed down near the cowboys. Everything could be loaded into one wagon that she would drive.

Jane looked at the gold tie bar and its matching cuff links with the tiny diamond set in each one with the initial G engraved in each piece. This and Peter's Bible was all she had left that had belonged to Opal's father. These meager items would be passed on to Opal when she was older and settled in her own home. She had Samuel's silver tie bar and cuff links, Bible, and the guns they still used. Sam would keep the guns and Bible and Ruby would get the tie bar and cuff links. She carefully wrapped each item and placed them securely in one of the trunks.

Sam would drive one of Jim's wagons. Jim had suggested Opal practice driving a wagon in case they needed a relief driver.

Opal was a bit reluctant as she was afraid of large farm animals. She willingly would do any farm chore except milk the cow. It wasn't because she was lazy, but Jane could sense her fear every time Opal tried to force herself to go near the milk cow. Although she did the other chores Opal believed she was supposed to have been a town girl instead of a farm girl.

Driving the wagon was an intimidating task for Opal the first few times she drove with Sam beside her. After driving the team and wagon on several trips to town or just over to the Armstrongs' she seemed to gain more confidence.

SETH ARRIVED IN MID-MARCH AND TWO DAYS LATER THEY were all ready to head west.

Jane was so excited to see Seth again but the urgency of preparing for the move kept them from spending more than a few fleeting minutes together. Occasionally she would notice him looking at her, but they would only exchange a smile or a wave. She wondered if she was reading too much into some of his glances. She had been married and recognized the look a man gives a woman when he is interested in her as more than just a friend. At times it seemed that was the look he was sending to her. Did she want their friendship to become more than just that? she questioned herself. The thought of sharing him with the army was too frightening. She must keep her feelings for Seth in check, she cautioned herself.

Jim, Seth, and one of the men would wrangle the two hundred and fifty head of cattle. Two other hands and Sam would be driving Jim's three wagons. The cattle would go first and then the wagons. One of the men, with Bea as a passenger, would drive the lead wagon then Jane; Sam would follow Jane and the other man would drive the last wagon. Jim figured, if they made fifteen to sixteen miles a day, they would be there in eight or nine days, barring any problems and that would be making good time.

Jane and the children became so excited about the impending trip that, for two nights before they left, they all found it hard to sleep.

Chapter Eleven

The evening before they left Erath County Jane and the children said good-bye to their neighbors and friends. They took some of the household items they didn't have room for to the Johnson family. Ruby gave one of her two rag dolls to her best friend, Susie Johnson. Sam and Billy both fought back tears when it came time to part. They promised to write letters and still be best friends. It was both a sad time and an exciting time.

Opal gave Maggie Powers one of her favorite brooches. It was a delicate butterfly with pretty, lavender stones that shimmered in the sunlight. Maggie promised she would think of Opal each time she wore Opal's special gift.

On the morning they left Jane took a final walk through their tiny house after the children were in the wagon. She felt a tear escape and roll gently down her cheek as many memories came flooding back. Now the memories were like shadows of past dreams that did not quite seem real. Jane gently pulled the front door shut and did not dare look back as Sam drove their wagon toward the Armstrong place.

As the early morning glow of the impending sunrise splashed yellow and orange across the eastern sky the Armstrong and Parker families started their journey west. The chill in the early morning air was invigorating. Jim, Seth, and Hank led, herding the cattle, and following close behind were the four wagons.

Opal and Ruby walked beside the wagon Jane was driving. Ruby sang and played with the rag doll she had gotten for Christmas. Her child's voice sounded sweet as it drifted on the morning breeze. Opal and Sam would take turns driving the team and wagon. A team of horses pulled each wagon and an extra team was ready in the event they were needed. The morning passed quickly. About noon they took a quick lunch rest, and Jane had cold meat, sliced oranges, and fresh bread ready for everyone.

By late afternoon everyone was tired, dusty, and ready for a break from the constant jostling of the wagons as they traveled mile after mile over the rough terrain. They made camp in a clearing by a small creek.

Jane worried about how Bea was holding up being bounced about in the wagon all day. Bea assured her that she was making out fine, but Jane had her doubts.

Jane and Opal prepared a large pot of stew. By the time everything was cleaned and preparations for breakfast were made everyone seemed ready to turn in for the night. Jane and the girls laid their mattress by the wagon and the girls were soon asleep.

Jane sat beneath a tree trying to relax before going to bed. Seth walked over and handed her a cup of steaming hot coffee and sat down beside her.

"Well, what do you think of traveling with a wagon train?" he teased with a slight smile.

Jane turned and looked at him in the pale light from the campfire. "I'm glad we're only going to west Texas and not California. Every bone and muscle in my body aches. I'm worried about your mother, but she swears she is doing fine."

"Ma's never been one to complain, that's for sure."

"I guess you're used to riding for hours over all kinds of country, so this probably doesn't bother you," Jane stated, with a bit of envy in her voice.

"Yeah, it's pretty routine," he answered. He poured out the remains of his coffee and stood, giving Jane his hand to help her up. "You better get some sleep. It's another long day tomorrow." Seth wanted to give her a goodnight kiss, but there were too many prying eyes nearby for such a display of affection.

Jane watched Seth standing beside the campfire talking to a couple of the men. She realized that at the right time and under the right conditions he might become an irresistible temptation.

Jane felt she had just drifted off when she awoke to the low rumble of voices by the campfire and smelled the fresh aroma of coffee. She quickly dressed and woke Opal to help prepare breakfast. By sunup everything was packed and ready to continue their journey. The next two days seemed much like the first. Endless miles of rough trails, by noon the days were quite warm, and by evening they were all covered with what seemed like several layers of dirt. They had just crossed into Eastland County when they stopped for the night.

After the supper dishes were cleaned Jane made a fresh pot of coffee for the men. Seth poured himself a cup and offered one to Jane. They took their coffee and found a flat rock to sit on a short distance from the campfire. This was the first time they had been alone to visit since Seth's return. Jane thought about the evenings they had sat on her front porch after supper and just talked. She had missed that quiet time and Seth's companionship.

"Do you think you'll like being stationed at Fort Clark?"

"Yeah, I'm interested in getting to know some of the black Seminole Indian scouts and hope they'll help me improve my tracking skills."

"You mean black soldiers are there too." Jane sounded surprised.

Seth looked at Jane and smiled. "Yes, and they are one of the most elite fighting forces in the army. They have a remarkable history of engaging in numerous fierce battles and never losing a man. I would consider it a privilege to be trained by them," Seth answered.

"Oh, I just didn't know they had black soldiers mixed in with the white soldiers."

"They have their quarters and we have ours." Seth stretched his legs and looked up at the darkening sky. He wanted Jane to understand more about how the army worked but wasn't sure exactly how to go about it without boring her to death.

They talked about how she planned to get started with her new business venture. Jane was very excited, but, at the same time, Seth felt there was a bit of apprehension underlying her outward appearance.

Seth wanted to gently broach the subject of Jane considering an alternative to her current plans, but he just hadn't quite worked it out in his mind how to best approach the matter.

Seth wished they were farther from the campfire so he could sit closer to Jane and at least hold her hand and maybe even—. Best not be thinking along those lines as it wasn't likely they would have a chance to be alone on this trip.

When they finished their coffee, they said good night, as they knew morning would come all too quickly.

When they woke on the fourth morning the sky was overcast and a chilly wind was coming from the north. They found their rain gear and prepared for what looked to be a wet day ahead. Within an hour the drizzle began and continued all day with a few heavier showers. The wind picked up and the temperature dropped to an uncomfortable chill.

They reached the railroad tracks about noon and began trailing along beside it toward Albany. Early in the afternoon Jim decided to put the wagons in front as the cattle were leaving the now sodden ground a muddy bog. That made traveling a bit easier.

Mid-afternoon they heard the whistle of a train in the distance up ahead and could see the black smoke rising from its smokestack. Jim rode up to caution them about the train possibly startling the horses. As the train grew nearer the wagons pulled as far away from the tracks as they could without becoming tangled in the brush. The engineer did not blow the whistle again, and the train rumbled past with little disturbance to the horses or cattle. The passengers waved vigorously, and the wagon party waved in return.

The chill seemed to seep into Jane's bones. Jane worried that Bea must be suffering greatly from the cold. Jane hoped it wouldn't make her or anyone sick. The men hung a tarp off the side of the lead wagon so Jane could prepare the evening meal. They left their mattress inside the wagon and the men spread their bedrolls inside two of Jim's wagons. Everyone was ready to turn in early.

Jane, Opal, and Ruby climbed into the wagon and huddled together trying to get warm. Eventually warmth and sleep overtook them.

On the fifth day the rain continued, and their progress seemed even slower than the previous day.

Jane had put Ruby inside the covered wagon for the second day. Late in the morning suddenly Ruby let out a yell, making Jane jump.

"Yaks! I'm sick of this rain. I want to get out of this wagon and RUN!" Ruby almost shouted.

"Ruby, calm down, you can't get out in the rain and make yourself sick," Jane scolded her.

"I know," Ruby replied, a bit dejected. "When is it ever going to stop?"

"I wish I knew. No one likes to travel in this mess, but there isn't much we can do but just keep going," was about all Jane could tell her daughter.

When they camped that evening, Jim estimated they had only traveled ten miles, but that put them ten miles closer to their destination.

When they awoke everyone was glad to see the beginning of streaks of bright yellow and oranges lighting the morning sky. The wind had calmed during the night and it looked as though the rain had passed. The ground was still soaked but if the sun came out it would soon dry and traveling would become better than the past couple of days.

By noon the sun was shining full force and the day had warmed considerably. Ruby and Opal walked along beside the wagons as they continued toward Albany. Jim estimated they would be there in three days or maybe a little less if the weather continued to hold.

Mile after mile passed slowly. Jane's spirit lifted now that the sun was shining bright, and they were making better time.

By mid-afternoon of the seventh day the weather was warm enough that everyone shed their wraps and enjoyed feeling the warmth of the sun.

As they rumbled along, they heard dogs barking in the distance. Thinking they were passing a farm or ranch house that was hidden by scrubby growth of trees and underbrush they paid little attention to the barking even when it grew louder. Then suddenly out of the brush a pack of four big mangy, wild dogs emerged. Several had open sores on their bare skin. Without warning they launched a brutal attack on the team of horses pulling Sam's wagon. The dogs were barking, growling, and biting at the horses' legs in a frantic melee.

Jane watched in horror as the horses began to lurch and could hear their loud screams of pain when the dogs bit and ripped the flesh from their legs in their bloodthirsty attack.

Sam was working hard to hold the team as he shouted at the dogs trying to scare them away. His shouts were ignored by the savage dogs as they continued their fierce attack by ripping the flesh from the horses' legs and coming back to attack again. The stench of the sweating dogs, their foul-smelling breath, mingled with the fresh smell of the horses' blood permeated the air. Blood covered the dogs' frothing mouths and splattered their ragged bodies. The ground, as well as the horses, was spotted with globs of bright crimson blood.

Sam hated having to hold the horses but was afraid if he let them run the dogs might attack the other horses and possibly some of the cattle.

Opal had been about to take the reins from Sam when the attack began. She managed to grab a table leg, about the size of a bat, from the back of the wagon. She would swing it wildly at any dog within her reach, but her efforts were mostly in vain. Then suddenly one of the larger dogs made a hard lurch toward her, and she hit it with a crushing blow to the side of its head. The table leg snapped in two just as the wild-eyed dog fell to the ground. Opal reached into the back of the wagon and grabbed another table leg to use for their defense.

Jane turned her wagon to go back to try to help although she had no idea what she could do. Then she saw Luis bringing his wagon forward past Sam. Luis shot the dog that Opal had knocked to the ground just as it started to get up again. Luis motioned for Jane to go forward away from the wild attack. Jane felt her heart sink but knew she had to keep her team and Ruby safe. Just as Luis passed her, Jim and Seth came riding like the wind toward Sam and Opal. Jane felt some relief knowing the two men were going to their aid. Jane watched the frenzied attack from the distance, and it seemed her heart would stop beating at any minute. A terrified Ruby clung to her mother.

Ruby could feel her body shaking and then realized she was shaking because her mother was shaking.

Seth and Jim rode toward the ferocious attack with their Colt 45 pistols drawn. Jim veered to the right side of the wagon and Seth to the left. The men would angle their horses in order to get a clear shot at one of the dogs. After several attempts Jim killed one of the dogs and Seth killed one more. The last dog headed for the brush with Seth in hot pursuit. Within seconds another shot rang out and, shortly after, Seth returned.

"I got the last one," he shouted to Jim and the others.

"Stay back," Jim called out. "I have to shoot the horses."

One shot rang out and another close behind it. The two horses gave a final hard lurch forward as they tumbled to the ground in their final seconds of pain. Their fall caused the wagon to suddenly lurch forward, yanking Sam forward over the front of the wagon. He hit the ground with a loud thud. To everyone's horror the wagon rolled over Sam.

Time seemed to be frozen for a few seconds. There was no sound. No one moved.

Jim and Seth simultaneously dismounted and ran to Sam's still body lying halfway beneath the wagon.

"Sam, Sam!" they both called.

"Can you hear me, Sam?" Seth asked, as he gently laid his hand on Sam's leg.

It seemed like an eternity before Sam groaned and scarcely moved his leg.

"Be still, boy," Jim said in a strained voice.

Jim and Seth exchanged a worried look.

"Sam, can you hear me?" Seth asked again.

Sam managed a weak, "Yeah, I hear you."

"Just lie still for a few minutes. Let us see how bad you're hurt," Seth tried to sound calm, but his insides were tied in a knot from fear Sam was badly hurt.

Jane pulled her wagon alongside and jumped to the ground. She looked pale and her eyes appeared huge with fright.

She ran to where Sam lay. Jim moved aside so Jane could be close to her son.

"Sam, Sam," Jane called his name in as even a tone as she could manage in order not to alarm him.

"Mama, are the dogs dead?" Sam murmured.

"Yes, they are all dead! You were so brave to hold the horses the way you did," Jane told him with pride and relief in her voice. Sam amazed her at times with his maturity and that made it hard to remember he was still just a boy.

Sam attempted to sit up, but Jane and Seth both quickly reached to restrain him.

"Hold still, partner," Seth told him.

"Let us check you out a bit to see if anything is broken before you go moving around too much," Seth continued.

Seth and Jane did a thorough examination of Sam's extremities. Although the wagon had gone over him just above the waist, he didn't appear badly injured.

"I'm going to move you out from under the wagon," Seth told Sam.

After gently poking above Sam's waist, Seth told Jane to bind him just in case some ribs were broken. "We'll have a doctor check him as soon as we reach Albany."

They made as comfortable a bed as possible in the back of Jane's wagon and Ruby rode with Opal in the wagon Sam and she had been driving.

Chapter Twelve

Albany came into view between the low-lying hills late the next afternoon. Jim decided he had misjudged the distance, but it was a welcome site to them all.

They found a holding pen for the cattle and left the wagons nearby. Luis said he would rather stay with the wagons than go on into town.

A congenial doctor in his mid-fifties, well-seasoned to mishaps of travelers and cowboys, tended to Sam and declared it was a miracle he had no broken ribs.

"Lucky for him he's a bit skinny," the doctor surmised. "The wagon probably tilted just as it rolled over him and kept most of its weight off Sam. He'll be sore a few more days but then as good as new."

Jim got two rooms at one of the nicer hotels. Each room had two big feather beds. The men took one room and the ladies the other. He paid extra for each one to have a bath in fresh warm water. It was a luxury each one enjoyed, even the two cowboys that rarely bathed.

Shortly before dark Jane and the girls decided to take a walk in one of the nicer neighborhoods near the hotel and then meet the men for supper in the hotel dining room.

"Oh, Mama, look at these beautiful houses and their flower

gardens. Do you think we will ever have enough money for a house like this?" a wistful Ruby asked.

Jane looked at the large two-story homes with big front porches. Some had decorative shutters beside their huge downstairs windows. Most had a porch swing and several chairs for sitting out in nice weather. A few residents were already sitting on their elegant porches and waved or nodded politely as the women passed.

"I doubt it, Ruby. I would be happy with a small house that is all our own," Jane said with a wistful sigh.

They continued to walk and noticed that each block seemed to bring smaller, less affluent homes.

"Look," Opal said excitedly, as she pointed to a small house across the next street. It was painted white with white brick planter boxes on each side of the wide front steps leading up to the porch. The porch wrapped around the sides and front of the house giving it a larger look. At the corner of the porch a white swing hung, and two wicker rocking chairs sat nearby. Several large pecan trees shaded the house.

"Oh, I like that house too," Ruby pointed enthusiastically. "Could we have a house like that one, Mama?"

"That would be just about perfect for us if we can make enough money with the vegetable garden business," Jane agreed. She didn't want to give the girls false hope for their future but wanted to believe someday they could live in such a fine house, even if it was more modest than the first elegant homes they had seen.

When Jane and the girls entered the dining room Seth noticed how the light seemed to make Jane's freshly washed auburn hair sparkle in the brightly lit room. She looked refreshed and relaxed. He knew she was relieved Sam hadn't suffered any serious injuries in the wagon accident. If he hadn't known better, he would have thought she and Opal were sisters, not mother and daughter. He motioned her to sit in the chair next to his. She felt a little self-conscious at his obvious gesture but took her seat and thanked him for assisting her with her chair. No one seemed to think anything of Seth's being sure Jane sat beside him.

As Jane had approached the table, she noticed several women eyeing Seth as he waited for her. Now, he was clean shaven, had a fresh haircut, and looked very appealing in his freshly ironed blue shirt and clean pants. She caught a whiff of his spicy aftershave and liked the light fragrance. Seth was a fine-looking man, and Jane had often wondered how he had managed to stay single this long. It was a bit unusual for a man in his thirties to have never married, but she felt it inappropriate to pry into his private life.

They enjoyed the luxury of a hot meal while seated in chairs at a table with a white tablecloth. It seemed it had been ages since they had enjoyed a meal seated at a table.

They talked during the meal much as they used to do sitting on her front porch. When the others had finished and were about to leave, Seth asked Jane to join him in another cup of coffee. She hesitated but again no one seemed to mind. They talked about the trip and, finally, Seth asked, "Are you still sure you want to try your hand at starting your own business?"

"Oh yes, I truly feel I can make a go of it and give my family a permanent home for a change," Jane answered without hesitation.

Seth could see the excitement shining in her eyes.

"The girls and I just took a walk and saw some beautiful homes, and there was a smaller house with a wrap-around porch and white brick flower planters beside the front steps. It looked like the perfect kind of house for us someday," she said almost dreamily.

Seth could see Jane's eyes sparkle as she talked about the house. He wished that was the kind of house he could offer her but, if she should fall for him as he hoped, it would be a very different house on some army post. It would not be a permanent home. There was no telling when the army might decide to transfer him and no telling where it might be.

Seth listened and thought for a few minutes. He didn't want to put a damper on her dreams but also knew things didn't always work out as we intended. "I hope it all works out, Jane, but have you thought about what to do in case it doesn't?" he had to ask.

Jane lowered her gaze and shook her head slightly. "No, not yet, I guess I'll just have to cross that bridge if it comes to that," she answered.

Seth could see the lines of worry crease her forehead. He didn't want to curb her big plans and for some reason this didn't seem like the place or time to discuss other possibilities he had been thinking about.

EARLY THE NEXT MORNING THEY LEFT ALBANY HEADED west to the Clear Fork of the Brazos River. Jim said they should reach the river a little early but would go ahead and camp there. That would be their last night to camp on the trail, and then they would make it to their new home in Jones County. Home would be a tent for a while, but at least it would be in one place.

Seth had ridden ahead to find which side of the river would be the best place to camp that night. Shortly before they reached Lieb's crossing they saw Seth riding back to meet them.

"The river is on the rise but two of the Swager Creek ranch hands happened to be there checking the water level and said we need to cross it today as it has been steadily rising since morning. If we wait, we may have to wait several more days," Seth reported to the anxious group.

Seth's words sent a shock of terror through Jane. A vision of Peter's colorless, swollen body after it was dragged from the flooding Trinity River flashed into her mind. She felt herself begin to shake.

"How, how deep is it?" she managed to ask.

Seth looked at her face and saw the deep concern in her eyes. He remembered what had happened to her first husband and understood her worries.

"Hard for me to say, I think we have to depend on the Swager Creek hands to guide us across since they have lived here for years. I don't believe they would put us in undue danger."

Jim seemed to be studying the small rocks on the ground as he listened to what Seth had to say. When Seth finished speaking, he raised his head and looked at each person.

"We will take every precaution to get everyone and the cattle across safe. That is if everyone agrees. It will be hard to wait several days as we don't have provisions for that long, but I could ride back to Albany and get enough to tide us over if that is what you want to do."

No one spoke right away. Finally, Luis spoke up.

"I'm ready to go since them fellers thinks we can go ahead and cross," he said, with no specific emotion in his speech.

"Me too," the other driver agreed.

Jim looked at Jane. "Don't let anyone else sway you. You tell me what you think you can do."

Jane took a deep breath, "I trust your judgment, Jim. I'm worried about Sam and Opal being able to make the crossing since Sam's not quite up to par."

"Seth and I or one of the Swager Creek men will be right there beside them. You know we'll do everything in our power to get them safely across," Jim answered. He looked Jane square in the face so she would not doubt his word.

Jane remained silent for several seconds and then nodded her head in the direction of the river. "I reckon we better get started," was all she said.

Jim and Seth rode ahead to start the cattle across the river first and then the wagons would follow.

The two hired hands were waiting when the wagons rolled up near the crossing. Seth rode over to the wagons with them and introduced each man to the wagon party.

"This is John and Chaw," Seth nodded toward each man as he gave their name.

John, the older man, with his piercing black eyes and skin that looked like old leather, fitted the part of a seasoned ranch hand, one who had seen the good and the bad in ranching, people, the seasons, and the world in general.

It was obvious as to Chaw's name, as his jaw protruded in a round knot indicating a large chew of tobacco tucked into his jaw. He looked even more unkempt than Luis. The color of his clothing was almost unidentifiable; his long brown scraggly hair stuck out from under, what might have been at one time, a black felt cowboy hat. His face was mostly covered in unkept whiskers and mustache that all blended together.

John and Chaw nodded politely to each lady and man as they were introduced. When Opal was introduced, Chaw set his eyes on her and went no further. When Seth had finished the introductions, Chaw continued to stare at Opal.

Jane could see Opal was a bit uneasy with his obvious attention and so was she.

Several seconds passed and then Chaw politely tipped his hat toward Opal and said in a most sincere tone, "Miss Opal, you are about the prettiest young lady I have laid eyes on in many a day."

Everyone remained in a stunned silence.

Before Seth or any of the men or anyone else could intervene on Opal's behalf, she smiled sweetly at Chaw and graciously said, "Thank you, Mr. Chaw, that is the nicest compliment I have received in many a day."

"Welcome," was Chaw's only reply. He turned his horse and rode toward the river.

Jane felt a swell of pride in her daughter. It was true that Opal was developing into a rare beauty, and Jane was glad to know her looks hadn't gone to her head. Jane wondered if perhaps Opal had reminded Chaw of a long-lost love or some other woman that had been special in his life. It was strange what prompted some folks to do such unexpected things.

When Jim motioned the wagons to move forward, Jane was unprepared for the sight that greeted them. She saw the last of the cattle battling their way toward the far shore through the brownish-red muddy water. The steady roar of the rolling water grated on her nerves. She felt her heart begin to beat faster and sweat break out over her entire body although the evening was growing cooler.

Jim saw the look on Jane's face and wondered if she would be able to cross the river after all. Somehow, they had to get all of the wagons across. He didn't know how they could manage to have some of the wagons on one side and the others and the cattle on the other side.

Jim rode toward Jane's wagon. "Jane, you can do it," he said in a tone that made her want to believe him.

Jane just looked at him with rounded eyes and moved her mouth, but no words came out. Then she seemed to gain some control and shook her head to indicate her doubts.

Jim spoke in a sterner voice. "Jane, Seth and John will be with you and Chaw and I will be right behind you with Sam and Opal. Don't be afraid, everybody's going to make it across just fine."

Jane took a deep breath and swallowed hard. Then she gently moved the reins so the horses would move forward.

John rode up and grabbed hold of one horse's bridle and slowly led the team into the swirling muddy water. Seth rode along the side of the wagon and tied a rope to the back to help hold it steady.

Slowly they moved into the rolling stream. Jane could feel the sway of the wagon as the water lapped at the bottom. The rough water made the wagon bounce as it had done on the bumpy trail. Ruby sat beside her mother holding a wad of her dress in one hand and clutching the seat with the other until her knuckles turned white. Jane could hear Ruby breathing hard as though she had been running for miles beside the wagon. Once in a while the wagon would give a violent shake when it got caught in a stronger current that bounced it harder on the rocky river bottom. Jane could only see the backs of the horses and the dark red swirling water as it lapped against the wagon. Their progress seemed to be at a snail's pace, but finally she could focus on the muddy embankment several yards ahead. Then she noticed the depth of the water was receding and soon they were headed up the low grade on the far side of the river.

Jane let out her breath and wondered if she had even breathed during the crossing. She smiled at Ruby and gently said, "We made it."

John let go of the horses and motioned her to continue up the grade to the top of the embankment. When she reached the top bank, she looked back and saw Sam and Opal were already near the middle of the river. She watched intently as they made the same slow progress through the dark red whirling water. Jim and Chaw were leading their wagon just as Seth and John had led hers. Seth and John were almost to the far bank ready to escort Luis across.

Suddenly something happened and Sam's wagon gave a violet lurch and swung into the current. The sudden movement caused Opal to tumble into the river and disappear beneath its murky waters. *She's drowning just like her father,* her mind screamed, and her heart pounded even faster as sheer panic overtook Jane.

Jane could hear screaming but did not realize it was she that was screaming. Almost instantly Bea and Hank were beside her wagon.

"Oh, dear Lord," Jane heard Bea shriek.

Jane could hear the men yelling above the constant roar of the river.

Just as Seth and John reached the east bank Seth heard Jim shouting and looked around to see the wagon had turned in the rushing current. He could see Sam still on the wagon seat, but where was Opal? Jim was frantically pointing toward the water and then Seth realized Opal had fallen into the rolling mud red river. His heart seemed to stick in his throat. He could hear screaming from the far riverbank above the roar of the water. He knew it was Jane screaming in sheer terror.

She saw Seth and John moving as quickly as they could through the swift water toward the wagon. The seconds seemed to drag as Jane's eyes frantically searched the tumbling water for any sign of Opal.

Seth diligently watched the water behind the wagon too for any sign of Opal. Then she bobbed up just behind the wagon and grabbed for it but missed by a few inches. She disappeared again but soon came up frantically fighting being swept downstream. Seth could see the terror in her eyes as she tried desperately to grab the wagon. Then she was sucked under again and Seth felt the panic building within himself. He maneuvered his horse ever forward toward where he had last seen Opal. Seth had his rope in his hand ready to fling a lifeline to Opal when she reappeared, if she reappeared again. He fought the thought of losing her. It seemed like an eternity later when Opal bobbed to the surface several yards downstream, and Seth called her name to get her attention. As soon as she looked at him, he threw the rope and prayed she would grab it. The rope disappeared beneath the whirling water and Seth feared she had missed it. Then he felt the tug and knew she had found it indeed. He gently pulled her toward him, calling out, "Hold on, don't let go! Hold on a little longer!"

Jane watched as Seth scooped Opal out of the water and onto his horse. She could see John, Chaw, and Jim pulling with all their might on the wagon to turn it back in position to continue toward the shore.

Seth reached the shore first and rode up the embankment to let Opal off beside Jane's wagon.

"She's fine, just a bit wet," he said with a slight grin that showed his relief in delivering Opal alive and well to her mother.

Jane closed her eyes and said a silent prayer of thanks for her daughter's safe return. Then she managed to give Seth a teary-eyed smile of thanks.

They all breathed a sigh of relief when the last wagon was safely across the river. They thanked John and Chaw profusely and watched them return to the other side of the Clear Fork and ride out of sight.

After Opal and Ruby turned in for the night and Sam was out riding first shift with one of the cowboys, the other adults sat around the campfire talking about the day's events. Jane was relieved to hear there were no more rivers to cross, just a couple of creeks that would probably be running normal by the next afternoon. Eventually, everyone rose and parted to their separate wagons. Seth walked the short distance with Jane to her wagon.

"Are you doing all right now?" he asked with concern. "I know Opal falling in the river gave you a real fright."

Jane paused briefly then answered, "I'll be fine. It just brought back the horrible memories of when her father drowned." As she said the words she turned toward Seth and he took her in his arms. "Oh, Seth, I'm so grateful you were there today," she said as she nestled in his arms for security.

"I'm glad I was too," he answered as he brushed her cheek with a tender kiss. Then his lips moved to caress hers, but he did not push for a more intimate response under the circumstances. "Now rest, it will be morning soon and the last day of our journey."

WHEN JANE AWOKE BEFORE DAWN, SHE DID NOT HAVE TO see the river to know John and Chaw had been right about it coming up more as she could clearly hear its loud roar.

As the eastern sky began to brighten Jane and Seth walked the short distance to the top of the embankment. It was plain to see the river was twice as wide and likely twice as deep as the day before as its muddy waters continued to churn in the early morning light.

Jane shivered when she saw the undulating waters and Seth gently put his arm around her to comfort her. She turned her head slightly looking up at him and he lowered his head until their lips met. Then he was holding her against his solid body and the softness of her curves pressed against him. The kiss that had begun as a matter of comfort had turned into one of undeniable passion. The softness of their touch had suddenly become pressing with a turbulent ardor. The two were lost in their own world until Jane heard Ruby calling her name.

Seth gave a moan of regret that the kiss was interrupted. This might have led to the time for him to tell Jane how he felt about her, that he loved her, and wanted to provide the best home he could for her and the children.

Jane slowly pulled away from his embrace as though she too regretted the constant summons she heard from Ruby.

Ruby came running in their direction half out of breath. "Opal got burned trying to start the breakfast!" Ruby shouted.

Jane and Seth did not hesitate but ran toward the chuck wagon to find Opal sitting on a keg with a wet towel wrapped around her hand. She looked up as they approached.

"I don't think it's going to be too bad. I didn't realize how hot the handle of the skillet was and grabbed it to move it from the fire," she explained. "Bea wrapped a wet towel around my hand and has gone to find some salve to put on the burn."

"Why didn't you wait for me?" Jane asked, a bit flustered.

"I didn't know where you were, and I knew it was time to get breakfast started," Opal explained.

"Here's the salve," Bea handed the jar to Jane to put on the burn.

"I don't think it will blister up, just be a bit painful for a while," Bea said.

Jane quickly took over the chore of finishing the breakfast. As she worked, she wondered if it was ever meant to be that she would again have the strength of a man to rely on, and to know the passion a man and a woman could share. She knew she could easily learn to care for Seth, but it seemed their dreams were too far apart.

Several others had walked to the crest of the riverbank to look at the swiftly rolling water. Everyone was glad they had crossed the day before, and Jane hoped she never had to cross another river unless it was on a boat or on a bridge.

The land west of the river was almost flat. It was covered in grass tinged with green as spring had arrived. The scattered clumps of scrubby mesquite trees were covered in their lacy green fringe, a sure sign that winter had passed. Yellow and red wildflowers dotted the countryside adding a little color to what might have been a monotonous landscape. The wide blue sky and brilliant sunlight seemed to be giving them a warm welcome. This last leg of their travel was the easiest of the entire trip.

Mid-afternoon they spotted the small settlement up ahead and Jim told them their property was just south of the village.

Everyone seemed to feel giddy with excitement and some of the men gave an occasional YEE-HAW or YA-HOO as they neared their new home.

Home, my own land, Jane thought, *what a wonderful sound.*

Chapter Thirteen

They pitched their tents on the south side of the creek in a wide flat area dotted with sparse sprigs of new spring grass. The creek separated Jane's ten acres from the rest of Jim's ranch. There were several nice size mesquite and willow trees that offered some shade for the tents.

Jane's land started about a quarter of a mile south of the settlement and stretched toward the creek. She planned to build her house on the side nearest the town but for now, would camp with the Armstrongs as a tent wouldn't offer much protection from rowdy cowboys on Saturday night. She didn't want to risk a repeat of what had happened last year in Erath County.

Jane was happy they were in a permanent place and hoped this was the last move she would ever have to make except into her house once it was built. First, they would have to clear the land and get it ready for fall planting. She had agreed to help at the ranch until school was out in the afternoon, and then she would meet the children on their land to start clearing.

After supper on the second evening, Jane moved her chair near the creek and was enjoying a few minutes of solitude. Jane had appreciated the beauty of the trees and hills in Erath County but decided she liked the flatter terrain making it easier to see the breadth of the sky. She gazed in awe across the creek at her ten acres of land. Oh, what hopes and dreams she had for that piece of property.

In the quiet of the late evening Jane's thoughts turned to those dreams. A pretty, little white house, like the one they had seen in Albany, with its wrap around porch would look ever so nice sitting near the road. They would dig a cellar not only for a place of protection from storms but a place to store canned goods. If the garden produced enough, she would probably have some vegetables left over for canning for their use and some to sell during the winter. That would help her income during the off-season. Jane was also thinking of adding some pear, plumb, and peach trees next year, and some fig bushes too. Her lips curved into a satisfied smile and her eyes sparkled as she dreamed about the possibilities ahead. Maybe she and the children would finally really have security in this new place. A home of their own, a way to provide for her family, that was what Jane desired. At last, her dreams and desires appeared to be within her grasp.

As she stood to go get her shawl since the evening was growing cooler, she saw Seth approaching bringing her wrap and a chair for him.

"Thought you might need your shawl by now," he said with an easy smile. "Mind if I join you for a spell?"

Jane enjoyed seeing Seth smile. It enhanced his fine looks and showed the dimple in his left cheek. Seeing the dimple reminded her of an impish little boy. Although Seth maintained his almost boyish good looks, his forceful presence left no doubt about his manhood. Seth was generally good-natured, but Jane was very aware of an air of rugged strength that one would not want to provoke.

"Thanks, and please do come sit. It is so pleasant here. I like being able to really see the sky. The sunset is quite nice this evening," Jane said, as she looked to the west at the splashes of deep orange and purple above the far horizon.

"I thought maybe you were feeling like one of the children of Israel," Seth said with a teasing grin.

"How's that?" Jane asked with a thoughtful look.

"I was thinking maybe you felt like you had been wandering in the wilderness and were looking across the creek at your promised land," Seth teased.

Jane laughed at his analogy. "I guess that's about right. I do find it hard to believe this land is really mine and I will build my home there someday."

Seth cleared his throat as he reached for Jane's hand. He held it gently and turned slightly on his chair, so he was facing her. "It's yours if that is really what you want," he said in a more serious tone. "Jane, there is something I've wanted to speak to you about but just hadn't found the right time or words. This may not be the right time either, but I feel I need to speak up," he said, as he gazed into her eyes.

Jane felt her heart give a small quiver when she saw the anxious expression on his face and his words sounded so serious.

"I have grown very fond of you and your children over the past months. Although I haven't courted you proper, I do feel deep in my heart that in time we could grow to truly love one another. I realize army life might not be your first choice for yourself and the children, but I could provide a good home for your family and schooling for the children. You would soon make good friends at the post and wouldn't be too lonely when I'm away," he paused looking anxiously at Jane for some indication of her feelings toward what he was trying to say.

Jane lowered her head and seemed to be studying their joined hands. Then she rose and walked to the edge of the creek with her back toward Seth. She was gazing across the creek at her promised land.

"I don't mean for you to marry me and come with me now but to think on it for the future." He didn't want her to feel he was expecting too much at one time. "We can write letters and when you feel you're ready I will come for you and the children."

As he spoke Jane had turned her head to the side to show she was listening. Seth could see her profile against the darkening sky but could not begin to guess at her thoughts.

Jane turned and walked slowly back to her chair. She sat and gently took Seth's hand in hers. She lifted her head so he could see her face.

"Oh, Seth," she almost whispered. "I'm not concerned with the proper courting. I feel truly honored for you to consider me for your wife, but I'm afraid I would never be any good as an army man's wife. Every time you rode out, I would be wondering if you would come back riding straddle that horse or strapped across his back," she said with a note of sadness in her voice.

Seth started to speak but she quickly placed the fingers of her other hand to his lips as a sign for him to not speak.

"I've buried two good men, good husbands, and I don't think I could survive burying another," Jane said with pleading in her voice for his understanding. "It doesn't seem fair; you desire the adventure of knowing what's over the next hill or around the next bend in the road, and I desire a place to set down roots and let them dig deep into this Texas dirt. Why do you suppose we have such different needs for our lives?"

Seth sat quietly for several moments letting Jane's words sink in. Then he leaned forward and brushed a light kiss against her cheek. "It's a puzzle to me, Jane. I could stay but I'm afraid that in time I would grow to resent not being able to follow my longing for adventure and then—," he let the sentence die before he said he would resent her. He supposed he was being selfish to want his life the way he wanted it and hope Jane would want him enough to give up her dream.

Seth gathered his thoughts and said instead, "I do understand, Jane. I would never want to make you unhappy."

Jane smiled in appreciation. "We will remain friends, won't we? I would hate to think we can't remain friends," Jane said anxiously.

Seth squeezed her hand gently, "Yes, we will always remain friends." Her answer was not what he had hoped for, but he too would hate to think they couldn't remain friends.

On Sunday they all attended the little church in town and met most of their new neighbors. The square unpainted building didn't look much like a church. There was no steeple with a bell to signal it was time for Sunday services. There were no tall windows like the church they had attended in Erath County. But Jane reminded herself the building did not make the church; the people made the church.

They soon learned that on the first Sunday of the month the Methodist preacher rode forty miles from Albany to hold services. The next Sunday a Baptist preacher came from Abilene to hold services. On the third Sunday one of the local men would direct services and on the fourth Sunday another preacher from Abilene would conduct the services. No one was quite sure about the religious affiliation of the fourth Sunday's minister, but he was a good hellfire and damnation style preacher.

They were a friendly lot and made the newcomers feel most welcome. After the morning service everyone spread their dinner and all shared. They insisted the newcomers stay and share the meal. Jane was more than grateful for their invitation and satisfied to see her children quickly adjusting to their new home.

Opal met several girls and a couple of boys near her age. The girls were seated on a quilt in the sparse shade of a large oak tree. The new leaves were still too small to provide the thick shade that would come later in the summer.

Ruby quickly made two new friends. They told her all about Miss

Bird, their teacher, and Mr. Porter, the upper grades' teacher. The girls said the two were sweet on one another, as Miss Bird would giggle at anything Mr. Porter said.

Sam was soon playing marbles with several boys and talking fishing and hunting. One of the boys rather favored his friend in Erath County, Billy Johnson. Jane hoped he had found a new best friend.

On Tuesday morning Seth said his good-byes once again. This time he found Jane alone near her tent getting ready to wash clothes.

They just stood looking at one another, not quite knowing what to say or how to act. After a few moments, Seth stepped close and took Jane in his arms, something he had hoped to do for eternity. He knew this would likely be the last time he would hold her close for a long time, if ever again. Although she had refused his proposal, he still had a glimmer of hope that she might change her mind. The business venture might not be all she had expected. Any number of things could happen to make her change her mind. He was willing to bide his time.

Jane savored Seth holding her in his strong arms. She could smell the clean odor of his bath soap and gently laid her cheek against his cheek feeling the slight stubble of his beard. He seemed so familiar, so comfortable and secure, like she felt when she was wrapped in her favorite quilt. For a few fleeting seconds she questioned her decision of not marrying him. He was probably her last hope for a husband that could learn to love her and she him. Although not a vain woman Jane knew that in a few years her looks would fade, her waist would grow thick, and what man would desire her then? she wondered.

They did not speak, just held one another for a while. Then Seth brushed her cheek with his lips and found her mouth. Their lips met in a sweet kiss that ended all too soon for them both.

"Good-bye, Jane," was all he said. Then he turned and walked away.

The sound of Seth's good-bye made Jane tremble and then the tears came in torrents. She did not make a sound, as she did not want anyone to know she was crying or that she felt her heart might break. Seth's departure was almost as hard as when she had lost Peter and Samuel, except Seth lived.

Chapter Fourteen

Seth rode one of the older horses south to Abilene, where he sold it and the rigging for a fair price. Later that afternoon he boarded the train headed south for San Antonio.

He had bought a ticket for a regular car and sat looking at miles and miles of the gently sloping countryside roll by. An occasional farm instead of the natural vegetation broke the scenery and sparse livestock dotted the landscape. In a few hours darkness obliterated the surroundings. The conductor lit the dim lamps. Seth moved to an empty seat near a lamp but found reading the newspaper he had bought in Abilene next to impossible. Finally, he laid the paper aside and tried to fit his lanky body into a comfortable position in hopes he could sleep. His efforts proved to be futile.

The conductor came by and offered him a pillow. Seth propped the pillow in the corner between the back of the seat and the window to support his head. He slept intermittently, usually waking after some strange dream. Some dreams were mixed events of his past army life and some involved Jane. Jane, the enigma that haunted his nights and filled much of his waking hours, he thought, as he repositioned the pillow and tried to return to sleep.

Eventually, the long night turned to the gray light of early morning. The conductor happened by and told Seth they would be stopping soon for about half an hour and directed him to a café near the railroad station where he could get a good breakfast and strong coffee.

As Seth stepped down from the train, he was met by a morning chill in the air that felt good after hours pent-up in the train car.

Maybe he should just get off this train at the next stop and go back home, send a letter of resignation to the army and learn to be content as a rancher and farmer, and have Jane in his life forever. The thought became so overwhelming that when the train slowed and pulled to a stop, he reached for his valise but remained seated with his hand on the handle but did not rise, did not get off the train, did not return home. He just sat there until the train started to move again and he finally let his hand drop from the handle of his satchel. The train moved on toward San Antonio and so did Seth.

In San Antonio he had a six-hour layover before catching the train west that would deliver him to Fort Clark. He walked up and down several streets of the old town that was quickly becoming a city. Seth was intrigued by the architecture of many of the older buildings. He walked to the Alamo and stood a long time visualizing the horrific fight that had taken all of the lives of its defenders, heroic men that fought to the death for their principles and to give this great state a chance to become even greater.

After a long walk, he located a decent looking restaurant and ordered a steak.

Again, he was almost overwhelmed with the desire to take the train back north and send the Post Commander a letter of regrets. He stood beside the railroad tracks as a brisk north wind blew in his face. He always hated riding into the wind. Perhaps that was an omen. Again, he anguished over his decision but in the end, he boarded the train headed west.

Seth asked the conductor to let him know when they were near Fort Clark.

When the word came, he picked up his satchel and walked up the aisle to the men's latrine. In about ten minutes Major Seth Armstrong emerged. He looked striking in his dress uniform, drawing the attention of the other passengers. As he walked back to his seat several men gave him a smart salute although they were not in uniform. Several ladies followed his every move with wide eyes and one young woman slowly licked her lips as he passed. When he took his seat, he saw the young woman was still staring at him with obvious interest. He smiled at her. She turned to the older woman beside her and whispered something in her ear as she giggled excitedly.

When the conductor called out "Fort Clark next stop," Seth was relieved to see the flirt did not rise to get off the train. He looked out the window and was met with openness like he had scarcely seen before. To say Fort Clark lay in the middle of nowhere was an understatement. There was a sparse settlement just outside the fort. Few trees dotted the landscape; lots of sage brush, cactus, and scrubby cedar filled the vast expanse. It appeared to be a harsh land. But for some unexplainable reason Seth immediately felt a kinship with this forlorn place.

As he stepped down from the train he put on his hat and walked the quarter of a mile to the fort headquarters.

Shortly after his arrival at the fort, Seth tried to volunteer for service in the war against Spain but his request was denied. He was told his services were needed at Fort Clark in helping keep a lid on the constant problems between the Texas ranchers along the border and the Mexican bandits and American outlaws that often raided their ranches stealing livestock, burning their homes, and attacking their families in the most brutal ways possible. He was a bit disappointed but could understand his commander's decision.

Seth settled into the routine of life at the fort and met a varied group of soldiers. Some had spent their entire life in the army and found this place no more or less desirable than many others where they had served. The new recruits hated the fort and its isolation to any town big enough where they could kick up their heels on Saturday night. The small village offered little in that accord except Miss Bella's Bar and brothel though few mentioned the latter part of the establishment offerings, it was common knowledge among the troops.

Seth was assigned a fine group of men for patrol and several of the black Seminole buffalo soldiers as trackers. It did not take long for them to prove their reputation as the finest trackers he had ever met. Seth worked hard to gain their confidence in hopes of learning as much about tracking as they were willing to teach him. It took a while for him to gain their trust, but, once that gap had been breached, he began to reap the harvest of their vast knowledge.

As a result of the raids by the Mexican banditos and American outlaws, sporadic gun battles between the ranchers and the culprits broke out. The troops tried to quash these outbursts as quickly as possible, but the territory they were expected to patrol covered several hundred miles. The vast area was also a favorite hideout for American outlaws. They could hold up in an immense array of caves that filled the landscape west of Fort Clark toward the Devils and Pecos Rivers. If the army or other law enforcement got too close, they could skedaddle across the Rio Grande to Mexico where they knew they were safe.

The small settlement of Del Rio lay about thirty-five miles west of Fort Clark on the San Felipe Creek and Rio Grande. The country west of there, some fifty or more miles to the Pecos River and north along the Devils River, was rugged and made it hard to travel over its rough terrain and through the craggy hills. Seth was probably one of the few that saw a rare beauty in this harsh land.

They often camped along the rivers, and the pictographs painted on the caves' walls and on the sides of the cliffs fascinated him.

Once they came across five archaeologists studying some of the pictographs along the Devils River. Seth spent the better part of the afternoon trying to learn as much as he could about the crude paintings left by the Indians years ago. It was hard to imagine the life they had led in this harsh land, but when the Indians had inhabited this area it was rich with buffalo, deer, and antelope. The rivers and streams had probably been teeming with plenty of fish.

Each time Seth returned from patrol he anxiously searched through his thin stack of mail for a letter from Jane. When he found one, he would read it over and over for a hint that she might be changing her mind about their relationship.

Dear Seth,

I'm sorry it has taken me so long to answer your last letter. I'm so glad to hear you like your assignment and the men under your command. It seems your wish to learn tracking skills from the black Seminole trackers is coming true. That's wonderful.

Things here are going fine but we stay busy from early morning to about bedtime. The garden plot is growing bigger every day. We should be able to plant an enormous garden with plenty of vegetables left over for canning. What we don't eat ourselves I can easily sell.

The cellar is almost finished. Opal still turns her nose up at having to live in it this winter. Sam is opting for a tent unless the weather gets really bad. Ruby is happy with whatever is going on. All of them have made good friends and that helps as we settle into our new surroundings.

Your folks are doing well. Even your Mother seems to feel better in this drier country.

We all miss you and think of you often. Be careful and may God protect and bless you.

Yours sincerely,

Jane

Each time he was more disappointed. Her letters were full of the progress they were making. After several months, he admitted she had not changed her mind nor was she likely to, it seemed. He often lay awake at night wondering if he should go home before some other fellow came along and claimed her.

Seth had not joined in the general dance held once a month at the post for all enlisted men and their spouses. He had only attended the stuffy dinner parties he was expected to attend due to his rank.

One of his sergeants, Owen Sparks, told him about a dance that night and suggested he come and socialize for a change.

"They have lively music for dancin' and good eats too. There's plenty of gals to go around. Some are young ladies from the village that come and some of the farm girls too. It'd do you good," he suggested with a big grin.

"You think it would, huh," Seth responded with a grin of his own.

"Yeah, I see you sittin' in here by the lamp light readin' most nights. A feller your age should be out chasin' the perty gals afore he gets too old."

Seth laughed, "Well, I'm not exactly ready for my rocking chair just yet. Okay, I'll give it a try," he agreed with little enthusiasm.

"Good fer you," the good-natured sergeant smiled again showing his stained teeth from using too much tobacco.

Seth strolled across the parade ground toward the pavilion where the dance was already underway.

"Well, well, look who finally decided to join life at the fort," fellow officer Major Clarence Huff called as he approached Seth.

"Evening, Major Huff," Seth greeted his fellow officer.

"Yes, Sergeant Sparks talked me into giving it a try with a promise of lots of pretty girls to dance with and good food too," he answered with a grin.

"Well, as a matter of fact, he's quite right, there always seem to be plenty of both to help entertain us poor lonesome soldier boys," he laughed.

Seth had heard through general talk that Major Huff was vastly sought after by the lovely young ladies as he was a handsome man, with chestnut brown hair, same color well-trimmed mustache, and piercing green eyes. He appeared well-mannered and quite charming with the ladies.

As the two men entered the pavilion several young ladies immediately made their way in their direction.

Major Huff half whispered, "If you've changed your mind you'd better run now."

Seth chuckled, "I believe I can hold my own with this group."

Within minutes he found himself whirling around the floor first with one lovely young woman and then another. Each was eager to introduce herself but, unfortunately, he forgot most of their names by the end of the dance. He was curious enough to ask where they had come from to attend the dance, as it seemed like an abundance of young women for such an isolated place. Some lived on the fort with their families, some were from the small village, and others were local ranchers' daughters that came for miles but stayed overnight with friends on the fort or in town. Seth thought most were too young for him to become too interested in but there were a few a bit older. Two were local teachers, two more were widows, and one owned a dress shop in the village. None particularly grabbed his attention but could perhaps provide some compatible companionship.

The temperature in the room became warm, and at last Seth made his way toward the refreshment table, eyeing the punch bowl as he approached. Then he looked up at the woman serving the punch. She was stunning. She was tall, with a mass of brown hair that looked like thick rich chocolate flowing from the crown of her head down around her face in wavy strands. Her large brown eyes were enriched with thick dark lashes; her mouth was full and painted a soft rose color.

Seth felt something he had not experienced in a long time, interest in a woman besides Jane. It was a new experience. It was one he found that he welcomed since he had realized Jane did not appear to be changing her mind about their future.

At his approach she looked up and gave him a delightful smile. "Good evening, Major. Would you care for something to quench your thirst on this warm evening?" she questioned in a pleasant manner.

"Yes, thank you. It certainly has become warm in here," he replied with a smile as he reached for the cup she offered. When their fingers brushed, he felt a tingle reinforcing his interest in the lovely lady.

"Mrs. O'Conner, would you fetch more cakes from the kitchen? It seems the pieces of your chocolate cake are flying off the plate," a middle-aged woman addressed the younger woman.

"Of course," she agreed pleasantly as she picked up the almost empty plate. "Please excuse me, Major," she said as she turned away.

Mrs., he thought, wouldn't you know such a lovely woman would already be taken and he must have imagined the tingle of interest that occurred when their fingers touched.

Seth turned and ambled away to find a chair where he could sit and watch the dancing while he enjoyed the refreshing punch. The dancers whirled past, and he tried to pick out some interesting young woman to ask for a dance, but none struck his interest as the woman serving punch had done. He glanced back toward the refreshment table and saw she had returned to her post at the punch bowl. It crossed his mind to go get a refill but decided it would only be a futile action. He continued sipping the punch and scrutinizing the dancers.

Seth had finally decided to ask one of the teachers for a dance. Before he could move he was startled to hear a soft voice near his ear say, "Major Armstrong," he looked around to find the lovely punch bowl lady standing beside him.

"I thought you might enjoy some of the sandwiches and a piece of the chocolate cake I made before it's all gone," she said with an amiable smile.

Seth was startled to hear her call him by name.

"Thank you, Mrs. O'Conner. Isn't that the name I heard the lady call you by?"

"I'm Kathryn O'Conner," she said and extended her hand to shake his.

"It is a pleasure to meet you and thank you for the plate of delicious looking treats," he said a bit ill at ease knowing she was a married woman. If it had been one of the single women making such a gesture it wouldn't have bothered him.

"If you need anything else, please, let me or one of the other hostesses know," she said as she turned to take her place once more. Before her departure she asked, "Aren't you new at the post? I haven't seen you at any of the other socials," she added.

"I've been here several months but haven't been to any of the general socials until tonight."

"Well, hopefully you'll enjoy the evening and come to more," she smiled before she returned to her duties.

SETH DIDN'T RUN INTO SERGEANT SPARKS FOR SEVERAL days. He was sitting on the veranda that ran the length of the unmarried officers' quarters, in the late evening, reading before the last of the light faded into dusk.

"Evenin', Major," came a cheerful greeting.

Seth looked up to see Sergeant Sparks walking in his direction. "Evening, Sergeant," Seth returned his greeting.

"Been wonderin' how you liked the social the other night."

"Oh, it was a pleasant enough way to spend an evening," Seth replied with moderate enthusiasm.

"Well, sir, you should give it another try this comin' Saturday night. There's gonna be a band out of Uvalde come and I hear they are real good. They throw in an extra dance when they can get some good entertainment. Probably bring some of those beauties from Uvalde too," Sparks added a bit excited.

"Well, I'll think about it. I leave on patrol Sunday afternoon so can't get too worn out from dancing too much," Seth said in a teasing manner.

Sparks laughed at Seth's remark.

"Well, sir, I believe I'm assigned to your patrol, but I plan to dance holes in the bottoms of my shoes 'cause it will sure be a while afore we get back to civilization."

Seth laughed, "You are likely right on that subject, Sergeant."

Seth did go to the dance for a while, but he did not see the attractive Mrs. O'Conner or anyone else that sparked his interest enough to hang around too long, not even the gals from Uvalde.

Chapter Fifteen

They left the fort shortly after the noon meal and traveled west toward Del Rio. Rumors abounded about the Mexican bandits causing more trouble for the ranchers in that vicinity, and the army wanted to keep a constant presence to discourage their activities.

It was mid-August and the heat seemed to intensify a little more every day. Mid-afternoon they took a short respite beside a small creek and let the horses refresh themselves. Seth studied the surrounding countryside. To the north there were some low-lying mountains that faded into hills further west. To the south there were also rolling hills with a few higher peaks. Ahead the land seemed fairly flat for long stretches. The wagon road they were following made traveling easier this far. Past Del Rio the country became rugged often causing patrols, or anyone for that matter, to go several miles out of their way to reach a certain point. High cliffs were common along long stretches of the Devils River and in places along the Rio Grande. The valleys often turned into narrow, jagged ravines slowing their progress.

The problem was they never knew at what point they might encounter bandits, and the chase through the rough country filled with thorny brush and cactus made tracking them even harder. The bandits were usually in small groups of less than twenty men and would often split up to make it harder for the soldiers to capture them. Of course, once they reached the Rio Grande the chase was over.

They camped several nights along their westward trek. Now they were deep in Val Verde County scouting along the lower Devils River country. Riding was slow due to the narrow trails and thick undergrowth. Two of the Seminole scouts rode back to report they had spotted a group of Mexicans moving a herd of cattle toward the Rio Grande about two miles or so up ahead. One of the scouts had been able to get close enough to see the brand on the cattle and said they belonged to the Wagner Ranch located about fifteen miles up the Devils River. The patrol would have to step it up in order to catch up with them before they crossed the Rio Grande to safety.

Seth gave the command, and they picked up their pace. It seemed every thorny bush reached out to snag their shirtsleeves or britches as they rode past. They couldn't slow down if they expected to catch up with the suspicious Mexicans. Soon they caught up with the scouts waiting for the patrol. They reported the Mexicans seemed nervous and appeared on guard. Seth asked if part of the patrol could move around them unseen and be waiting near the river while the others trailed behind to catch them by surprise.

The scouts talked it over and decided it was possible for half of the troop to work their way around to the east and make it to the river ahead of the Mexicans.

"If they get suspicious, they will stampede the herd or just leave them behind and hightail it to the river or head for the caves," Sergeant Sparks told Seth.

"Yeah, and if we meet them at the river with no stolen cattle, we won't have any reason to detain them," Seth answered.

"Sergeant Sparks, you take half of the men and work your way around and be careful to not let anyone see you. We'll trail them far enough back for them to not know we are here but close enough to reach the river before they are ready to cross."

The scouts were divided between the two groups to keep them informed as to the movement of the outlaws.

The afternoon seemed to drag before they were all in place and ready to confront the outlaws just before they reached the river.

As soon as the Mexicans saw the army troop ahead of them, they began to fire and try to stampede the cattle in their direction. They quickly realized they were also being attacked from the rear. The situation burst into an all-out melee. The bandits were not sure which way to head, whether to try to cross the river, head west toward the cave country, or stand their ground and take on the army attacking from the front and rear. Guns blazed; cattle scattered in all directions; men fell, some dead, some wounded, and others trying to take cover behind the nearest pile of rocks. The battle raged on for over half an hour. At the end, the troops were able to capture five bandits and find three more dead and two severely wounded. Several apparently made it across the river and the rest headed for the caves.

The army fared better. They had three men with non-life-threatening wounds. The patrol waiting near the river had pursued several Mexicans all the way to the Rio Grande and watched in disgust as they crossed. As they reached the middle, one turned and fired on the patrol bringing down two men. One was dead when he hit the gravelly riverbank and the other was severely wounded. When the other soldiers tried to reach the wounded man, the four Mexicans took pot shots at them from behind an outcropping of rocks on the Mexico side of the river.

After several unsuccessful attempts to reach the fallen soldier one of the men returned to report what was taking place at the river. By then Seth's patrol had secured the prisoners and tended to their wounded. Seth left Lieutenant Pike in charge and followed the soldier back to the river to assess the situation.

Seth was appalled when he saw the wounded soldier lying on the muddy riverbank on his back with bright crimsoned stains on his shirt, upper arm, and face. He could tell the other man was dead. Anger built inside him when he heard the Mexicans call out taunts. "Come get your wounded. What kind of soldiers are you to leave a wounded man to broil in the hot sun?" they would question and laugh at the helpless soldiers. "Give us your prisoners and we'll let you have him," they jeered.

"If he can just hang on until dark, we can get them both," Seth told Sergeant Sparks.

Sergeant Sparks spat chewing tobacco in the direction of the Mexicans and swore. "Them dirty bastards will wait until last light and likely finish the job. They ain't gonna let us have him. They know we ain't gonna let them have them prisoners; they just tauntin' us, Major."

Seth knew deep in his gut the sergeant was probably right. He sat for a while assessing the situation and trying to figure a way to retrieve the two men without getting anyone else hurt or worse, killed. As he looked at the far bank, which actually wasn't all that far due to the lack of rain, he noticed how dry the tall grass had become a few feet above the water's edge. He could see the grass covered the bank and seemed to creep up into the rocks behind which the bandits were hiding. Then a plan formed in his mind, probably not the greatest plan but possibly good enough to give them a chance to retrieve the men; he spoke.

"Sergeant Sparks, how good are the Seminole scouts with bows and arrows?"

The sergeant looked at Seth with a puzzled expression. "Well, sir, they're good at huntin' deer and small game. It's a sight to see how accurate they can shoot an arrow."

"Send one of the men back to camp and have them find out if one or more of the scouts can shoot flaming arrows across the river and set that patch of grass on fire. If they can, we have a chance. Once the grass catches fire and starts to really smoke we'll send a volley of rifle fire at the same time. Maybe, just maybe, we can get those men without getting shot. Tell Lieutenant Pike to move camp back as far as he can travel before dark. We need to be as far from this river as possible tonight."

Sergeant Sparks slapped his knee with his hand and let out a low laugh. "By damn, Major, I think you're onto somethin'. I'll go since I know just what you want."

After the sergeant left, Seth told the others about his plan to rescue the one soldier and retrieve the body of the other man. Four soldiers immediately volunteered to go after their fallen comrades.

The wait wasn't long until Sergeant Sparks reappeared with three of the Seminole scouts.

"They say these are the best shots with the bows and they even have stuff to light the arrows," Sparks reported.

The three scouts exchanged a brief glance and slight smile. "Where do you want the fires lit?" one of them asked.

Seth pointed to three places that should catch and quickly spread.

"We'll start there and help it spread by filling in between those points," one of the other scouts told Seth.

"As soon as the fire gets going, we are going to send a volley of shots toward those rocks and hope we can retrieve those two men," he nodded in the direction of the men lying beside the river. One was still alive, as he would occasionally lift his hand slightly for the soldiers to see but not the Mexicans.

"Good thing we still practice old ways of battle, huh, white eyes," one of the scouts looked toward Sergeant Sparks with a slight smile.

"Let's just see if you boys can put on the fireworks show we need," the sergeant spat a stream of chewing tobacco between the scout's feet.

The scout looked at the puddle of tobacco juice between his feet and raised his eyes to meet Sparks' gaze. "May have to practice scalping smart-ass white man too," he said with a somber expression.

Sparks whipped off his hat exposing his baldhead gleaming with sweat in the sunlight. "No self-respectin' 'Injin would wear this ugly thing around on his belt," he said with a laugh as he replaced his hat.

The three scouts laughed raucously.

"You're right," one said, still laughing. "I sure as hell wouldn't want to carry that ugly bald thing around."

Seth chuckled too at their good-natured banter. He understood a brief amount of harmless teasing brought some relief to the seriousness of the situation.

"Take your positions and when I give the signal you scouts let loose with three rounds of arrows. When the blaze gets started enough to cause sufficient smoke, I'll give the signal for you others to fire at the rocks or anyone that moves. You four men be ready to run."

As soon as Seth gave the signal, the Seminoles fired volleys of the flaming arrows into the dry grass. It didn't take long before the slight breeze fanned the flames and smoke began to fill the air. They heard coughing and cursing from the far side of the river. Seth gave the second signal for the soldiers to fire their weapons and the four men ran like the devil himself was right on their heels. They retrieved the two men and returned to the safety of the low-lying rocks.

Seth ordered all but himself and four men to move back to safety while they kept up the attack to be sure the Mexicans would stay on their side of the river. After a while it became apparent the bandits had fled. Seth and the men joined the others for the trek back to camp reaching it just at nightfall.

Heavy guards were posted that night. Early the next morning six cowboys from the Wagner Ranch rode in looking for the stolen cattle. They were told about the army's encounter with the Mexicans.

"I'm afraid your cattle may be scattered all over this end of the county," Seth told them.

"We'll find 'em and keep a keen eye out for more trouble," one of the cowboys answered.

They broke camp and began the long journey back to Fort Clark. It was slow going with the prisoners having to walk, as they didn't have enough horses for them to ride.

About three hours into the return trip Sergeant Sparks approached Major Armstrong. "Sir, I'd like to ask permission to take the wounded soldier, Private Carlson, to Del Rio to the doctor. The Doc has a three-bed hospital right there in his house where Carlson can stay till he's better. He ain't gonna make it back to the fort at the slow pace we're movin'."

Seth knew Sparks was right in his assessment of the young man's chances of surviving the forty-five miles or more back to Fort Clark. It might even be a miracle if he survived the ten miles to Del Rio but at least that was a better chance.

"Permission granted," Seth answered. "Take four men with you, then meet up with us as soon as you can."

Seth felt better about the decision of letting Sparks take the young man to Del Rio. He wished the other man had made it too. Occasionally when he rode to the back of the line he would pass the horse carrying the fallen soldier's body, which caused Jane's words to reverberate through his head.

"Each time you rode out I'd be wondering if you'd come back straddle that horse or tied across his back."

He tried to think of other things, even the letter he would have to write to the man's family, but his thoughts returned over and over to Jane's words. He had understood what Jane was saying at the time she refused his proposal, but now he seemed to appreciate the depths of her feelings even more.

Chapter Sixteen

Seth stood on the veranda taking advantage of the good light while inspecting the snagged and ripped pants he had worn on patrol. His sewing skills were poor at best. He could manage to sew a button in the correct place and make some minor repair that was located in some obscure place that wouldn't likely be seen by the human eye. These pants were far beyond his expertise.

"Mornin', Major," came Sergeant Sparks' usual cheerful greeting followed by a smart salute.

"Good morning, Sergeant Sparks," Seth returned with an answering salute.

"I see you are inspecting the damage the brush did to your britches," Sparks observed.

"Yes, I don't know if they are worth the repair or if I should just spring for a new pair."

"Oh, why buy new ones? They'll just come out looking just like 'em next time you go out."

"Does the post have a seamstress that could repair such a mess?"

"I wouldn't waste my time with either of the post seamstresses. One is slow as molasses in January and the other's work is average at best. Take 'em into the village to Mrs. O'Conner. She can sew 'em up so's you can hardly tell they was ripped all to he—, uh, pieces."

"Mrs. O'Conner, I believe I met her at the dance you talked me into attending a month or so ago. She was serving punch."

"Yep, that be her," Sparks confirmed. "She is a fine sewing lady."

"Where does she live?"

"Just stay on the main road leadin' into the village. She lives in a little white house on the corner just past the general store."

"Thanks, Sparks, I think I'll see about her sewing before I buy new ones."

Later that afternoon Seth walked into the village with his parcel of sewing tucked under his arm. He posted a letter to his folks as he passed the post office. A pang of guilt tugged at his conscience for not writing to Jane. He had reached a point of not knowing exactly what to write to Jane, so he included greetings to her and the children in the letter to his parents. It appeared their relationship had become strictly friendship and there wasn't much going on in his life to share. He certainly didn't want to divulge the gory details of their recent patrol to Jane.

The small white house on the next corner facing west looked inviting with a porch across the front and honeysuckle vines running up trellises to provide afternoon shade. A dark headed girl of about six sat in the porch swing gently moving it as she sang to her rag doll. The scene brought back memories of Ruby when he had first met Jane and her children. Hanging from the eave above the steps was a sign that simply read, SEAMSTRESS.

"Hello," Seth greeted before he entered the yard so he wouldn't startle the child.

She looked up, smiled, and returned his greeting. "Hello," she called in her sweet child's voice. Apparently, she was accustomed to people bringing sewing as she looked at the bundle he carried under his arm. "Do you have sewin' for my mama?" she asked before he could say more.

"Yes, I do," he answered as he walked toward the house.

The child jumped from the swing and skipped to the front door. She put her face against the screen and called to her mother.

"A man is here with sewin'."

Just as Seth reached the bottom step Mrs. O'Conner appeared in the doorway. She gently opened the door as the child stepped back.

"Hello, Major Armstrong," she greeted in a pleasant manner. "Please come in."

Seth noticed the strong resemblance between mother and daughter. They shared the same lustrous dark hair, large dark eyes, and the same Cupid's bow mouth.

"Thank you," Seth replied as he removed his hat.

"This is my daughter, Kate," Mrs. O'Conner said as she nodded toward the child.

"A pleasure to meet you, Kate," Seth said with a smile and held out his hand to give her small one a friendly shake.

Kate shook his hand with more vigor than he expected.

"Let me take those from you and see what repairs need to be made."

Seth handed her two pairs of pants and one shirt. One pair of pants was in such disrepair that he doubted she could salvage them, but if she was as good with needle and thread as Sparks had indicated there was hope for the other items.

Mrs. O'Conner held up the shirt, inspected it carefully and laid it aside. She took the first pair of pants and repeated her inspection. When she unfolded the second pair of pants, she held them at arm's length and looked at Seth with an inquiring grin.

"Looks like you've been in the Devils River or Pecos River country."

"Yes, Ma'am. I doubt you can do much for those," he nodded toward the trousers she was still holding.

She looked at the pants once again and smiled. "Believe it or not,

Major, I have seen worse and been able to repair them," she replied with confidence.

"Whatever you can do will be an improvement, and I'll be sure to wear them on next patrol," Seth answered knowing there was a limit to repairing the same pants again.

"Please, sit for a moment and I'll explain how I do my work," she indicated a chair near the front window. "Would you care for a cup of tea? I just brewed a fresh pot," she asked pleasantly.

"Thank you, Ma'am, that sounds fine."

Seth watched her retreat to the other room and could hear her moving about in what he assumed to be the kitchen. Kate's pleasant little voice reached him as she had resumed swinging and singing to her doll. As he took in his surroundings, he noticed a small picture of a man in a lieutenant's uniform sitting on the mantle. He rose and walked the few steps to get a closer look to see if he had seen him at the post. Mrs. O'Conner returned with the tea just as he replaced the picture.

"I assume this is your husband," he nodded toward the picture.

"Yes, that is Jackson."

"I don't seem to recall seeing him at the fort. What is his position there?" he asked thinking he may have some office assignment.

Mrs. O'Conner looked at him with a mild expression of surprise. "My husband was killed about," she paused to think of the time that had passed, "fourteen months ago. He was on patrol near the Pecos River when they were attacked by a gang of bandits from Mexico," she simply stated as she handed Seth his cup of tea.

"My condolences, Ma'am, I did not mean to pry," Seth said as he resumed his seat.

Mrs. O'Conner gave a short laugh. "I'm surprised no one told you. It seems these unfortunate incidents are the topic of many conversations forever. I was sorry to hear about the man being killed on your patrol and another severely injured. It is good you left him in Del Rio he probably has a better chance to survive than if you had brought him all the way back here," she said, with a touch of sadness that was clearly apparent in her eyes as they misted with tears.

She cleared her throat. "Now let me tell you how I run my business. I do the work in the order it is received. A man of rank does not move ahead just because he has rank. I also sew for the general public and often have dresses to make that take a considerable amount of time. Let's see, your things should be ready by Tuesday evening."

"I understand and I wouldn't fault you for being so fair. Tuesday will be fine. I'll pick them up about four o'clock if that is convenient. Thank you for the refreshing tea," Seth said as he rose to leave.

"You're welcome, Major. Four o'clock Tuesday will be fine."

Seth walked back to the post already anticipating seeing the lovely widow, Mrs. O'Conner, on Tuesday. He would like to ask if it was too soon for him to spend some time with her and her daughter. He thought back to the first time he had kissed Jane only to learn he had moved too quickly as her husband had not been gone a year at that time. He had waited what he thought to be a respectful length of time and found it was too late. By then circumstances had set her mind on a different path she seemed determined to follow. He did not want to make the same mistake with Mrs. O'Conner. He did not want to pursue her too soon nor did he want to wait too long. If she accepted his approach, then he would have to take his time in being sure she was all he had hoped to find in a woman.

PROMPTLY AT FOUR O'CLOCK ON TUESDAY AFTERNOON SETH knocked at the front door of Mrs. O'Conner's house.

She appeared and in a soft voice invited him inside.

"Kate is still napping," she explained. "I think she isn't quite up to par as she normally doesn't sleep this long in the afternoon, but children seem to bounce back quickly from little illnesses," she said as she walked to a table where she kept stacks of repaired clothing. She turned with a slight smile and unfolded the pair of pants that Seth had doubted she could repair. "What do you think, Major, will they pass muster?"

Seth took the trousers and stared in amazement at the quality of her repair work. He didn't try to hide his smile of approval. "Your sewing is remarkable. I would never have believed those pants could turn out looking half this good. No wonder you came so highly recommended."

"Oh, may I ask who recommended me?"

"Sergeant Sparks."

She broke into a delightful smile that lit her face and made her eyes twinkle. "The sergeant has been a wonderful friend since Jackson died. He's sent me a tremendous amount of business from the fort to help me out," she said with obvious fondness for Sergeant Sparks. "The sergeant was on patrol with Jackson when he was killed. They had become good friends and it was a difficult time for him too," she said with empathy.

Sergeant Sparks seemed to have ingratiated himself to many people no matter their rank or station in life. Seth had certainly gained respect for the sergeant. Patrolling with him several times showed his dedication to getting everyone back alive if at all possible.

Seth wanted to veer the subject away from the present topic so he could approach her about accepting a dance from him. Standing this close he caught a pleasant whiff of some flowery scent that seemed to suit the lovely woman.

"I suppose there will be a dance this Saturday night since it is the third Saturday in the month. That seems to be the pattern for the general dances."

"Yes, you're right."

Seth hesitated a moment, gathered his courage and continued. "Will you be helping at the refreshment table?"

"Yes, I plan to assist with the refreshments."

"Will you be serving more of that delicious chocolate cake?" he asked with a glint of humor.

Kathryn seemed pleased that he remembered her chocolate cake with favor. "Yes, and I'll make sure you get a nice big piece," she said with obvious pleasure.

"I will certainly be looking forward to enjoying such a treat. Needless to say, most of the food at the mess is nothing like home cooking."

Seth rose to leave with his parcel of repaired clothing. Kathryn followed him to the front door to say good-bye.

Seth put on his hat as he reached the edge of the porch. He turned and asked, "I hope to not be out of place to ask if it is too soon to ask you for a dance Saturday night."

Kathryn studied him for a moment. "No, Major Armstrong, it's not too soon to ask me for a dance. That sounds delightful as it has been a long time since I've danced," she answered with an engaging smile.

"I'll certainly look forward to Saturday night," Seth answered with renewed eagerness as he turned to leave.

"Major," she called.

Seth turned.

"My name is Kathryn."

Seth grinned and simply said, "My name is Seth."

KATHRYN WATCHED SETH STROLL LEISURELY TOWARD THE post until he was out of sight. He is a fine-looking man and seems to have an agreeable personality, she thought. It seems strange that a man like him has never married, she mused, or perhaps he has, and something happened. As Kathryn turned to go check on Kate, Sergeant Sparks came to mind. The next time she saw him she would very carefully try to find out more about Seth. She suspected that if anyone knew much about Seth's background it would be the sergeant.

Chapter Seventeen

By the middle of April things had settled into a routine at the ranch, so Jane and the children started clearing their land. That turned out to be far harder work than Jane had anticipated. She bought a plow and old mule from a man planning to head farther west. Jane would meet the children after school, and they would put in several hours of hard work in the hot afternoon temperature. The heat of most days had already reached into the low nineties. The wind seemed to never cease blowing, which in some ways was a blessing.

Sam would plow the hard ground, and Jane and the girls would clean the grass and weeds from the plowed dirt. They would grab a clump of grass and pound it against the hard ground to loosen the dirt from the roots. Billows of red dirt surrounded them, getting into their noses and eyes until they could hardly breathe or see. However, Jane experienced a sense of elation each time she felt the dirt sifting through her fingers. Clearing the land was a slow process, but Jane felt a moment of satisfaction at the end of each day when she saw their progress. By late evening they were tired, sweaty, grimy, and hungry when they trudged back to the ranch for supper and to help finish the evening chores.

Everyone had been worried that Seth might get sent to the war against the Spanish, that was, everyone but Seth. He even tried to volunteer but his request was denied. In his first letters to his parents and his letter to Jane, from Fort Clark, it was evident he was disappointed to not be included in the tumultuous uproar.

Springtime and early summer thunderstorms periodically rolled across the land giving it much needed moisture and temporarily cooling the increasingly hot air.

One evening in late June, just as Jane and Ruby were finishing cleaning the evening dishes, the sky began to darken. They could see a dark cloud on the northern horizon with rapid flashes of lightning dancing in the distance.

Jim hollered, "Looks like a bad one coming; better finish up and get in our tent."

Jim had recently built a wood frame with a roof that stood about two feet above their tent to give Bea a cooler place to rest during the day. It offered what little protection they had from a storm. Jane just hoped it would be enough as this did look like a bad storm coming in fast. The sky had turned almost black with a greenish tint that surely meant there was likely to be hail in the storm.

Everyone scurried around the yard lowering the other tents, weighting them down with rocks and pieces of wood. The wind picked up and the smell of approaching rain filled the air. Soon they were battling the increasing wind to get everything battened down before the full force of the storm hit.

Just as Jane and Ruby reached Bea's tent where she and Opal were making room for everyone to fit inside, huge drops of rain began to pound the hard earth sending splatters of red mud flying. Jim, Sam, and the two cowboys came running into the tent just as the first hailstones began to fall. At first, they were small but soon grew larger and larger. The sound was almost deafening as they pounded the shelter roof and slammed into the sides of the tent.

Loud crashes of thunder started in the north and boomed overhead as it rolled toward the south. Streaks of lightning lit the sky and everything surrounding their tent.

Ruby was excited about the flashes of lightning that seemed to illuminate the bouncing hailstones. She laughed and squealed with delight when the lightning was exceptionally bright and when she spotted a particularly large hailstone. "Look at that big one, Mama," she would squeal. "Oh, look, there is a bigger one," Ruby pointed to each new large hailstone.

"Ruby, you silly twit, those are dangerous," Opal scolded.

"Yeah," Sam put in. "Just think how that would feel if it hit you on your noggin," Sam said, as he whacked her on her head.

"Ouch, that hurt," Ruby complained.

"That's enough, Sam," Jane gave Sam the look that meant to stop.

Jane marveled at Ruby's childlike innocence by not realizing the danger they were in. She prayed silently for their safety through this storm. Jane held Ruby's hand to be sure in her excitement she didn't dart out into the storm to retrieve a particularly large hailstone.

The storm raged on for almost an hour, lessening at times and then regaining its strength. Finally, it passed on to the south and they dispersed to set up the other tents again. Soon everything was quiet. Jane and the girls snuggled under a light blanket to ward off the night chill the storm had left behind. Jane lay awake for some time longing for a house where they would have a measure of safety. She finally fell asleep listening to the distant snores coming from the other tents.

The heat of summer strengthened making it miserable to work outside in the afternoon. Bea suggested Jane and the girls leave the ranch chores as soon as they cleaned up from breakfast and go work their land until the afternoon heat became unbearable.

Sam would lead the mule and once again attempt to plow the hard, dry earth. On occasions it became a battle of wills between Sam and the mule he had named Jack. At times they would dig around the base of a small mesquite tree, tie a rope to it, and pull it out with the mule. Opal and Ruby would hoe the prickly pear and gingerly drag it to the brush pile. The girls would let out an ear-splitting squeal and run when a snake would come slithering out of the cactus pile. It was good they were vigilant as they killed two rattlesnakes and one copperhead. The others were of the harmless variety, but Opal insisted they be killed too. Jane was proud of how hard the children worked to help get ready to plant a big fall garden.

Jane had begun to think ahead and plan for the winter months. She would need a place to store canned goods and she didn't want her family to spend the winter in a tent. After much thought, she decided the solution would be to dig a cellar or dugout for them to winter in and to also have a place for the excess canned goods.

Jim had been talking about finding someone to build a house, and Jane hoped he would do it soon for Bea's sake. Jane could see the living conditions were wearing on Bea, but she would never complain.

One evening after supper, in late July, Jim called everyone over to sit in the shade of one of the large cottonwood trees near the creek.

"I have good news," Jim began. "I heard about a man that's a good builder that I am going to see. Right now, he's building a place near where we crossed the Clear Fork River. I plan to ride there tomorrow to talk to him."

"Who is he?" Bea asked as she looked at Jane with a measure of excitement lighting her sallow face.

"Fellow by the name of Hyrum Wharmund. Mr. Lungreen, at the general store, told me about him. Lungreen says when Wharmund builds a house there is hardly enough scraps left over for kindling to build a fire. I believe he has a helper too."

Bea smiled and clapped her hands. "That is good news. I sure hope he can start soon, don't you, Jane?"

"I surely do," Jane answered with a sigh of relief in her voice. "I have been worried about you spending the winter in a tent."

"Oh, I'd be all right," Bea answered, but didn't sound too convincing and Jane knew better. Bea tried hard to put a good face on things so Jim wouldn't worry about her.

Jane cleared her throat, "I've been thinking ahead and have decided I'm going to dig a cellar for us to winter in and have a place to store the canned goods from the fall garden."

Jane saw the look of despair on Opal's face as she announced her plan. Bea looked disappointed too.

"Oh, Mama, not a dugout," Opal almost wailed. "First we live in a tent and now a dugout! Won't we ever have a house again?" Opal moaned as though it were too degrading to think about.

"Oh, no," Bea protested. "You and the children can live here until you build a house."

"I know we could but it's getting harder and harder to do the work that needs to be done here and there," Jane said nodding her head in the direction of her own property. She hoped Bea and Jim would understand. Opal's reaction to her announcement did not surprise Jane.

"I feel bad that I'm not doing more here, and I think you need some help that can be here all the time. I worry about you, Bea, when I'm away so much," Jane said as she gave her dear friend's hand a gentle squeeze.

"Why can't that man build us a house when he builds theirs?" Opal pleaded.

"I need to save some more money before I can have a house built. If the fall garden does well then, in the spring, I should have enough money for a house," Jane patiently explained. "It will be just a simple house, Opal, not one of those fancy ones like we saw in Albany."

"Like the last one we saw with the porch all the way around?" Ruby asked with excitement. "Then we can have a porch swing where I can swing my dolls."

"Yes, more like the last one," Jane answered, hoping it would be that nice.

Bea started to protest more but Jim interrupted her.

"Now, Bea, we knew there would come a time when Jane and the children would need their own place again. Then he turned to look at Jane. "Just know any time you need to come back we will make room somehow."

Jane stood up and gave them both a hug. "You've been so good to us and I will never forget it. Any time you need any of us to help we will be here," Jane said with a catch in her voice.

"I think a dugout will be fun for a while," Ruby piped up.

"Ruby, you think everything is fun; you even like hailstorms," Opal almost spat at her sister.

"It won't be so bad," Sam tried to soothe Opal. "It'll be closer to town. You can go see your friends more when we live in town."

"Yeah, Opal, it won't be so bad and just for a few months," Ruby joined in with Sam trying to reassure her sister.

HYRUM WHARMUND, A ROBUST GERMAN FELLOW IN HIS mid-thirties, and his helper, Slim, arrived in early August. Jim had drawn a simple plan for a square house with four rooms, built on pier and beam, with porches all the way across the front and back. There would be a fireplace in the parlor, a big kitchen, and two bedrooms. Bea wanted the house to face east so the bedrooms would have the southeast breeze at night in summer and a buffer against the cold north winds in the winter. When Hyrum and Slim finished the house, they would build a bunkhouse and barn.

Lungreen had been right about Wharmund's building ability. When he finished there was scarcely enough wood left over to build a decent campfire. The house and outbuildings were well-built and sturdy. They would likely outlast any of them.

Jane spoke to Hyrum about building her house the next spring and he promised he would return the next year to see if she was ready to build.

Jane and the children began digging the cellar. She marked off a twelve-by twenty-foot area. When it was deep enough, she would hire someone to build in the walls and make floor to ceiling shelves along one side and across the back wall for the canned goods. It would have enough room for a small wood heater, Jane's bed, bunk beds, and the dining table and chairs.

Sam decided he would sleep in a tent unless the weather was really cold. Otherwise, the females could have the cellar. Not that he minded living in the cellar, but he felt he was getting too big to be stuck with the women all the time. His body was changing, and he didn't want his mother and especially his sisters to notice the difference.

ONE MORNING JANE HAD MADE A TRIP TO THE GENERAL store and returned with a few supplies she needed at the ranch. Opal and Ruby were taking turns digging and Sam, with the mule hitched to the plow, was clearing some more land for the garden. Sam was almost at the far end of a row as Jane approached to tell him to come help dig. As she got closer, she could hear him talking.

Jane paused to hear what he was saying. It came as a shock when she understood his words.

"Damn-it, Jack, stop pullin' to the right! Damn, Jack, you old jack-ass, I said quit pullin' to the right!" Sam emphasized each word as he wrestled to make the mule pull straight.

"Sam!" Jane called in surprise. "Is that the kind of language you've been learning from the cowboys?"

Sam turned with a shocked look on his face. "I didn't hear you coming, Mama."

Jane gave him a stern look. "Well, is that what you learn from hanging around the cowboys?" she insisted he answer her question.

Sam didn't want to get the men in trouble, as he knew they didn't mean for him to be repeating the things he heard them say. The men were his friends. They taught him things a boy needed to know and, since he didn't have a pa, Jim and the men were all kind of like a pa.

"They say stuff once in a while, but they don't make me say it. If they hear me say stuff they get after me. It's not their fault," Sam defended the men.

Jane looked at Sam for several seconds. She believed what he said about the hired hands as they seemed respectful but were just men. Sam was growing up fast. She had to depend on him for a lot of things Peter or Samuel would have done.

"Well, just watch what you're saying," Jane warned Sam. "Besides, Jack don't understand anyway."

THE CELLAR, WHICH WAS MORE OF A DUGOUT, WAS finished by the middle of September. The man she hired to finish the inside made the roof about two and a half feet above ground with a small window by the front door. It had a solid door like a cellar and a screen door at the bottom of the steps to keep out flies and mosquitoes. Dirt was piled over the sides and top except for the small window and door. Then Jane had the man build a shelter like the one Jim had put over Bea's tent for her cook stove and some tables for a place to process the canned goods.

Sam pitched his tent just a few feet from the cellar door. It would certainly do until the next spring, Jane thought as she looked with pride at the progress they had made.

The fall garden flourished. There was intermittent rain and between rains they hauled water from the creek to water the tender plants. By mid-October the garden began to produce in profusion. Jane would take a wagonload of vegetables to town a couple of times a week and spend the remainder of her time canning.

Near the end of October Jane was delighted when a letter arrived from Seth. She realized she had not heard from him since early July. She opened the letter and began to read with interest his stories of life at the fort. He always had a funny story or two to share. Then he wrote, *"I have met a very nice lady who lives in the settlement near the fort. She takes in sewing to support herself and her six-year-old daughter. Her husband was a soldier and was killed a little over a year ago. I know you would like her; her name is Kathryn, and her daughter is Kate. She reminds me of Ruby. Kate likes to swing and sing to her rag doll. Kathryn is a kind lady and often helps with social dances at the post. Mother wrote that you had finished the cellar and moved in. She misses you and the children, but the new lady you found to help her seems to be working out well. Hope the fall garden does extremely well and you can build your house next spring. Give my best to the children. Don't worry too much about Sam using a few profane words. It is all part of a boy growing up. I remember Mama washing my mouth out with lye soap more than once when I was growing up. He is a fine boy, and I am sure you have nothing to worry about.*

Yours truly,

Seth"

Jane folded the pages and sat for a long time thinking of Seth. She remembered their few encounters when he held her in his arms and the few amorous kisses they shared. Now, did he hold Kathryn in his arms and kiss her with that same tenderness laced with passion? she wondered. Jane closed her eyes and could almost smell the scent of his soap. Had she made a mistake by not accepting his proposal? Should she write and tell him she might change her mind? No, she had made her decision, the right decision. There was no need for her to have these feelings. Feelings of what, could it be jealously? No, no, she would not allow herself to have those feelings!

Chapter Eighteen

Despite the blustering cold north wind Jane needed to get out of the cellar for a while. She put on her heavy winter coat and warmest headscarf and walked to the general store. There were few people out on such a disagreeable day. As she entered the general store Mr. Lungreen greeted her warmly.

"Mrs. Parker, you are just the person I've wanted to see," the tall vigorous storekeeper greeted her. His warm smile made Jane feel at ease. Charles Lungreen was a pleasant looking man in his fifties with wavy brown hair with a few strands of gray that fell over his broad forehead almost reaching his full eyebrows. He had large brown eyes that seemed to take in everything at once.

He had been one of the earliest businessmen to settle in this area, opening his first store in a tent. It had not taken long for his business to outgrow the tent, so he had built the first part of this store. A year later he had doubled the size, and even now it seemed to be bursting at its seams.

"Oh, why is that Mr. Lungreen," Jane asked curiously. She had known Mr. Lungreen since moving to the area but could not imagine why he would want to see her.

"Please, come join me in a cup of coffee. I just made a fresh pot a short time ago," he invited as he led the way to the back of the store. He had an elevated office so he could see what was going on in the entire store.

Jane followed Mr. Lungreen and mounted the six steps leading to his office. A large, cluttered desk with an equally large wood chair facing the store took up half of the space. There was a wood stove and a couple of other chairs nearby. Jane seated herself near the heater, glad for its warmth.

"I only have sugar for the coffee," Mr. Lungreen said a little apologetically.

"I don't need anything in my coffee, thank you."

Lungreen handed Jane a full cup of hot coffee sitting on a matching saucer and poured another for himself. He turned the desk chair sideways so he was facing Jane, but he could still survey the store, and seated himself by the desk.

"I'm sure you are wondering just why I have wanted to see you, Mrs. Parker," Lungreen began.

"Yes, I am a bit curious," Jane confessed.

"Opal told me you are planning on building a house this spring when Mr. Wharmund returns."

"Yes, that's right."

"May I ask when you expect Mr. Wharmund to return?"

"Oh, I expect he will show up in late April or May."

"Good, good," Lungreen said with a broad smile lighting his face.

"Do you want him to build something for you while he's here?" Jane asked still curious.

"Yes, I do, but only if you agree to my plan," Lungreen answered still smiling.

Before Jane could ask any further questions, he continued. "Mrs. Parker, the railroad is coming soon, within a year if not sooner. I know this because some of the hands from the Swenson Ranch were in the store last week and told me Mr. Swenson had sealed the deal with the

Texas Central Railroad to extend the track from Albany to here. The next day I rode out to the ranch and, indeed, Mr. Swenson confirmed what they had told me."

"That is exciting news," Jane said as she realized more people would be flooding into their area and her business should really boom.

"Yes, indeed, the surveyors should be coming within a month or so to lay out the route for the railroad and to set up a real town."

"I'm glad to hear that; we need a plan before too many people get here and just build willy-nilly," Jane put in.

"I have a business proposal that I hope will be of interest to you, Mrs. Parker."

Jane could not imagine what Mr. Lungreen had in mind unless he wanted her to expand her gardening business and sell directly to him.

Mr. Lungreen continued, "People will be pouring into this area, and, as I said before, it will soon become an official town. They will need a decent place to stay until they can get established. There will also be businesspeople and cattlemen coming and going and they too will need a decent place to stay and take good meals. That is where you and I can work together and both make a tidy profit," Lungreen paused so Jane could take in all he was telling her.

Jane could hardly imagine just what Mr. Lungreen was proposing. "I will only have a house big enough for my own family. I don't think I could be of any help to those people," Jane told him a bit perplexed.

"Mrs. Parker, that's where I come into the picture. My business has done very well, and I have managed to set aside a rather tidy sum of money. My plan is to assist you in building not only a home for you and your children but a fine boarding house to help accommodate those newcomers," Lungreen told Jane with even a broader smile.

Jane sat stunned into silence as Mr. Lungreen's business proposal buzzed around in her head. At last, she gathered her thoughts enough to ask a few questions.

"Can you explain to me just how this business venture would work?"

Lungreen launched into great detail about the amount of money each one would invest, and the prices Jane should charge for lodging and meals. Then he explained how she would pay him back, and eventually she would own the boarding house and all of its profits would be hers.

Jane nodded and asked more questions as he proceeded in his explanation. At last, Jane felt she had a good grasp of the proposal.

"Mr. Lungreen, you have taken me quite by surprise with all this and I do need time to think it over," Jane told him at last.

"Of course, of course, take all the time you need." He reached into the desk and withdrew several sheets of paper with figures and estimates written neatly on them. "I have written it all out for you to study over, and feel free to seek Mr. Armstrong's advice if you wish."

"Thank you, I will study these figures and think it over carefully, Mr. Lungreen. I'll let you know in plenty of time before Mr. Wharmund gets here," Jane said as she rose to leave.

As Jane walked back to the cellar, she hardly noticed the cold wind whipping at her coat. She could just imagine a large white house, like one of those two story houses they had seen in Albany, sitting on her property. She could run a boarding house and take care of the gardening and canning. The garden would provide nearly all of the food for the meals. She might need some help with the cleaning and laundry but there would be plenty of women willing to do those chores. This idea might be the right thing to do just in case there was a time when the garden didn't produce well, and Jane knew that could happen for any number of reasons.

She wondered what the children would think of the idea of them having a boarding house. Likely Ruby and Sam wouldn't mind and probably Opal would love the idea of living in a big house.

She would most assuredly go show Jim the figures and talk it over with him and Bea. Jane felt a wave of excitement wash over her. Since Seth's last letter she had felt a bit down. Perhaps this was just what she needed to take her mind off Seth. Her mind shouldn't be on Seth anyway. She had had her chance with Seth and turned it down. Seth had his own life to live and that didn't include her, she told herself for the hundredth time.

DURING THE NEXT TEN DAYS JANE MADE SEVERAL TRIPS TO the Armstrong Ranch and talked extensively with Jim and Bea about the boarding house. Jim liked Mr. Lungreen and felt he had made Jane a fair business proposition. He and Bea felt it would be the right thing for Jane to do.

One evening, after making her decision, Jane called the children to sit at the table after supper. She told them about Mr. Lungreen's business proposition, and that Bea and Jim agreed it would be a good idea.

"Oh, Mama, I can hardly believe we will really have a fine big house to live in," Opal emanated with excitement. "Will it look like the grand houses we saw in Albany with their wide porches, tall columns, and huge windows with the pretty shutters?" she asked with obvious anticipation.

"Do you think we would have room for a kitten?" Ruby wanted to know.

"Cats belong outside, so they don't scratch stuff," Sam stated without hesitation.

"Sam's right, no cats in the house, some of the guests might not like having animals inside," Jane told Ruby. "We'll see about a kitten or puppy later on."

"I'd rather have a dog so I can teach him to hunt," Sam said.

"You get a dog and I'll get a kitten; they can be friends," Ruby suggested, not giving up on the idea of a kitten.

"Will we each have our own room?" Opal wanted to know.

"No, you and Ruby will share a room with me, and Sam will have his own room next to us. All of the other rooms will be rented out."

Opal looked a bit disappointed but didn't argue since she was so elated about the big house.

Sam started to chuckle, then he burst into laughter so hard that he almost toppled his chair over backward.

"What's so funny, Sam?" Ruby asked, starting to giggle at his laughter.

Sam shook his head and held up one hand to signal for Ruby to give him a chance to get his laughter under control. He calmed his laughter and looked at his mother and sisters. "Just think, here we are living in a dugout and before long we'll be living in a mansion. Now, ain't that funny?" he asked and started laughing again.

They all caught his spirit and began to laugh with him. Life did seem to deal some strange twists and turns.

The next morning when the children started to school Jane walked with them as far as Mr. Lungreen's store. He was delighted when Jane accepted his business proposition. He started drawing plans for the house as Jane told him what she wanted to be included. Mr. Lungreen said Jane should plan a trip to Fort Worth to order wallpaper, paint, and proper furniture for the boarding house. Jane's head swam with the ideas, and plans changed somewhat from time to time. By the end of March, they had worked out the final plans. When Hyrum Wharmund and Slim arrived, they were ready to begin. Supplies were brought from Abilene to start building. Jane and Sam drove the wagon to Albany and took the train to Fort Worth to buy the other supplies. The most exciting additions were the two bathing rooms to be fitted with large clawfoot bathtubs, flush toilets, and hand-washing sinks. This indeed spoke of being a house of quality.

The boarding house was finished in late June and *The Parker House* opened for business July 1, 1899.

It was a large white two-story house with a wraparound porch. The eaves of the porch were decorated with white latticework to add a touch of elegance. There were eight bedrooms upstairs and four bedrooms downstairs along with a large parlor, dining room, big kitchen, and the two bathing rooms. The parlor was finished in rich shades of green wallpaper, with deep rich wood tones around the windows and fireplace and two floor-to-ceiling bookcases flanked each side of the double doors leading to the dining room. The large dining room held two large walnut tables, seating twelve people each, with matching ladder-back chairs. Jane, Opal, and Ruby shared a large bedroom, with pink and red roses on the wallpaper, on the front southeast corner of the house, and Sam had a smaller bedroom, done in shades of blue, next to their room. The other ten rooms, done in greens, golds, and blues, were for rent and quickly filled. Jane hired one woman to help with cooking and another for laundry. Both helped with housekeeping when not otherwise occupied.

Jane decided to leave the outhouse in case of emergencies but did have it painted white to match the newly constructed boarding house.

They settled into the new house and things soon worked into a daily routine. Sam got a puppy to train for hunting and Ruby got a calico kitten she named Prissy. Opal was overjoyed with the new house and constantly invited her friends over to enjoy a delicious meal and play parlor games in the evening. From time to time several of the guests would join the young people in the games. Jane would savor a few minutes of quiet by sitting on one of the chairs on the porch or swinging gently in one of the porch swings for a short time after the evening meal.

Along with getting the boarding house ready to open, Jane had expanded the garden and it was producing quite well. By evening she fell into bed exhausted but satisfied with the great strides she and the children had made in their lives.

Jane wondered what Peter or Samuel would think if they could see their family now. She felt certain they would both be amazed at how well things had turned out. They had been so poor in material things back then but rich in love. She vaguely wondered if there always had to be a trade-off. Were you either given love or possessions? That couldn't be right, she thought. She knew several people that seemed to have both.

JANE, ALONG WITH EVERYONE IN THE COMMUNITY WAS abuzz with the surveyors' activities. At a town meeting it was announced that the town would be laid out with a central square with businesses framing it. Streets were laid out for blocks in every direction. The railroad would enter the town south of the central square and run east to west about two blocks south of the square. This was certainly to *The Parker House's* advantage as it could be clearly seen south of the railroad tracks as the train approached the depot. The stockyards would be located farther to the west.

Chapter Nineteen

"Mama, Mama! I just saw Seth and some lady drive by headed for Uncle Jim and Aunt Bea's ranch," Ruby shouted as she bounded through the front door late one afternoon in August.

Jane wiped her hands on her apron and walked briskly to the front door only to see the back of a buggy in the distance, headed south.

"Are you sure it was Seth?"

"Yes, I'd know Seth anywhere," Ruby answered assuredly, with her bright blue eyes twinkling and her red curls bobbing as she shook her head in the affirmative.

"Did he wave or say hello?"

"He didn't see me; I was sitting beside the house playing with Prissy, but I know it was him. Can we go see?"

"Not today, it's getting late, and he'll need some time to visit with Jim and Bea," Jane answered still wondering if Ruby was right.

"Who do you think the lady would be?"

"I don't know but I suppose we'll find out soon enough," Jane said as she returned to her kitchen chores. Jane recalled the letters from Seth had been far apart and he had not mentioned the woman he had met but that one time, she thought for a minute, last October. She had assumed the relationship had not developed or perhaps this was someone different. Ruby could have been mistaken, Jane thought, as she continued preparing the evening meal.

Mid-morning the next day Henry Beard, one of Jim's ranch hands, stopped by on his way to town.

"Mornin', Mrs. Parker," he called as he walked up the front steps.

"Morning, Henry, come on in and have a cup of coffee," Jane invited.

"Thanks, that sounds good. The Armstrongs want you and the children to come for supper tonight. Seth and his lady got home late yesterday afternoon."

"Who is the lady?" Jane asked with a pang of dread as to what his answer might be.

"Don't rightly know but I guess we'll all find out tonight as the ranch hands are invited to supper too."

"Tell them we'll be there, and I'll bring two chocolate pies. I know they are Seth's favorite," Jane said with a smile, although her heart seemed to be growing heavy for some reason she didn't want to think about.

About four o'clock she and the children bathed and dressed in their nicest clothes. Sam hitched the horse to the wagon, and they drove to the Armstrong Ranch.

As they pulled into the yard Seth stepped out onto the front porch and greeted them with a big wave and called, "Hello!"

Ruby was the first to reach him as he grabbed her up in a big hug and swung her around.

"My, but you have grown since I saw you last. You are about grown now," he teased.

He reached for Sam's hand and gave Opal a big hug as well. Then he greeted Jane with a smile and friendly but discrete hug as well.

Jane could still feel the strength in Seth's arms, although he did not hold her close as he had before he left for Fort Clark. She caught a faint whiff of his familiar smell. A longing burned inside her heart, but she knew it was her own fault that now he likely belonged to another woman.

Seth released her and smiled, "Come in, come in. I want you to meet my family," he said as he opened the door.

Jane felt her heart plummet but kept a smile on her face, as she had no right to be anything but happy for Seth.

A rather tall, slender woman with big brown eyes and dark brown hair pulled up in a bun came forward with her hands outstretched in greeting. She had a pretty face and warm smile that lit her expressive eyes.

"This is my wife, Kathryn," Seth said with obvious delight.

"This must be Jane and her children. Let's see," she said as she reached one hand to greet Jane and the other to greet each of the children. "This must be Opal, and Ruby, and Sam," she said as she shook each hand with a warm greeting.

"Yes," Seth answered. "Jane and her family have become very dear and a part of our family," Seth said, but did not indicate in any way that he had expressed deeper feelings for Jane at one time.

A little girl about six or seven, with her mother's looks, came skipping into the room followed closely by Bea.

"This is my daughter, Kate," Kathryn said as Kate came to stand by her mother and Seth.

"Seth is my new daddy," Kate announced to the group.

"Congratulations," Jane said to Kate and then to Seth and Kathryn. "When did you marry?"

"Three weeks ago," Seth answered. "I didn't want to leave them behind when I came for a visit, so we decided to go ahead and marry and surprise everyone," Seth said as he smiled fondly at Kathryn and gently patted Kate's shoulder.

"It was quite a surprise too," Bea added with a smile that indicated her approval.

"This calls for a celebration I'd say," Jim said as he winked at Kathryn.

"Thank you for making me and Kate feel so welcome," Kathryn answered as she smiled at everyone.

"Let's sit and visit a while before we eat," Bea suggested.

"Opal, you and Ruby go bring in the pies," Jane told the girls.

"I sure hope at least one is chocolate meringue," Seth said as he gazed longingly toward the wagon.

"Both are chocolate meringue," Jane answered.

"I will have to get your recipe," Kathryn told Jane. "I have heard so much about Jane's delicious chocolate meringue pies."

"I'll be happy to give you the recipe," Jane replied without hesitation as she sensed Kathryn was genuine in her request.

When Opal and Ruby were seated Kate inched her way nearer and nearer and was soon seated between the two girls. Before long, Ruby and Kate were talking and giggling as thought they had known one another forever.

"Jane, I was shocked to see the huge house standing on your property and the sign for *The Parker House.* Pa and Mama told me about your new business venture, but I had no idea the house would be so big and elegant," Seth said as they were all seated in the parlor.

"You and Kathryn, and Kate, must come see it as soon as you have time."

"We have six days of time before we have to return to the fort," Seth answered as he slipped his arm lovingly around Kathryn.

"Why don't all of you come tomorrow evening and stay for supper?" Jane invited.

"Wow, you won't believe how big it is," Ruby told them excitedly. "Mama, Opal, and I have a h-u-g-e room and Sam has his very own room. There are lots of other rooms that people rent," Ruby went on gesturing with her hands to indicate how big the rooms were. "We get to meet lots of new people and hear stories about where they have traveled. Some people plan to live here but some just come to do business."

"I get to invite my friends over to play parlor games in the evening as there's plenty of room for a bunch of us," Opal added pleased to let the others know she had acquired lots of friends.

Seth turned to Sam. "Well, Sam, what do you think of the big new house?"

"It's fine, I like having my own room. It beats sleeping in a tent," Sam shrugged his shoulders. "I mostly spend my time outside working in the garden. We're going to make the garden even bigger next year," he added with a bit of pride.

As everyone chatted Seth thought Jane looked good but there was something about her eyes that made her look, perhaps, tired, he thought. She had taken on a huge responsibility, but he could tell she was pleased with the results. He had waited for quite some time for some indication from Jane that she had changed her mind about his proposal, but none came. Even after he met Kathryn, he had to give himself time to put his feelings for Jane to rest. Slowly his feelings for Kathryn became more and more important and he realized he had indeed fallen in love with her. Seth felt contented as he sat with his arm around Kathryn and listened to the flow of the conversation with Jane and the others.

The evening progressed pleasantly, but Jane felt wrung out when it was over and time to leave. Kathryn walked out on the front porch with Seth to say good night to the departing guests and told them again how glad she was to meet them at last and looked forward to seeing them and the new boarding house the next day.

Opal, Ruby, and Sam chatted all the way home, but Jane sat quietly trying to put her feelings into perspective. She was happy Seth had found such a pleasant woman for a wife and truly hoped they would be happy together. At the same time, she felt she had lost something very dear and knew that even their friendship would never be the same again.

Jane had kept each of Seth's letters, but now it was time to put them away. First, she sat up later than usual reading each one again. She laughed at the funny stories and savored his few words of affection. She could not bring herself to throw them away just yet. She knew it was her own doing that caused him to find another, but it still left a vast emptiness in her heart that she doubted would ever be filled by another man.

They had visited several times with Seth and his new family before they returned to Fort Clark. Jane had truly come to like Kathryn and found Kate to be a delightful child. They promised to write letters and Jane knew she would, although it would be somehow on a different level than when it was just she and Seth writing to one another.

Chapter Twenty

As word spread about the coming railroad, people continued to come to the area to settle, and the boarding house was constantly full into the fall. The fall garden had done as well as the spring garden and Jane spent hours canning. After school and on weekends Opal and Ruby were a great help with the canning. As fall was turning to winter the cellar shelves were becoming full.

One Saturday morning Opal and Jane were busy preparing the jars to can tomatoes when, for some unexplainable reason, one of the jars burst and a large piece of glass jabbed into Opal's right hand cutting a deep gash from the heel into the palm. Blood spurted profusely as Jane removed the piece of glass. She quickly wrapped Opal's hand with a clean white dishcloth and had her hold her hand above her head. The blood quickly soaked the cloth and began to run down her arm soaking the sleeve of her dress.

Jane ran to the door and yelled for Sam to hitch the horse to the wagon so she could take Opal to the new doctor in town.

By the time the two women pulled up in front of the crude wooden building that housed a barber shop on one side and the new doctor's office on the other, blood had soaked a third towel. Opal looked a bit pale as Jane bounded out of the wagon and pounded on the door to the office belonging to Aidan McKaskel, Medical Doctor.

Doctor McKaskel opened the door quickly taking in the scene before him. Before Jane could tell him what had happened, he was beside the wagon lifting Opal to the ground. He gently escorted Opal into his office and lifted her onto the examining table.

Noticing her pale color, he suggested, "Perhaps you should lie down to let me examine this wound."

Doctor McKaskel, likely in his late twenties stood near six feet tall, slender build, reddish-blond wavy hair cut short, and pale green eyes. Most anyone would agree Doctor McKaskel was a handsome man.

As Jane listened to him speak gently but authoritatively to Opal while he cleaned and stitched the ugly gash in her hand, she noticed his easy manner when attending a patient. He wanted to know how the accident happened and asked Opal several questions in a calming voice. It occurred to Jane that every single female in the county would soon have some ailment or another just for the chance to meet the new young, good-looking doctor.

Jane felt relieved she didn't need to worry just yet as Opal was a bit young and had to finish this year in school before she got any notions about marriage. Then it occurred to Jane that Opal was slightly older than she had been when she and Peter married. She hoped Opal would wait a few more years before marriage. She seemed so young yet, or had she matured more than Jane had noticed? Jane wondered.

"There, that should heal up and hardly leave a scar," Doctor McKaskel said with a look of pride in his work as he finished with Opal's hand. "Let me put on a clean dressing and you will be all finished here," he said and smiled assuredly at Opal.

"Thank you, Doctor," Opal said still sounding a bit weak.

Aidan turned to Jane. "Bring her back in a couple of days for me to check to be sure there is no infection. You can change the dressing daily and put some of this ointment on the wound."

"How much do I owe you, Doctor?" Jane asked.

"Well, Mrs. Parker, I have already heard you serve the best food around at the boarding house so how about one fine meal as payment?" Aidan asked, hoping Mrs. Parker would be agreeable.

"That sounds like more than a fair price to me," Jane answered. "Come any time you're ready for that meal. On Tuesday nights we have pot roast with fresh vegetables and lemon meringue or chocolate meringue pie for dessert," Jane told him with a note of pride.

Aidan burst into a big smile and his green eyes brightened at the thought of a delicious home-cooked meal. "I'll see you Tuesday evening for supper. I'll just check Opal's hand then. No more canning for a while for you, Opal," he told her with a conspiratorial wink.

Aidan walked the women out to the wagon and helped Opal up onto the wagon seat.

As soon as they were out of earshot Opal turned to Jane, "Mama, did you notice how handsome Doctor McKaskel is?"

"Yes, he is right nice-looking but don't go getting any ideas; besides, he's too old for you," Jane answered.

"Oh, Mama, he can't be more that twenty-five and I'm seventeen; that's not too old," Opal argued.

"For now, it is. You have to finish school. Besides he might be married or have a fiancée somewhere," Jane tried to sound reasonable.

"He didn't have on a wedding ring and who knows about a fiancée," Opal answered with a wistful look and sigh.

When Aidan arrived for supper on Tuesday evening, he looked near exhaustion. He had delivered two babies, both in the middle of the night, in the country miles apart. Then he drove his buggy to another farm to set a broken leg and had seen six patients in his office between Saturday morning when he had tended to Opal and Tuesday evening.

"Let me have a look at your hand, Opal," he said as he sat down in the parlor before supper was served.

Opal sat beside him and held out her hand. "You look really tired, Doctor McKaskel," Opal observed as she noticed the dark circles under his eyes.

"I am indeed," he said as he removed the bandage. "I have been a busy fellow since I saw you last. I thought my practice here would get off to a slow start, but it doesn't seem that is the case."

"There are going to be more and more people coming here when the railroad gets here in a few months," Opal warned him.

"Well, I surely hope one or two of them are doctors," Aidan said with a tired smile.

"May I ask where you are from?" Opal asked a bit shyly.

"I am from South Carolina originally. My parents, two brothers, two sisters, and I moved to Kentucky when I was about seven. I just finished medical school a few months ago and decided to seek my fortune in Texas. When I got to Fort Worth, I heard about the railroad expanding west because of some big ranch wanting it to ship their cattle and decided to come see what this area had to offer. I was a bit surprised to find this many people already here with no official town established yet."

Opal brightened as she told him about the surveyors. "Some of the surveyors ate supper here last evening and they told Mama the town will be named Stamford, after Mr. McHarg's hometown of Stamford, Connecticut."

"Who is Mr. McHarg?"

"He's the President of the Texas Central Railroad that's coming here," Opal told him, feeling important that she knew more about the subject than he did.

"Oh, I see. I figured they would have named it Swenson after the ranchers that persuaded them to extend the line from Albany," Aidan observed.

"That's what most folks thought but Mama said the Swensons had probably just been glad to get the railroad and weren't going to argue with Mr. McHarg over the name of the town."

"That sounds reasonable to me," Aidan said as he realized he was still holding Opal's hand although he had finished replacing the bandage. She was the prettiest girl he had seen since moving here but was still in school and that meant she was too young for him. Once she finished school, if she didn't have a serious beau, he might be interested in getting to know her better.

"By the way, I need to find someone to help me around the office. Do you think your mother would know of some lady interested in being a doctor's assistant?"

"You'll have to ask Mama but if I were out of school I'd love to train to be your assistant," Opal said, hoping he would ask her to anyway.

Aidan looked at the lovely young Opal and thought about the complications that could cause in his life. She possessed a rare beauty and had a pleasing disposition. Working closely with Opal might impose a burdensome temptation on his part to not succumb to her charms. If he became involved with a girl still in school, it would be a scandal that could ruin his career before it got started. He could wait for her to finish school. Besides, she was too young and innocent to be exposed to some of the problems he had to deal with.

"School is of the utmost importance for now, Opal. Once you have finished, I am sure you will find any number of things that interest you."

He didn't want to dissuade her, but he did need a more mature woman for his assistant.

Jane knew of two possibilities for Doctor McKaskel to approach about the position.

Aidan enjoyed the meal so much that he made arrangements to take three meals a week at the boarding house. This would most likely keep him healthy and from starving as he wasn't much of a cook. That was especially pleasing to Opal as that would give her more chances to see Doctor McKaskel than any of the other girls who were sure to fall madly in love with him.

AIDAN HIRED ISABELL GLENWOOD AS HIS ASSISTANT. Isabell was in her mid-forties, slightly plump, with strands of gray running through her chestnut brown hair. She was a pleasant woman and very efficient.

Aidan's practice continued to flourish but, somehow, he managed to tend most who called on him day or night. Isabell soon became competent to handle many of the folks' minor needs that came to the office. Aidan found himself always anticipating his next visit to the boarding house, not so much for the delicious, nourishing food as for the opportunity to spend a few minutes or more with Opal. All the while he reminded himself of her youth and would never allow himself to act inappropriately with her in any manner.

At least by dining at the boarding house several times a week he could keep abreast of Opal's latest boyfriend or boyfriends. For the most part they did seem boyish and immature. Once in a while he would join in the parlor games, which gave him another opportunity to be around Opal.

He was pleased to find her to be lively but kind to everyone. She made sure each person was included in the activities. You might say she was the perfect hostess.

Chapter Twenty-One

1900

The town was in a frenzy in early February 1900 when the Texas Central Railroad finally arrived. Almost everyone in town and many from the surrounding area were on hand to see the first train steam into the station. On February 13, under blue skies and unusually warm temperatures, the first passenger train arrived and was welcomed with a grandiose celebration. Splendid speeches were delivered by a goodly number of the leading citizens; they had compiled a band that played vigorously, off key as much as on key but no one seemed to mind. They had horse races up and down Swenson Street that bordered the west side of the town square. The local citizens furnished dinner on the ground and the celebration concluded with dancing in the streets. The town of Stamford had truly been launched into the new century.

Business at The Parker House was so brisk that Jane even rented out the cellar and allowed folks to sleep on the porch that had no other place of refuge from sleeping under the stars. She always managed to squeeze women with children inside somewhere. Sam finally set up his tent in the back yard and often gave up his room to those women.

Two of the boarders were twin sisters, Miss Tressie and Miss Essie Hamlin. Miss Tressie was to teach the first through third grades at the new school and Miss Essie, through some unfortunate early childhood disease, was left blind. No one was quite certain what had gone wrong with Essie's eyesight, but it started to fade when she was about three years of age, and by the time she was twelve she was totally blind. Tressie had taken it upon herself to learn Braille so she could teach her sister to read and write. They were not particularly pretty women, but they were not ugly either, just rather plain in their features. They had light brown hair, small brown eyes, and pale complexions. Their saving grace was their exuberant personalities. No matter the chore or pleasure they undertook, they did it in high spirits.

At first Jane was concerned about Essie staying at the boarding house all day while Tressie was teaching, but she soon discovered there were many things Essie could do to not only pass the day but that were most helpful to Jane. Essie had taught herself to efficiently dust furniture without knocking anything off the table or dresser, make a bed minus the wrinkles, wash clothes, and do a little cooking and she loved to shell peas or snap beans.

The two ladies were soon among the most popular dinner companions as they both could carry on a delightful conversation on numerous topics.

One evening after supper, Mr. Lungreen told Jane he was expanding his general store business. With all of the new folks arriving he just didn't have enough space to stock everything they needed. He chuckled and then added that he also had plans in the works to open a lumberyard.

"How in the world will you be able to manage so much?" Jane asked concerned.

"I wrote to my sister in Virginia, and she is sending her son, Maxwell, to help me out for a while."

"Is Maxwell good at business?"

"I truly hope so," Lungreen said with a slight shake of his head and pensive expression. "Maxwell must be about twenty-two by now. He has never quite found his niche in life and Emily, my sister, is hoping this experience will give him some direction and I do need help."

"Well, hopefully it will work out for both of you."

"I was wondering if you could spare Opal to help out in the store on Saturdays until I can find some reliable help after Maxwell arrives. I know you are busy here, but since it isn't gardening time just yet, I thought perhaps you could do without her help just on Saturdays. That's such a demanding day at the store," Mr. Lungreen explained, almost pleading.

"Well," Jane pondered his request. "I know she would like to earn some extra money, and I could let her help out until planting time."

"I truly appreciate this favor, Jane," Lungreen gave her a warm smile of gratitude.

"I believe I'm going to have to hire some help with the gardening anyway. It's getting bigger and those fruit trees just arrived that we'll have to get planted. We've been working every spare minute to get the holes dug, and we need to start cleaning the garden for spring planting," Jane told him, thinking of all the work that lay ahead.

Lungreen sat quietly for several minutes pondering the situation. Jane could tell when he was thinking things through by the slight frown lines that appeared across his otherwise smooth forehead.

"Jane, would you consider hiring a man of color?" Lungreen finally asked a bit reluctantly, not knowing how she might feel toward blacks.

Jane was somewhat surprised by his question as she had not seen any men of color in town. Then it was her turn to think over his question. "Yes, I would consider it if he were a man of good rapport," Jane answered honestly. "But I haven't seen any men of color in town." Jane added, a bit puzzled by his question.

"There are several families camped out west of town a ways and two of the men came to the store asking about work. They said they would work at most anything. One man in particular struck me as an upstanding man and I believe a hard worker."

"Well, do you think I should send Sam to fetch him to come talk to me about working here?" Jane asked, still with some reservation since Lungreen didn't really know the man that well.

"Tell Sam to come get me before time to open the store tomorrow and we'll ride out there together."

The next morning Sam left just after breakfast and was back home within an hour. He told his mother the man would be along in a bit to talk to her about the job as he headed out to start planting more trees.

His back was straight as an arrow; he was tall and lean with a muscular build. He wore a straw hat, faded blue cotton shirt, and overalls. His feet were bare even in February. He was black.

Jane saw him coming down the road as she and Ruby sat on the porch, in spite of the chill, for a short respite before starting their daily cleaning. He turned up the path to the front porch, stopped at the bottom of the steps, and politely removed his hat.

Jane rose and walked to the top of the steps with Ruby right beside her.

"I be Blackie Jones," he said in a deep rumbling voice.

Before Jane could say anything, Ruby bent over and let out a roar of belly laughter. "Do they call you Blackie 'cause you're black?" Ruby asked in spite of her laughter.

Jane was so stunned by Ruby's sudden outburst that it took her several seconds to collect her thoughts. She would not tolerate such behavior even toward a person of color.

"Ruby Parker, you apologize to Mr. Jones for being so rude," Jane admonished her.

Ruby looked at her mother in surprise. "I didn't mean to be rude, but I just wondered why someone would be named Blackie unless it's 'cause he's black," Ruby tried to defend herself.

"Well, it was rude! A person's name is a person's name. They should be proud of it and not have others make light of it," Jane persisted in a stern tone of voice.

"Oh, well, I'm sorry," Ruby finally said a bit flippantly.

Blackie watched and listened to the exchange between Mother and daughter. He instantly knew he wanted to work for Mrs. Jane Parker. She was a true lady to his way of thinking. He suspected Ruby was just a curious child that didn't mean no harm.

Ruby turned and retreated to one of the porch swings. She could still hear everything being said but wasn't as likely to get in trouble listening from a distance.

"Mezer Lungreen and yu boy say yu needin' some help here," Blackie stated his purpose for being on Mrs. Parker's property.

"Yes, yes, I do," Jane answered. "Do you know much about gardening, Mr. Jones?"

Blackie kept his eyes on Jane as he answered, "Yez'um, I knowed some about gardenin'. I raizes a garden ever year and worked for a man in East Texas 'bout ten years that raized a big garden with all kinds of vegetables and fruit trees too," he nodded toward the trees being planted.

Jane watched Blackie Jones as he talked, and she liked his manner. After some further discussion Jane told him to be there by sunup the next morning. Blackie was there by sunup the next morning and for many years to follow. He worked until sundown and never complained about anything Jane asked of him. Jane became more and more impressed with Blackie's knowledge of plants although he could not read a word for information. Jane admired his stamina for long hours of work in the blazing sun or freezing cold. She did see to it that Blackie always had appropriate work shoes. They soon developed a lasting mutual respect and satisfying working relationship.

It didn't take long for Ruby to come to thoroughly like Blackie. He could manage to get more work out of Ruby than anyone else and she never complained. When she worked in the house it was often a different story. Ruby wasn't a lazy child but she just much preferred being outside to inside.

Chapter Twenty-Two

Maxwell Covington arrived on the train in late February and came immediately with his uncle to the boarding house for dinner. After introductions he entertained the entire group of dinner guests with flamboyant descriptions of his trip west. Max, as he preferred to be called, not only possessed a winning personality but was quite handsome to boot. His black hair was neatly trimmed in the latest style worn in more urban areas, his brown eyes danced as he talked, and he possessed an attractive physique that complimented his six-foot frame.

Opal was awestruck once again. Two incredibly handsome, well-bred, young men arriving in town within such a short time. Just wait until she told the girls at school about Max Covington. They wouldn't know whether to go shopping or be sick. The beauty of it was that both would be taking meals regularly at the boarding house.

Max and Opal quickly developed camaraderie at work and at play. He escorted her to the Saturday night dances on the square and they sat together in church on Sunday for the first several weeks. Then Max began to spread his wings, so to speak, and often escorted some other attractive young lady to the dances or to church on Sunday. Opal was not entirely jealous of Max's attention to the other girls as they often went together as a foursome. Several young men vied for her attention, so she was rarely without an escort for dances, parties, or church. Much to her chagrin, if she couldn't have most of Max's attention then she preferred the attention of Doctor Aidan McKaskel to that of the schoolboys, but he never asked her out or even for a dance.

Aidan found his visits to the boarding house both a pleasure and a torment. He relished Opal's pleasant company and enjoyed their discussions on numerous topics. It was apparent she was exceptionally bright and that would be a real plus in his book when he decided to seek a wife. It was her young age that kept him from swooping her away from all of her other prospective suitors. It would never do for the town's doctor to be courting a schoolgirl. He was counting the months until she graduated, as that would change everything.

Well, it would change everything if Max didn't claim her first. He didn't seem to have any qualms about dating a schoolgirl although he was a businessman.

When Aidan came for meals, Opal always tried to have some important question in mind so she could ask for his opinion. She would spend hours thinking of some interesting topic to discuss in an attempt to gain his attention. He was always pleasant and seemed to enjoy their discussion but that was that. Opal struggled trying to discover why it was so easy to have the other fellows' attention but not Aidan's.

One afternoon, near the end of the school year, Opal dropped by Max's rooms his uncle had built over the store to invite him to a party the next evening. She climbed the steps, tapped on the door and opened it, at the same time sticking her head inside and calling out a cheerful, "Hi, Max." Then she froze.

Max whirled to face her. Opal was met with a view of his open shirt, revealing his bare chest, and his shirttail hanging halfway out of his trousers. Something about his face looked different. Standing behind him was a woman she did not know, whose bodice was in much the same condition as Max's shirt.

Before either could utter a word, Opal whirled, ran down the stairs, rounded the corner of the building, and kept on running as fast as she could run. When she was well away from the building, she finally slowed to a walk to catch her breath. She felt as though her face was on fire. Opal was inadequately prepared to fully comprehend what she had just witnessed, but she knew she had interrupted a very intimate moment between a man and a woman. Why, oh, why had she just opened the door without waiting for Max to answer? she condemned herself, feeling embarrassed at her own careless behavior. How could she ever look at him again knowing what she now knew? Would he be so angry with her that he wouldn't ever want to be around her again? she wondered.

Should she talk to her mother about what happened? No, maybe not. Her mother would surely scold her for going to Max's room in the first place. Perhaps she should keep what she saw to herself and see how Max acted the next time they were together.

The next time wasn't long in coming as Max and his uncle arrived at the boarding house several hours later for dinner. Max was his usual amiable self.

After the meal Opal retreated to the front porch where she took up snapping the beans Ruby had brought from the garden. Minutes later Max slipped out the door and joined her on the swing.

He didn't bother with small talk but leaned close.

"Opal, I am sorry you came at the wrong time today. I know you were embarrassed by what you saw, but I do hope you will keep it to yourself," Max said in a low voice so as to not be overheard.

"I'm sorry too. I, I, just didn't think, well, I never expected," she floundered trying to put proper words to her jumbled thoughts.

"Look, Opal, these things just happen sometimes. It wasn't planned, it just happened," he shrugged with a slight chuckle. "I had seen her at the store several times and she was lonely, that's all. It didn't mean anything," he shrugged.

"But, Max, it's a sin to do what you were doing," Opal whispered in a desperate attempt to make him see the error of his ways.

Max gave a soft chortle. "If two people agree to what they want to do together it isn't a sin," he looked at her with a smug expression.

"The preacher says it is," Opal insisted.

Max straightened and looked directly at Opal. "Well, I have never been much on going to church until I came here, and I damn sure don't need some hell-fire preacher telling me what's a sin!" Max stated angrily.

Opal looked at him in shock. She realized that she did not know Max very well after all. He might be charming and handsome, but he was a heathen, she thought as she stared at him in astonishment.

Max threw back his head and laughed, "Opal, Opal, you are so innocent. Here you are almost eighteen and know nothing about men. A lot of girls your age are already married and have babies."

Opal was deeply wounded by his laughter and stinging remarks. "I intend to remain innocent, as you put it, until I am a married woman," she spat as she stood up to leave.

Max reached for her hand before she could make her escape. "Don't be mad. In a way it's refreshing to know someone like you."

Opal remained standing just in case she decided to leave. "Don't try to tell me all of the other girls act like she was acting with you," Opal said, still stung by his remarks.

Max looked thoughtful, "No, not all, but I think you would be surprised to know what some of your friends do."

"What do they do?" she challenged.

Max stood up and before Opal realized his intent, he pulled her snug against him and gave her a searing kiss. Opal was so shocked she momentarily opened her mouth slightly. Suddenly his tongue darted into her mouth caressing her tongue. Her instinct was to bite him for such brazen behavior but instead she gave him a firm shove. He let her go but glared at her.

"You are a baby," he hissed. Then he brushed past her and walked briskly toward town.

Opal watched his retreating back and suddenly decided she didn't much care for Max after all.

SEVERAL EVENINGS LATER WHEN AIDAN CAME FOR DINNER, he noticed Opal's subdued mood. After the meal he found her sitting on the front porch swing snapping beans.

"Mind if I join you?" he asked as he stepped out onto the porch.

Opal noticed how exceptional he looked tonight. She had never seen him wear the black slacks and pastel green shirt before. The color of his shirt accented his green eyes.

"Sure, want to snap some beans?" she asked with a smile.

"No thanks, I'm not much of a beans snapper," he replied as he took his seat on the swing.

Opal caught the aroma of his clean smelling aftershave. It made her want to scoot a little closer to him but she knew that would be considered acting too forward.

"The weather has really been sweltering lately," he commented.

"Yes, it has," Opal agreed.

"I noticed at supper you didn't seem your usual cheerful self. Are you feeling poorly because of the heat?" Aidan asked with a look of unease.

"I feel fine."

"Is something bothering you?" he asked, unwilling to let the subject drop.

"No, everything is, is," then she paused.

Aidan looked at Opal waiting for her to finish.

Opal ducked her head slightly and let out a long breath. Then she looked at Aidan with tears swimming in her eyes.

"Oh, Aidan, I may have done something awful," she confessed with a tremor in her voice.

Aidan felt his gut tighten at her words. Dear Lord, don't let it be what I think she may be going to confess, he thought. Not my sweet Opal. Well, she's not my Opal, but I would certainly like her to be mine and I don't think I can bear hearing what she may have to say, he reflected, as he waited on edge to hear what she might have done.

"Does it involve a young man?" he asked hardly daring to look at her.

Opal sat in silence for several moments and then nodded her head in the affirmative.

Aidan felt his heart would surely stop beating at any moment. Being a doctor, he put on his professional face and continued. "Opal, you can tell me anything, and it will be held in the strictest of confidence," he tried to sound reassuring and professional. Professional, yes, he was professional, but he was also a man likely in love with the young woman seated beside him.

Opal looked at him as a few tears seeped from her lovely eyes and rolled down her pink cheeks. She launched into a lengthy description of what she had witnessed when she went to see Max. Then she told about their conversation of several days ago and him kissing her in such a shameless manner.

"I didn't like the way he kissed me, sticking his tongue in my mouth and all, and I shoved him away. Then he glared at me and called me a baby!" she ended her account of what had happened.

Aidan sat quietly letting her story sink in with a great sense of relief. After several minutes, he asked, "Why do you think you did something awful?"

"Going to Max's room and just opening the door! If I hadn't done that none of the rest of this would have happened. I really liked Max, as a friend you know, but now, well, I don't think I like him at all anymore." She didn't want Aidan to know she had kind of had a crush on Max since she couldn't seem to get his attention.

"I see," Aidan said and agreed that going to Max's room was a mistake. Perhaps it was lucky the other woman was there, or Max may have misconstrued Opal's intentions and taken more advantage than he did by the kiss he gave her on the front porch. Aidan knew he felt great relief that what Opal termed "awful" wasn't so awful after all.

"We all do things at times without thinking it through. You have learned an important lesson about thinking about your actions ahead of time," Aidan offered in an attempt to put her mind at ease.

"So, when will you turn eighteen?" he asked.

"In two more months," Opal said with exasperation, as though she thought that was a lifetime away.

"Well, that isn't so far off." Aidan would like to have parted with a kiss but felt it too risky after the recent unfortunate encounter she had experienced with Max. He could wait and, when the time was right, he would go slowly in introducing Opal to the more grown-up ways of men and women. He wondered if any of the boys he had seen her with at the dances had ever given her more than a quick peck on the cheek but thought better of asking. He doubted any of them had gotten too far with Opal after what she had just told him.

Aidan rose and walked slowly down the steps. At the bottom he turned and looked at Opal. "Don't think too harshly of Max, he's really not such a bad sort. Some men find it harder to control their passions than others." He looked thoughtful then added, "I think he has the idea now that he needs to respect you, and if he forgets, just let me know," he said and continued on down the path leading to the road.

Opal watched Aidan climb into his buggy and drive toward town. She was smitten with him all over again. For a while Max had clouded her vision, but it was clear again as to which man she would choose if given the chance. Oh, how she longed for her eighteenth birthday to arrive. Maybe Aidan would think of her as a more grown-up woman when she turned eighteen, she mused.

Chapter Twenty-Three

Aidan did not wait for Opal's eighteenth birthday but, as soon as school was finished, he was the first to ask to escort her to the Saturday night dance. He was the first to ask to accompany her to many of the following dances and parties. When he was available, he sat by her in church on Sunday.

Opal was happy with Aidan's undivided attention and knew she was falling madly in love with the handsome doctor and prayed he was falling madly in love with her.

The summer had been extraordinarily hot and just as dry. The spring garden soon withered under the unyielding summer heat. The fall garden didn't fare much better, so Jane's profits were down about one-third from the previous year. She was thankful, once again, that she and Charles Lungreen had become business partners in the boarding house as that business remained solid.

Charles' new businesses kept him so busy that he didn't make it to dinner as often as he had in previous days. Max almost never came to dinner, as rumor had it he was entwined with one female after another, and knew Opal had no desire for his company. Her eyes were only for Aidan.

Just before Christmas a letter arrived from Kathryn with the news they were expecting a baby in the spring. Seth had been promoted to a higher rank and seemed pleased with his new assignment. He was still gone from home for days at a time, which Kathryn, like any good wife, dreaded to see.

Jane rarely thought about Seth anymore, and when she did it was in connection with his wife and stepdaughter and now soon to be his own child. She was happy for him but wondered if she would ever reach a point of wanting to marry again. If she ever did, she knew in her heart it would have to be a man of Seth's character.

CHRISTMAS MORNING AIDAN ARRIVED EARLY WITH A lovely gift box exquisitely wrapped. He and Opal sat in the parlor away from the guests who were already at breakfast.

Aidan took Opal's left hand and kissed it gently as he gazed at the beautiful face of the lovely young woman seated beside him. "Opal, do you know what would make this an absolutely perfect Christmas?" he asked.

Opal chuckled. "I think it's already perfect since we get to spend it together," she answered. Then she became more serious. "At least it will be perfect if you don't get called away."

Aidan chuckled. "That's true enough, but there is one more thing," he paused.

"What might that be?" Opal asked curiously.

Aidan slipped from the sofa and knelt before Opal. "If you will accept my proposal of marriage and this ring as a promise of our future life together," he said earnestly as he presented the lovely ring.

Opal's hands flew to her face as her eyes grew huge.

Suddenly, everyone in the dining room heard a squeal of delight and Opal's excited voice shouting, "Yes, Yes, Yes!"

Before anyone could move the couple appeared in the doorway with

Opal holding her hand so everyone could see the lovely solitaire diamond engagement ring.

Jane could plainly see the signs of love reflected on the couple's faces. She was delighted for Opal and grateful Aidan had not rushed her into marriage.

Jane still carried on their Christmas tradition. She baked a white cake and on Christmas morning it was sitting on the dining room table decorated with colorful hard candy. The family and several boarders thought it was the best cake they had ever tasted, almost as good as Jane's chocolate meringue pie. Jane felt certain now that Ruby was ten, she likely knew the true origin of Santa Claus, but Ruby pretended just the same, and so did everyone else.

Jane wondered what her life would be like in a few more years when Opal would be married, Sam already on the verge of manhood, and Ruby in her teens. She knew Christmas would be celebrated a bit differently, and the rest of her life would be different too. But to what extent would her life be so different, she pondered. Would Sam stay to oversee the orchard and garden business? Or would he want to strike out on his own? Sometimes he still talked about joining the army. Jane shivered with dread should that come to pass. She would constantly worry for Sam's safety, like most other mothers.

Ruby, Ruby, what would she be like in a few years? She could be such a handful at times and so independent. Then at other times she would still be so clingy. The changes seemed to weigh on Jane's mind more lately, or maybe it was something about the holidays that made her think about the years ahead. The years seemed to be passing faster now. Perhaps it was just that she was so busy most of the time that the days blended together until a holiday or birthday came along to remind her another year had passed. Here she was in her mid-thirties and in just a few years all three of the children would be grown with their own lives separate from hers. That meant many years of aloneness ahead. She didn't want to think of it as loneliness; that was too depressing. Aloneness sounded like a choice to either be alone or seek company, but loneliness sounded like you had no choice.

Jane stood up and walked to the kitchen. She put on a clean apron and started setting out the ingredients she needed to bake some pies. Baking always lifted her spirits, and she had wasted enough time dwelling on what might or might not lay ahead.

Chapter Twenty-Four

1901

Late one evening in February 1901, Jim sent word for Jane to come to the ranch as Bea had taken a turn for the worse. She put a change of clothes in a straw satchel, told Opal to take over her duties, and walked to the ranch, with a cold north wind to her back, arriving before night fall.

When Jane saw Bea's ashen pallor and heard her arduous breathing she turned to Jim. "Has Aidan been to see her?"

Jim nodded his head and spoke softly. "He was here about noon but said just to keep her comfortable." Jim looked at Jane with utter defeat reflected in his eyes. Jim looked older, tired, near exhaustion. Bea's health had been steadily declining since last fall and the uncertainty of her future was taking a toll on Jim.

"Go do your chores. I'll be right here by her side," Jane told Jim with a gentle shooing motion of her hand.

Jim moved to the side of the bed, leaned down, and gave Bea an adoring kiss on her cheek. "Honey Bea, I'll be back in about half an hour, gotta tend the livestock." He turned away before she could see the tears forming in his eyes.

Bea gave Jim a faint smile and her gaze followed him as he left the room. Then Bea turned her frail gaze toward Jane and gently reached out her trembling hand. Jane took her hand and held it until she closed her eyes. Bea's hand continued to jerk, and Jane let her own hand move with it. As Bea relaxed the violent shaking began to subside. As her eyes grew heavy her hand gave an occasional quiver and her breathing was less labored as she slipped into a tranquil sleep. Jane could not bring herself to let go so she continued to hold Bea's hand until she heard her breathe her last breath. Jane sat quietly letting the tears roll down her cheeks. The grief she felt for the loss of her dear friend engulfed her. The empathy she felt for Jim overwhelmed her. She knew the path he was about to tread all too well. She felt powerless to ease his pain.

When Jane heard Jim come in the back door she quickly let go of Bea's motionless hand, blotted the tears from her eyes and face, and met him halfway across the parlor. Jim did not have to ask; he saw his answer written on Jane's tear-stained face.

Word of Bea's passing spread quickly; by nine o'clock neighbors began to arrive bringing food and words of sympathy; and several people came prepared to sit all night with the body. Jane remained with the sitters, brewing strong coffee and speaking quietly to Jim about the funeral plans. She and two of the neighbor women prepared Bea's body and dressed her in her favorite navy-blue Sunday dress. When the coffin was ready Jane folded one of Bea's handmade quilts and laid it in the casket. Jane put a clean pillowslip on Bea's pillow, fluffed it, and laid it on the quilt. Jane, Jim, and one of the neighbors gently laid Bea on her bed of eternal rest.

Clementine Bea Collins Armstrong, age fifty-eight, was buried in a quickly constructed family cemetery, at three o'clock the next afternoon, with the Reverend Reginald Brothers officiating. The minister spoke words of Christian praise and kindness as the onlookers gazed at the plain wooden coffin constructed by several of the neighbor men. The mourners sang "Shall We Gather At The River" and "Amazing Grace." The coffin was gently lowered into the open earth and covered with the fresh turned dirt after Jim and the others had walked back to the house. Jane had stood by Jim's side during the service and walked beside him the short distance back to his home.

Sam stayed with Jim that night and Aidan escorted Jane and the girls back to the boarding house.

The next afternoon Jane walked to the ranch again with paper and pen tucked into the straw satchel. She would write the letters for Jim and carry them to the post office. It was one of the few things of comfort she could do for him, that and listen. She knew his pain, the loneliness that would soon set in. He would think of telling Bea the simplest thing and then remember again she was no longer waiting for him at home. He would grieve until he would feel he could not take another breath, but another breath would come anyway. Little by little he would begin to return to his normal routine and thinking of her would be less painful. The throbbing loneliness would become more bearable with time. Yes, time, time, the illusive healer of wounds, of loneliness, and broken hearts.

As Jane penned the letter to Seth, she thought how sad that Bea had been cheated out of knowing Seth's child and the child cheated out of knowing her grandmother, Bea. She knew Seth would take his mother's death hard and was glad he had Kathryn to comfort him. It would have broken her heart to think of him being alone when he received such sad news.

SETH RECOGNIZED JANE'S HANDWRITING WHEN HE WAS handed her letter. As he started toward the married men's quarters, he opened the letter and started to read. The words seemed to jump off the page into his heart and he almost fell to his knees with shock and grief. He could not finish reading the words, for the tears that filled his eyes blurred his vision.

He clutched the letter and quickened his pace to reach home, to reach Kathryn. The moment he entered their home Kathryn did not have to ask if something was wrong; when she saw the forlorn look on his face, she knew.

Seth sat in the nearest chair and handed the letter to Kathryn. She read it in spite of the tears that misted in her eyes and the quiver in her voice. She gently laid the letter on the table and put her arms around Seth. She just stood for a long time cradling him in her arms, holding him near her heart. He could feel the child inside her swollen stomach move. A life is taken a life is given, he thought as he took solace in Kathryn's embrace.

After a long while she spoke in a quiet voice. "When you are ready, we will write to your pa. He will need all of the support we can give although we are far away. Maybe we could arrange a visit before we move to El Paso," Kathryn suggested in her quiet, concerned manner.

IN MID-APRIL JIM RODE TO TOWN FOR SOME SUPPLIES AND found he had a letter from Seth. Jim rode to the boarding house for Jane to read the letter to him. He didn't want to be alone in case it was bad news. He was elated when he heard Seth and Kathryn had a baby girl, born April 2, 1901, and had named her Carolyn Bea. Jim was beginning to look better, but she wished Seth and his family could come for a visit before they moved all the way to El Paso. She knew it would really lift Jim's spirits to see his new granddaughter.

Chapter Twenty-Five

1902

Aidan's parents and youngest sister arrived by train on the third Sunday in March. On the fourth Sunday in March, after Sunday services, Aidan and Opal stepped to the front of the church and were united in holy matrimony before God and a large group of witnesses. Opal wore a lovely pink flowered print dress with white lace trim around the collar and ruffled sleeves. She wore a white hat with a matching band and bow made from the same material as her dress. She was a beautiful bride with her honey-blond hair falling in soft curls framing her lovely face and her blue eyes shone with bliss. Aidan looked even more striking in his new summer gray suit. His twinkling eyes were fixed firmly on his stunning bride throughout the ceremony.

Jane graciously invited the entire congregation to the boarding house for a picnic lunch to celebrate the couple's union.

Aidan's family departed on the Monday morning train, well pleased with their son's choice for his wife.

After the excitement of the wedding had passed life soon returned to its daily routine.

Jane wiped the sweat from her eyes with the sleeve of her cotton dress as she picked beans in the hot afternoon sun. The garden had certainly flourished this spring with the promise of a bountiful harvest into the summer. The rains had come just right all spring. She noticed a slight breeze picking up from the north and was thankful for its coolness.

School would soon be out, and she certainly needed Ruby's and Sam's help. It was about all she and Blackie could do to keep up with the work now. She even had Blackie bring one of his older boys to help once in a while so none of the produce would go to waste.

"Mama, Mama!" Jane heard Ruby calling from a distance.

Jane turned to see why Ruby sounded so excited and instantly knew. The northern sky was almost black with that strange greenish tint. She heard the first distant clap of thunder and saw several streaks of lightning at one time snake toward the ground. Jane picked up the two baskets that were almost full and started as fast as she could toward the house. She glanced over her shoulder to yell at Blackie but saw him coming not far behind her.

Jane could see Ruby closing the windows before she reached the porch.

"Come on in, Blackie, and put those things in the kitchen; we better head to the cellar as soon as we finish closing up!"

Normally Blackie did not come in through the front door, but he knew there was no time to balk at her instructions today. As he sat his baskets on the kitchen table, he turned to tell Jane, "I'll jes sit on the back porch; it should pass by fast."

Jane did not pause to argue. "No, you won't. You'll go to that cellar with the rest of us. Help Ruby finish closing the windows while I call the folks from upstairs," she ordered and was running up the steps before he could argue.

Several boarders were in their rooms but came running as soon as they heard the urgency in Jane's voice. As they hurriedly filed out the back door the storm was almost upon them. Blackie lifted the door to the cellar, and everyone scurried in just as the first huge raindrops started to fall.

Blackie lowered the door and perched on one of the steps. Jane lit a lantern that was always filled with kerosene and sitting on the old dining table.

"Mez Jane, where Miss Essie?" Blackie asked as he scrutinized the cellar occupants not seeing Essie.

"Oh, dear Lord!" Jane looked around with panic seizing her when she realized no one had brought Essie to the cellar.

"Quick, open the door so I can go get Essie!" Jane almost shouted.

Just as Blackie lifted the door a deluge of rain and hail hit with a violent force.

"Too late, you'll get yourself kilt goin' out in dis," Blackie told her as he peered through the crack in the door. "I'll go."

"No, you won't, if I'd get killed so would you!"

"We'll just pray that Essie will be all right until the storm passes," Jane told everyone, but her insides were quivering with fear.

The storm raged with pounding rain and hail that made conversation almost impossible. From time to time they could hear crashing and banging as though everything around was being torn to pieces. Jane feared everything would be in tatters if it survived at all.

The occupants murmured among themselves about leaving poor Essie behind, each person blaming themselves for not thinking of her need for help.

No one felt worse than Jane. She berated herself and prayed. She didn't ask that the boarding house survive except to protect Essie.

Jane dreaded to see what damage lay outside. She felt certain the garden was a total loss and wondered if the fruit trees even survived the onslaught. After what seemed like an unusually long time, the storm began to die away into the distance and the loud drumming of hail subsided. After what seemed like hours but was actually about one hour the storm moved on to the south.

Jane could feel her legs wobbling as she stood and spoke in a quivering voice, "Lift the door, Blackie, and let's see what has happened."

Blackie was the first to see the house was still standing. "House still dere," he said with relief in his voice.

Jane emerged behind him and then the others filed out. She hardly noticed anything but ran as fast as she could to the house. Blackie was right behind her. She entered the house calling, "Essie, Essie!"

"Here I am in the back hallway," they heard her answer.

Jane and Blackie found Essie lying on the floor with one foot turned at a precarious angle.

"Oh, Essie, what happened? I'm so sorry we forgot you needed help. You do so much on your own, I guess we just panicked and forgot," Jane gave a heartfelt apology.

"Don't blame yourself I must have tripped on something and down I went. Otherwise, I am fine, made it through the storm okay," Essie assured them.

Jane saw a small rug lying near the wall. One of the women must have dropped it when she went to put away the clean linens and rugs in the linen closet that was next to Essie's room.

"Help me get her to bed," Jane said to Blackie.

"Mez Jane, I think it would be easier if I just lift Miss Essie and carry her to her room if dat all right with Miss Essie," Blackie suggested.

Essie laughed. "It's just fine with me; I know you're black, but then everyone is the same color to me," Essie told them with another good-natured laugh.

After Essie was resting as comfortably as Jane could possibly make her, and Essie had listened to several more apologies, Jane sent Blackie to find Aidan or one of the other doctors to come see about Essie's ankle.

Then she joined the other tenants outside to see what damage had been done.

They all stood taking in the aftermath of the storm. Several boards had been ripped from the porch and the latticework was hanging at odd angles in several places. Jane noticed several broken windows and the part of the roof she could see looked heavily damaged. Then her gaze moved to the garden and she saw virtually nothing standing. The beautiful plants of an hour ago were beaten into the mud. All of their hours of hard, sometimes backbreaking work were gone in a few minutes. Even from a distance she could see tree branches down and others hanging perilously throughout the orchard.

"Oh, Mama," Ruby almost whispered in disbelief. "What are we going to do?"

Jane didn't answer immediately but finally said, "We're just going to work hard and put it all back together again." With that said she and several others headed toward the tool shed.

To Jane's amazement, over the next few days, even the boarders pitched in and helped clean up as much as they could around the property. Charles Lungreen arrived shortly after the storm passed and told Jane some of his workers would be there the next morning to make repairs, replace the broken windows, and replace the roof.

The rest of the town had faired about the same as Jane. The community came together, neighbor helping neighbor, and within a short time all traces of the storm were gone except for the lost gardens and damaged trees.

Charles had sent three men to replace the damaged roof and repaint the outside of the house. On the final day of their repair work Jane was in the kitchen preparing to bake some pies for dinner when she heard one of the men come in the back door.

"Mrs. Parker, could I get another glass of that refreshin' lemonade?" he asked.

"Of course, help yourself it's on the sideboard in the dining room," Jane told him and continued her work.

A few seconds later she felt the hair on the back of her neck prickle and realized the man was standing directly behind her. Before she could turn, he grabbed her in a bear hug, pinning her upper arms to her body, and whispered in a raspy voice, "What I'm hankerin' for most is a little kiss from such a pretty lady." With that he started to nuzzle her neck, and then the smell of alcohol filled her nostrils.

Jane was horrified at his intent. She did not hesitate to grab a handful of flour and with a swift hurl of her lower arm flung it over her shoulder hitting him in the face.

He immediately let go and stepped back uttering a curse. Jane turned on him landing several fierce blows on his arms with her wooden rolling pin.

"Get out of here!" she screamed at him as he was backing away from the onslaught of the rolling pin.

He bolted out the back door with Jane in fast pursuit.

"I didn't mean no harm!" he shouted back as he darted around the corner of the house.

Jane followed with the rolling pin drawn back ready to land more blows if necessary. "Get off my property and don't you ever come back around here!" she shouted as he put more distance between them.

Jane glanced up to see the other two men, perched on ladders, taking in the scene. As the man reached the road Jane got in one last word as she shouted again, "Keep on running, you old reprobate!"

When Jane returned to the kitchen she wondered again if there would ever be another man she could care about. Men of good character seemed in short supply, she thought as she continued her pie baking.

Chapter Twenty-Six

1905

Jane sat on the front porch gently swinging, letting the soft evening breeze soothe away the aches of the long day's work. She looked out at the vast garden and orchard that lay beyond the house. They were flourishing this year regardless of the summer heat. The rains had been good in the spring and occasional showers still moved through to keep things greener than usual.

Jane's thoughts wandered over the past several years. The boarding house had been her salvation through some years of drought, several hailstorms, and one horrendous dust storm that wiped out the garden and robbed the fruit trees of most of their crops. All in all, it hadn't been too bad, but if it hadn't been for the boarding house it undoubtedly could have been much worse.

Her thoughts turned to her eldest daughter, Opal. She and Aidan so desperately wanted to have children, but none had come. She and Aidan had been to several specialists in Dallas and San Antonio, but they had no explanation for Opal being barren. Jane hurt when she saw the disappointment in her daughter's eyes each month as her cycle started again. Year after year of hope was dashed time and time again. Jane was thinking of suggesting they consider adoption. But surely, they had thought about it themselves. Well, maybe it wouldn't hurt to mention it anyway, she rationalized.

The front door opened, and Ruby came to sit beside her mother on the swing. At almost fourteen, Ruby was blossoming into a lovely young woman. Her long red hair shown like a new copper penny a sprinkling of freckles on her fair skin gave her a wholesome look and her cornflower blue eyes often danced with mischief or merriment, depending on her mood at the moment. Jane rarely saw Ruby with a serious look.

Jane had also noticed Ruby's figure was filling out much to Ruby's chagrin. One morning Jane noticed Ruby wrapping her budding breasts to hold them as snug against her body as possible and still be able to breathe. Jane questioned Ruby about why she was binding herself so tight.

"The boys have been teasing the girls that have bouncing boobs and I certainly don't intend to give them anything to ogle and tease me about," Ruby answered indignantly.

"Ruby, your body is going to develop regardless of that binding you're doing. Besides I don't think that is very healthy, so you might as well get used to the idea of having breasts," Jane gently advised.

"It's just not fair," Ruby complained. "First mother nature springs the monthly curse on girls and then bouncing boobs. What will be next?"

Jane was glad her back was turned to Ruby as she couldn't suppress a smile as she thought, *oh, if you only knew.*

ONE NIGHT WHILE THEY WERE GETTING READY FOR BED Ruby asked, "Mama, do you know who Sam's keeping company with?"

"No, I don't suppose I do. Why do you ask?"

"Well, I wasn't exactly asking, I know who he's been seeing lately." Ruby loved to keep up with all of the latest gossip and was more than happy to share whatever she knew.

"Who?"

"That new girl in town, Susanna Stone. Her papa is the owner of the new bank that went in on the east side of the square. They are also the ones building that three-story mansion out on North Swenson Street. I hear Mr. Stone also owns banks in Abilene and Fort Worth. People say they're rolling rich," she finished with a haughty toss of her head.

"Um, well, there's nothing wrong with having lots of money, but is she a nice girl?" Jane wanted to know.

"I don't really know but since she's so rich I don't know what she sees in Sam," Ruby stated as though his status was all that should matter, but deep down she was afraid Sam would be the one let down when Susanna threw him over for some rich guy.

"Susanna is very pretty and dresses to the hilt all the time. She has fancy little parasols with lace or feather trims, and pretty little fans to match each dress. I've never seen her wear the same outfit twice. She looks at Sam with those big brown eyes and puts her fan over her mouth, fans it slightly, and kind of flutters her eyelashes. Then she takes the fan away and giggles or laughs at whatever Sam said. She acts like she is really smitten with him for now," Ruby finished seriously with a worried look.

"Well, if she is so rich, she will soon figure out that Sam is not and that will probably be the end of that. Rich stick with the rich," Jane stated.

"That's just what I'm afraid of. Sam's going to be the one really hurt. He's such a good person and really deserves better than what I am afraid he is likely to get from Susanna."

Jane was a bit surprised to hear Ruby's concern for her brother. They had usually gotten along well but it seemed a bit odd for a younger sister to take much notice of her brother's affairs.

Jane sat on the bed thinking about what Ruby had told her. "Well, Ruby, I certainly hope Sam isn't hurt by this girl. Maybe he will be the one to see the light and back away before things get too serious."

"Couldn't you talk to him, Mama?" Ruby almost pleaded. "He'll listen to you, but he would think I was just being nosy or jealous if I say anything."

"I think it would be best to wait and see if he says anything about this girl to me. Sam has a good head on his shoulders." Although Jane knew that was true, she also knew how one's head could be turned by the wrong person or in this case she was likely the most desirable young lady in town. Sam probably felt flattered at the pretty new rich girl's attention. This would soon pass she tried to reassure herself.

SUSANNA STONE LOOKED OUT THE THIRD-FLOOR WINDOW of their newly constructed elegant home on North Swenson Street. She watched several crude farm wagons headed toward the town square and two more headed away from the central business district. Each carried a variety of farm goods and was driven by men or young farm boys. She didn't see a single woman among the bunch. Several men rode horseback along the wide thoroughfare. Small clouds of dust filled the air and horse droppings dotted the street.

Why did they have to live in this God-forsaken cow town? she wondered. A scowl covered her ordinarily pretty face, and her lips were puckered in a pout as she considered her fate. Why did Papa insist she and her mother move here? He knew how much they loved living in Fort Worth where they could have decent shopping and go to the theater for entertainment. She was missing out on all of the summer parties. How was she supposed to catch a proper husband, correction, proper rich husband stuck off in the middle of nowhere? There was not one decent store on the square where they could shop; everything smelled like sweaty horses or cows, even most of the people smelled obnoxious.

If it weren't for Sam Parker, she would go stark raving mad. Maybe she should try that, she mused. Then Papa would let her mother take her back to Fort Worth to a real doctor, she brooded. Oh fiddlesticks, Papa would probably know she was just putting on an act. After all he had endured her mother's many years of putting on acts to get her way. Sometimes she just wore him down but then he could really get a stubborn streak and set his foot down. Once his foot was planted it would take a tornado to move it. She would have to think it over very carefully how to get Papa to change his mind.

She turned from the window and flopped on her freshly made bed and pounded her pillow with her fists. Then she rolled to her back to stare at the white ruffled canopy over her bed as though she expected an answer to this dilemma might be visible there. It wasn't.

A smile crossed her lips as her thoughts turned to Sam Parker. He was without a doubt the best-looking young man in town. His thick reddish-blond hair hung slightly over his forehead bringing attention to his captivating blue eyes. Yes, he was a fine-looking fellow with a body to match. Sam was tall, tan, and muscular from hours of work outside in the family produce business. A bit to her surprise Sam was also intelligent. He could carry on a clever conversation on a variety of topics. Sam also knew just the right words she liked to hear to flatter her ego. Well, for the present she would just have to be content with Sam's company, until she or her mother could think of a way to get back to civilization.

SAM WOULD GO MOST EVENINGS TO THE ELEGANT HOME OF Stephen and Margaret Stone to call on their only child, Susanna. After dinner they would walk out to the gazebo in the back garden for a bit of privacy. At times other couples would join them for several hours but would usually leave before sunset. Sam would linger on as darkness fell and shrouded them in a cloak that kept prying eyes at bay. They would soon venture into sharing fevered kisses, exploring, enticing, and tantalizing one another until they had worked themselves into a feverish frenzy of passion. She was wearing his favorite perfume that seemed to entice him even more. He had slowly moved his hand up the inside of her leg that felt like silk. When he ventured above her knee a few inches she clamped her legs together like a vice.

"Susanna, Susanna, how can we keep doing this and me resist your charms much longer," Sam spoke in a husky tone.

Susanna giggled and pretended she was about to pull away from his fierce embrace. She had managed to remove his hand from under her dress.

"Don't go yet," he begged. "I'll try to keep my hands away from where they shouldn't be," he feebly promised.

"Oh, Sam, it's just as hard for me to resist you," she purred. "I know if something happens and my daddy finds out," she paused, "there's no telling what he might do."

"I know, and I wouldn't blame him," Sam agreed.

They sat quietly for several moments. "Susanna, maybe we shouldn't see each other for a while. You know, give us time to think things over," Sam halfheartedly suggested.

Susanna jerked away from Sam's hold. "You just think I'm your entertainment!" she accused in her pouty manner.

"No, Susanna, that's not it," Sam protested.

"There's plenty of other guys just waiting for a chance to take me out," she fumed.

"I know that, Susanna. I know I'm not interested in any other girl." Then Sam asked, "Are you interested in some other guy?"

Susanna continued to scowl. "Not really, but there is so little to do here. I don't want to sit around here without you and nothing to do. I swear, I'd go crazy, crazy!"

"I know, but I'm afraid we will get carried away and may later regret what might happen," Sam said as he stood to leave. "I need to go, it's getting late," he said as he turned and walked slowly away. He half hoped Susanna would call for him to come back, but she didn't.

Later, Sam lay in his bed for hours dreaming of Susanna's soft skin, wondering just how far she would permit his hands to roam under her full skirts and touch her smooth, enticing legs. He knew about the ultimate reward from overhearing the cowboys talk but had not yet experienced the pleasures of which they bragged. He wanted Susanna but if she got in a family way, what then?

SUSANNA WOULD UNDRESS AND STAND NAKED BEFORE HER mirror admiring her lush young body and dream Sam was there with her, touching her in all of her secret places and someday, she knew he would.

One evening Susanna's parents announced they would be away for the evening but would return by ten o'clock.

They had only been gone a short time when Sam arrived not knowing he and Susanna would be alone.

Susanna smiled sweetly when she answered his knock and invited him in. "I'm glad you decided to drop by," she cooed. "You can help me eat some of these fancy sandwiches left from Mother's bridge club meeting. Would you like a glass of chilled wine?" she asked, like the perfect hostess.

That sounds fine," Sam answered. "I know it's been a while since I've been to see you, but things are super busy with the produce business right now," he quickly explained. He had half expected Susanna to refuse to see him after their last evening together about ten days ago.

Sam was so thirsty he had already finished his glass of wine when Susanna had only taken a few sips of hers. Susanna promptly refilled his glass.

They chatted as they enjoyed the dainty little sandwiches and more wine. Susanna swayed when she stood to get another bottle of wine.

"Oh, dear," she giggled. "I do believe that wine has me tipsy."

Sam stood to assist her and had much the same reaction. "Wow, that's potent stuff!" he chuckled.

Suddenly, they were embracing and kissing passionately.

"Sam, my parents will be gone until ten o'clock. This may be our best chance to, to, you know," Susanna whispered in a seductive manner.

Sam did not hesitate as he gave Susanna a wicked smile. He grabbed Susanna's hand as they almost raced up the two flights of stairs to the sanctuary of her third-floor bedroom. With great haste they finally fulfilled their desires of those many evenings of tormented passion they had shared in the gazebo. In that brief interval they discovered those magical feelings that men and women had been discovering for years.

Being young, they quickly came together again. They couldn't wait for another opportunity for their bodies to make that miraculous journey to that euphoric place only the two of them shared.

A week later Susanna's parents parted for what they termed a couple of hours.

The couple scarcely made it to the top floor before they had dispensed of their clothing and were wildly enjoying the splendid adventure of exploring one another's bodies.

Margaret Stone suddenly developed a terrible headache shortly after arriving at their destination. Stephen instructed their carriage driver to return his wife home and then come back for him in about an hour.

When Margaret entered the house and found the couple nowhere in sight, she peeked out the kitchen window and did not see them at the gazebo. She heard peals and squeals of laughter coming from above. Slowly she climbed the two flights of stairs encountering various articles of clothing strewn up to the third floor. As she climbed what seemed like the endless stairway, she picked up each article of clothing. The door to Susanna's bedroom stood ajar which provided her a view she never could have imagined. Her voluptuous daughter was frolicking in her white, pristine, canopy bed, worthy of only a virgin, with that Parker boy from—from—the wrong side of the tracks.

Margaret Stone flew into a rage like Susanna had never witnessed in her entire life. Margaret burst into Susanna's room. "Susanna Stone!" she shrieked. "You have disgraced us! Your father and I have worked hard for years to associate with the best families in society for you! We wanted the best for you!" she screamed. "We wanted you to marry well and enjoy the best of everything, everything!"

Susanna and Sam had remained in stunned and embarrassed silence during Margaret's tirade. They had managed to partially cover themselves from Margaret's view.

Susanna stared at her normally poised mother. Her pretty face was covered with red splotches and had become contorted, ugly, as she raged. Susanna felt herself begin to shake. She had never, ever felt afraid of either of her parents before, no matter how badly she had misbehaved. But she had to admit, this wasn't like anything she had ever done before.

Margaret took a deep breath in an attempt to calm herself. She flung their clothing toward them and through gritted teeth demanded they get dressed and come downstairs immediately.

When Stephen returned home, he found his household in a full-blown uproar.

By the end of the evening, when some semblance of calmness had returned, it had been decided, largely by Margaret Stone, that Sam and Susanna should marry soon, as no word of scandal should touch their family. After all, Margaret pointed out, what decent man of their class would settle for used goods.

Sam felt awful! He mostly blamed himself for letting things get so out of hand. Being the honorable person that he was, he decided he would marry Susanna without complaint and try his damnedest to fit into her world.

It had also been decided that Stephen would take his new son-in-law under his wing and teach him to be a first-rate businessman. Sam had no doubts he could do the job, but he also knew his heart was not in it.

Sam decided he would marry and then tell his mother and sisters. He didn't want them to know the full extent of his downfall. He knew they would disapprove, so it would just be best to say they had simply fallen hopelessly in love.

Two weeks later in a quiet ceremony the two were joined in holy matrimony for better or worse.

JANE WAS SHOCKED WHEN SAM BROUGHT HIS LOVELY NEW bride to meet her and the girls. She and the girls did not believe the falling in love story for one minute. As soon as the newlyweds left Opal and Ruby both questioned their story.

"I'd bet my new Sunday hat he got her pregnant," Opal fumed.

"If he did, it was her fault for flaunting herself in front of him," Ruby affirmed. "I'll never believe Sam took advantage of her, that's just not his way."

"Girls, we don't really know what brought on this sudden marriage but if she is expecting we'll soon find out," Jane soothed.

After Sam and Susanna departed, Jane sat on the porch in the quiet of the evening. Jane suspected her son had been lured into a marriage of youthful passion that would soon fade and he would be left with a hollow existence. Why, oh why hadn't Sam come and confided in her? They had always been able to talk, even about personal things. Perhaps as a young man he no longer felt he needed his mother's advice. Jane lowered her head and wept for her only son.

"Mama, what's wrong?" Ruby asked softly with concern, as she sat beside her mother and put her arm around her shaking shoulders.

Jane wiped the tears from her red eyes. "Ruby, I think you were right all along about Susanna. Whatever she did to get Sam to marry her, I'm afraid it will end in disaster."

After Jane had finished, Ruby sat quietly for several minutes apparently thinking about her brother's future with Susanna.

Then she turned and gave Jane a bright smile. "You don't ever have to worry about me leaving you, Mama. I plan to spend the rest of my life right here with you," Ruby assured her with a generous hug.

Jane gave her a faint smile. "I'm quite certain someday you'll fall in love, marry, and want a home of your own. I don't expect you to stay with me. I just want you to take your time and choose wisely before you marry," Jane answered and gave her youngest daughter an affectionate hug.

"Well, whoever I marry will just have to agree to live here because I'm telling you, I'm not leaving," Ruby emphasized again.

"We'll see, Ruby," was the only answer Jane could give.

Chapter Twenty-Seven

Jane didn't see much of Sam and Susanna. She missed her son. She tried to feel warmly toward Susanna but was given little encouragement by the young woman. She first heard from the town gossips that a couple of months after they married the entire family traveled to Fort Worth by train. The Stones had given the newlyweds an extravagant party so all of their friends could meet Susanna's new husband.

Jane and the girls were deeply hurt that Sam had not mentioned the event, but they had to hear about it from others.

When Sam came for a brief visit several days after they returned Jane asked him about his trip to Fort Worth.

"Oh, it was one tiresome thing after another," he said a bit frustrated. "We had to go shopping and then shopping some more to outfit me to meet their uppity friends. We were entertained at luncheons, small dinner parties, and then Stephen and Margaret threw one big fancy whing-ding to celebrate our marriage. I was damn glad when it was all over and we got on the train to come home," he said as though the trip had been of no more importance than going fishing or hunting.

"I see," was all Jane could find to say in response.

"I suppose Susanna is glad to get back to the peace and quiet too."

"Oh no, she and her mother are still in Fort Worth doing something. I don't know what's so damned fascinating about Fort Worth," Sam said with disgust. "It's too big and too much noise to suit me."

They sat in silence for several minutes. Sam looked down at his new shiny shoes, neatly pressed trousers made in the latest style, his clean hands, and felt like he did not even recognize the person dressed in these fine clothes. He cleared his throat and looked up at his mother.

"I miss being here with you, Mama. I miss working in the garden and orchard. I miss my old friends; I never see them anymore."

"Aren't you happy with Susanna?" Jane asked gently.

Sam sat quietly and looked down at his shoes again. Then he slowly shook his head in the negative. Then he whispered, "I don't really know, Mama. There's been so much change, especially for me, that I don't know what I'm thinking half of the time."

Sam looked thoughtful and then he said, "You remember when me and Seth went fishing while we still lived in Erath County and I caught that big bass," he spread his hands to demonstrate the size.

Jane nodded her head.

"Well, I feel kind of like that old bass. He fought and fought, and I pulled and tugged until I finally landed him. I feel like I'm that old bass and the Stones are pulling and tugging me in little by little. I don't think it'll matter how hard I fight they'll get me," he finished with a slight shake of his head. Jane could see the sadness reflected in his eyes. "Yes, they'll pull me right into their circle of rich, snobby friends."

Jane sat quietly for a while reflecting on the things Sam had just confided in her.

"Sam, only you can decide if you want to get caught and become like them. Maybe when Susanna gets back things will settle down and the two of you can make things work better between you."

"Maybe," Sam answered, but he had a strong gut feeling it wouldn't happen.

"Sam, I'm not meaning to interfere but be cautious about bringing any children into this marriage just yet," Jane advised.

Sam gave a snorting laugh that startled Jane.

"Oh, don't worry, Mama. Susanna's already made it perfectly clear that she don't want any sniveling kids to make her lose her figure. I noticed when we went to visit my friends, Charles and Maryanne, Susanna didn't even ask to hold their new baby, like most women would do. When Maryanne asked if she would like to hold the baby, Susanna said she better not as she had a slight sore throat, which was not true!"

Jane tried to give Susanna the benefit of the doubt. "It could be that she hasn't been around babies much and don't feel comfortable with small children."

Sam stretched as he stood to leave. He bent and kissed his mother on the cheek.

"Don't worry, Mama. I guess things will sort themselves out in time."

SUSANNA AND HER MOTHER RETURNED A WEEK LATER BUT things did not settle down between her and Sam. In fact, they seemed to daily slide toward some tremendous, yawning abyss of discontentment. No matter how hard Sam tried to fit into Susanna's expectations of a suitable husband he seemed to most often come up short. Her criticisms of him encompassed everything from using the wrong fork for a certain course at dinner, to misusing a word, to the shirt he had picked to wear. He simply could not please her, and he often caught disapproving glances from Margaret as well.

One evening he came to recognize that he was quickly becoming like his father-in-law. Mr. Stone often seemed to find some last-minute business to take care of at the bank to detain him from going home at quitting time. About four evenings a week he managed to slink into the dining room just as dinner was being served. Immediately after dinner he dismissed himself to his study where he began an evening of enjoying solitude with a bottle of fine scotch. The best part was he was well out of earshot of Susanna and Margaret.

Sam soon followed his father-in-law's lead and dismissed himself to the library, closed the door, and pretended to read, while he brooded over the situation, he found himself trapped in. At first, he never thought of drinking but after a while he discovered a brandy or two seemed like a good way to remove the tensions of the day and what awaited him in the bedroom. His and Susanna's relationship continued to slide toward that cavernous abyss.

Sam often lay awake wondering just what had so quickly cooled Susanna's ardor. Ever since she and her mother had returned from Fort Worth things had become progressively worse. Had that trip made her realize how different they were and that he would never likely fit into their group of uppity friends? There weren't that many snobbish people in Stamford yet but as the town grew there would probably be more. Sam knew he had no desire to fit in with them either, not even to please Susanna.

AIDAN AND OPAL SPENT CHRISTMAS MORNING WITH JANE and Ruby enjoying a quiet family breakfast and then exchanging gifts.

"I hear Sam and the Stones have gone to Fort Worth for the holidays," Opal said, as they were cleaning up the discarded giftwrappings.

"Yes, they came and brought that big box of chocolates for all of us," Jane nodded to a fancy box sitting on the buffet table.

Opal looked a bit disgusted, "My, oh my, that certainly took a lot of thought."

Jane just smiled. "I try to like that girl but am having to say some extra prayers on the subject."

"Let's take our coffee to the living room." When they were all seated Opal and Aidan smiled at one another and joined their hands.

"We wanted to tell you first before we go to Uncle Jim's that we are adopting a baby girl," Opal announced with such excitement that Jane could hear the thrill in her voice.

Ruby let out a squeal and Jane broke into a huge smile.

"I'm going to be an aunt," Ruby almost shouted with delight.

"That's wonderful news," Jane stood and went to them and engulfed the couple in a big hug.

"Tell us more about her, where did you find her?" Jane asked as she resumed her seat.

"One of Aidan's patients died shortly after giving birth to the little girl and the young father had no way to care for the child and work. He was so devastated by his wife's passing that he didn't even want to look at the child or give her a name."

"It is a sad case, but the man seems perfectly fine with us adopting her," Aidan added.

"Where is the baby now?"

"The Henrys are keeping her until we can get all of the adoption papers in order and signed. That should happen this coming week and then she is ours," Aidan beamed.

"Shall we bring your new granddaughter to lunch next Sunday?" Opal asked smiling.

"Oh, yes, yes. Don't wait until Sunday, bring her as soon as you get her," Jane was ecstatic with joy for Opal and Aidan and herself too.

"What are you going to name her?" Ruby wanted to know, secretly hoping they would name the baby after her.

"I believe we have settled on Amanda Jane," Aidan answered. "Amanda will be for my mother and Jane, of course, for you."

Ruby was a bit disappointed but still thrilled at being an aunt.

Before lunch they all climbed into Aidan's buggy and drove out to

Jim's for Christmas lunch. Several of the cowboys joined them and they enjoyed a large meal followed by visiting and games.

"Got a Christmas package and letter from Seth and family," Jim told them and handed the letter to Jane to read.

"I know this is out of the way, but will they get to come for a visit before they move to El Paso?" Jane asked as she unfolded the letter.

"No, maybe later in the year," he said. Jim was looking old. His hair was snow white and his face bore the wrinkles of time. "Sure wish they was moving closer instead of farther away," Jim lamented. "Them girls are growing up mighty fast. Kate's almost eleven and my little Honey Bea is going on four already. It's a darn shame the little boy didn't live," Jim said with a sad look. "I know Seth would really have loved having a son. The doc told them no more babies, too dangerous for Kathryn to have any more children."

"Yes, it is a shame about the little boy," Jane agreed. "I'm sure Seth would have loved having a son. He was always so good with Sam."

Chapter Twenty-Eight

1906

On Friday evening shortly after supper, Opal, Aidan, and baby Amanda arrived for their first visit to Gran Jane and Aunt Ruby. The two were almost as enamored with the delightful child as her new parents.

"Oh, what a wonderful way to start a new year," Jane declared, and they all agreed.

IT SEEMED JANE HAD JUST DRIFTED OFF TO SLEEP WHEN SHE heard the faintest knock on her bedroom door. She started to get up when she heard Sam call her name. Jane reached for the chain on her bedside lamp and the room was filled with a soft glow of light.

"What's the matter?" she asked, as she sat up and reached for her housecoat.

Sam sat on the side of the bed beside his mother and took several deep breaths.

Jane waited patiently for Sam to tell her the reason for his late-night visit.

"Mama, I've tried, and I've tried, but I just can't do it anymore." He sounded worn out, defeated. "I can't please Susanna, I can't please her mother, and although Mr. Stone never complains I doubt I please him either," he finished, and Jane noticed the dejected slump of his broad shoulders.

Jane gently reached out and put her arm around her grown son and held him close. "Sam," she said gently but firmly. "If you have done your best then that is all you can do. Now, let it go. Don't keep kicking yourself and letting them kick you, just let it go."

"I told Susanna to get a divorce and send the papers to you. I think I'm going to head out West but will let you know where to find me."

Jane dreaded to see Sam leave but decided it was for the best under the circumstances.

Three days later in the early hours, just as the sun blazed over the eastern horizon, Sam Parker rode west pulling a packhorse behind him. He had no idea where he was headed but he figured he would know it when he saw it.

Jane watched her son's departure until his figure faded into the distance and she could see him no longer. She felt a sorrowful ache in her heart for Sam. He was a good man but just made the wrong choice. All she could do for Sam was to pray for him and that she did.

JANE WALKED ALONG THE WEST SIDE OF THE TOWN SQUARE looking in various shop windows. There seemed to be new businesses opening constantly. The latest she noticed was a shoe repair shop. He should have a lucrative business, Jane thought.

Ruby had been talking about opening an upscale dress shop; she planned to cater to women and girls. It would have to wait a few weeks until she graduated. She had a good head for business and wasn't the least bit interested in attending the new college they were building. Ruby had built up quite a bank account from working for Jane and helping Charles Lungreen with bookkeeping for his businesses, so she had her own financing to get started.

Jane was amazed at how the town had grown in the past seven years and her businesses had grown too. She had expanded the garden and orchards to over twice their size when she had started. The boarding house was still bringing in excellent profits, and, if all continued well, she would have Charles Lungreen paid off in another year and a half. Then it would be solely hers. She would own all of her own businesses and a lovely home too. Jane thanked God daily for her family, good health, good friends, and good fortune.

At times she wondered what Peter or Samuel would think if they could see how well she had done. She realized it would probably have never happened if either of them had lived. She wondered what paths her life would have taken. It amazed even her how much she had accomplished when it had become necessary. However, she could not forget how she got her start. The reward money from the incident in Erath County and the money from her aunt and uncle's estate gave her the nest egg she needed, and the Armstrongs had taken her under their wing and helped her along.

Jane leisurely walked along the east side of the square browsing the displays in the store windows. She had been to Opal's to see how near they were to having their new house completed. It was a lovely two-story house with a porch all across the front and six large round columns supporting the eaves of the porch above the second floor. There was a small central balcony on the second floor over the front door. Dark blue decorative shutters flanked the windows. It would be a nice home for their growing family. Two children and another expected in a few months. Opal was a superb mother and she and Aidan adored one another. It made Jane feel happy to see how well Opal's life was turning out. After they adopted Amanda, about four months later, Opal was amazed to discover she was pregnant. Now with another on the way their big house would soon be full, Jane mused. Their life was full and overflowing with joy.

She expected before too long Ruby would find a man to make her just as happy. It still concerned Jane that Ruby insisted she would never leave her mother even when she married. Jane smiled slightly to herself. The poor man she married better be understanding of Ruby's obsession to remain with her mother.

"Howdy, Mrs. Parker," the new deputy greeted her and tipped his hat politely. Jane was jerked from her thoughts. She was amazed he would know her name.

He stood almost six-foot tall, muscular build, with light brown hair and a neatly trimmed mustache. His keen eyes were golden brown. Not a handsome man but not bad looking either, she thought.

She had heard Marshall Mills had hired another deputy as the town had grown so fast Mills and his two deputies couldn't keep up with the work. Marshal Mills kept a tight rein on things and didn't put up with troublemakers. This man looked like he could hold his own with just about anyone.

Jane smiled and extended her hand. "I don't believe I have had the pleasure to meet you. How did you know who I am?" she asked out of curiosity.

"Well, Ma'am, I have met you, but it has been a number of years ago," he stated with a sly smile as he took her hand in his large, rough hand.

"Indeed, well, I suppose you will have to refresh my memory as to where we met."

"I used to work for the Swager Creek outfit near Lueders and helped you and some others cross the Clear Fork when it was on a rise. One of your daughters fell in that muddy river and scared us all half to death."

Jane looked at the man in astonishment. "You are one of the men that helped us cross," she stated as she stared with obvious shock. His appearance was so changed she could hardly envision this man to be the disheveled cowboy with a big chew of tobacco in his jaw.

"Oh yes, you're Chaw," she remembered.

"Allow me to introduce myself, I'm Lester Barnes. Most folks call me Les."

"So nice to see you again, Les, or should I say Deputy Les?"

"I'll answer to either one. I hear you own the boarding house on the south side of town along with a big produce business and have done really well for yourself," Les commented.

"Yes, I own the produce business and went into partnership with Charles Lungreen on the boarding house, but it will be mine in less than two years." Jane was pleased to tell him of her good fortune.

"That's mighty fine, Mrs. Parker."

"Please call me Jane."

"Okay, Jane."

"I hope your family is all doing well."

"Oh yes, Opal, the one that fell in the river, is married to one of the local doctors and they have two children and are expecting another one soon. Sam has gone out west for a while and Ruby, my youngest, will graduate from high school next month. She plans to open a dress shop here on the square."

"That sounds mighty fine," Les answered amicably.

Jane thought for a minute. Then on an impulse she asked, "When is your next day off?"

"Tuesday."

"Why don't you come to dinner, compliments of the house and a small pay back for your help when we needed it to cross the river?"

Les broke into a pleased grin. "That sounds fine, but you really don't owe me a thing."

"Well, come anyway, you'll enjoy the food."

"I'm sure I will. I've heard it's the best in town and where they send us deputies to eat is nothin' to brag about."

Jane walked on a bit amazed at herself for inviting Les to dinner. She actually hardly knew the man. She hoped he didn't find her invitation too forward.

Tuesday evening Les came for dinner. He was dressed in new jeans and a green western-cut shirt; his boots were shined to perfection. Jane still had a hard time connecting him to the man they had met at the river.

Much to her surprise, he ate with proper manners and seemed at ease doing so. He carried on a pleasant conversation with the other guests seated nearby. Jane noticed more than once his eyes following her movements when she excused herself to fetch something for one of the guests or serve dessert and coffee. For some reason his attentiveness did not bother her, as it would have with most men. In fact, she found it rather pleasant to feel admired by a man like Les.

After the others departed, just the two of them lingered over a second cup of coffee. Conversation with Les seemed to come easily. "Have you been in law enforcement before?"

"Some years back I was a sheriff down in Brown County. After a few years I got fed up with the Saturday night drunks, wife beaters, and other low-lifers so I went north and worked on a big ranch in Throckmorton County. It was a good outfit but then I guess I got itchy feet again and went to work at Swager Creek. Mr. Swager is a fine feller, but once again I needed a change," he finished with a weary expression. "I heard the Marshal here was looking for another deputy so decided to give law enforcement another try. So here I am, well at least for a while," he smiled.

"I take it you don't have family," Jane commented after hearing about his wanderings.

"No, Ma'am, not anymore."

There was a brief silence.

"I'm sorry, I didn't mean to pry," Jane told him honestly.

Les looked down at his half empty cup, ran a finger over the fine linen tablecloth, and looked up. "I married once, she died in childbirth and the baby died too. I just never wanted to take a chance on going through that pain again," he said frankly. Jane could hear the lingering pain of long ago still reflected in his voice.

"I understand, I lost two husbands and one child too," Jane stated with a far-away look in her eyes.

"Life isn't always kind, is it?" Les asked as he gazed at Jane and they seemed to form some kind of bond. Neither could have described it, but it was there between them.

Les came to dinner most Tuesdays and got one Saturday night off duty a month. He would escort Jane to the opera house for some kind of stage show or to the dances on the square in the warmer months.

While they enjoyed one another's company Les did not push for a more permanent relationship. He would kiss her good night at her front door after escorting her home. The kisses they shared were pleasant but not passionate. This surprised Jane in a way. She did not mind Les kissing her. In fact, she rather enjoyed the close contact but was glad he did not try to get too close.

Jane also realized Les was a virile man when he held her close, but he never pushed the issue. At times Jane wondered with whom he satisfied those needs.

Les respected Jane. Nevertheless, at times he longed for a more serious relationship. At the same time Les knew he would not stay put in one place for the rest of his life. He also knew Jane was planted in this place like a strong oak tree.

As far as he was concerned, he would not have thought any less of Jane if she had permitted him to visit her bed occasionally, but he knew she wasn't likely to permit that to happen. Her life was too public running the boarding house.

He contented himself with occasional visits to a certain widow woman's house about a mile north of town. It was located in a secluded stand of mesquite trees that blocked the view of her house from anyone passing on the main road. Their arrangement worked well for both of them.

Les being a pragmatic man decided it was best to leave well enough alone.

Chapter Twenty-Nine

Ruby and Jane took the train to Fort Worth where Ruby lined up suppliers for her new dress shop. They spent four days in a whirl of buying the merchandise to stock it for her grand opening.

On July 15, 1907, Ruby opened the doors to *RUBY'S DRESS SHOP,* and in smaller letters the sign read, *For Ladies and Girls.* The sign was painted a pale green bordered with brown and the letters were ruby red.

Ruby was a natural salesperson as well as understanding the business end of keeping the books. Her shop was the new sensation in town. If Susanna Stone had still been in town, even she would have been impressed with the quality Ruby provided to the gentry as well as the working class of Stamford.

One evening in October, Ruby noticed a nice-looking young man perusing the items displayed in the window. She glanced his direction several times as she finished selling Mrs. Platt and her two daughters a new frock each for Thanksgiving and they also put three new dresses on lay-away for the Christmas season. When the customers were gone, Ruby noticed the young man was still walking slowly past her shop apparently still window-shopping. He was kind of cute, she thought as he opened the door.

"Come in and perhaps I can assist you in finding the perfect gift for," she paused, "your mother, sister, or perhaps your girlfriend," Ruby invited the prospective customer inside with an equally inviting smile.

The young man just stared at her for several seconds as though she were speaking a language he didn't understand. Then he yanked off his hat and muttered, "Thank you, Miss." He entered the store as though he were entering a foreign land. He looked around as though he was trying to spot another way out if the need arose. It was obvious he had never been in such a store before and wasn't sure just what was going to happen next.

Ruby smiled sweetly trying to put him at ease. "I'm Ruby Parker, the proprietor," she said as she extended her hand in a friendly gesture.

The young man looked at her hand and then took it in his much larger one and gave her a hardy handshake. He looked up and met her gaze with the most beautiful green eyes Ruby had ever seen, not that she had seen that many. His honey-colored blond hair was cut short, and he was clean-shaven. His features were firm but not harsh. He was not exactly handsome, but he was certainly good-looking. Ruby also noted that he stood several inches taller than her own five feet eight inches, which was rather tall for a girl.

Then she heard him speak in a smooth low-toned voice. "I'm Carl O'Dell. Do you own this shop?" he asked in near disbelief as he looked around at the obviously expensive dresses and accessories.

"Yes, I do. I worked for my mother and for Mr. Lungreen at the lumberyard the last three years I was in school and saved my money so I could open my own business," she told him, seeing he was impressed. "Are you new in town? I don't recall seeing you before."

"Yeah, we moved here about four months ago. My father is farming with two of my mother's brothers and I work on the farm too. We live out east of town at Ericksdahl."

"How did an Irishman get mixed up with all of those Swedish people?" Ruby asked with a charming smile.

"As for the Irish and the Swedish, well you see, a handsome Irish lad, almost as handsome as me, met a lovely Swedish *ung kvinna,* young woman, and fell hopelessly in love. The two married and I, Carl O'Dell, am their handsome, charming offspring along with seven more siblings," he told her with a good-natured laugh at his own wit.

She could definitely tell he was Irish and full of blarney as she watched his green eyes dance with merriment as he told her about his family.

"I see," Ruby responded with her own good-natured laugh. "Now if you tell me who you are shopping for, perhaps I can help you find just the right gift," Ruby said pleasantly.

"Oh, it's for my, my girlfriend. It's her birthday next week," Carl lied, as he didn't want to admit he didn't have a girlfriend and he had been hanging around outside in hopes of getting to meet the pretty young woman he had seen through the glass.

Ruby walked behind the jewelry display counter and asked, "Does she like jewelry?"

Carl looked at all of the sparkling jewelry displayed in the glass counter. "Oh yes, she adores pretty jewelry."

Ruby reached into the display case and sat several boxes containing lovely brooches on top for him to have a closer look.

"These are the types of brooches the younger women seem to prefer," she said in her business voice.

"They range in price," she said as she removed the lid to each box and turned it over so Carl could see the price of each piece.

He let out a short whistle when he looked at the price tags. "I don't have enough money for any of these yet," he said honestly.

Ruby gave him an encouraging smile. "You pick the one you like the best and we will set up a charge account, you know, like the farmers do at the lumberyard."

"You mean you do that too?"

"Yes, we will work out what you can pay down and then you can pay it out in monthly installments, but you get to take it with you now," she smiled again.

"You would trust me, someone you just met, to pay a little and take this lovely brooch with me. What if I never come back?" Carl asked a bit perplexed by her business methods.

Ruby gave her head a small toss, sending her shiny auburn hair gently swirling back over her shoulder. "Oh, I think you'll come back. If not, I know where most of the Swedes live."

Carl picked a lovely brooch with small pearls set as flowers and the center set with some iridescent stone that enhanced the flower. The delicate flowers were surrounded by lacy gold leaves.

Ruby gift-wrapped the small box for Carl. He left knowing he would return every chance he got until he could work up the nerve to ask her for a date.

Ruby strongly suspected there was no girlfriend and rather hoped she was right. Carl was the most handsome and charming guy she had ever met.

When he arrived with his payment in December, Ruby approached him about a Christmas gift for his girlfriend. He wanted to tell her the truth but had not figured out just yet what exactly to say that would sound plausible. He picked a gold brooch with matching earrings. The brooch was gold set with red stones, ruby red stones. Carl could just imagine how attractive the jewelry would look on Ruby. Here he was going deeper in debt just for an excuse to come see Ruby who likely only thought of him as another customer.

Carl gave much thought to the situation he had gotten himself into with the pretense of having a girlfriend. Before he went to make his payment in February, well aware Valentine's Day was approaching, he had made up a story to end this charade. He just hoped Ruby would believe it and he could stop spending his hard-earned money on things he had no use for. He had considered giving the jewelry to his mother for Christmas but knew it would not be to her liking. His sisters were too young for the pieces, so they were tucked away in the bottom of his underwear and sock drawer.

When he gave Ruby his payment and she inquired about a Valentine gift, he hung his head and put on what he hoped passed for a sad expression.

"She and I had a row. She turned to my cousin for comfort and the next thing we heard they had run away together. They sent word they got married in Albany and were headed for Waco to live," he said with the most forlorn look he could manage.

"Oh, how awful!" Ruby sympathized.

"May I ask, did she take the jewelry you gave her?"

Carl shrugged, "I suppose."

"Well, have someone look in her room and if they find it you can bring it back and won't owe another cent."

"But what if she wore it already?"

"As long as it looks undamaged, I can put it on the sale table," she said with understanding.

"Thank you," he said hardly above a whisper. "You are very kind."

Ruby still felt sorry for the poor fellow. He seemed so down in the dumps. Maybe there had been a girlfriend, she decided. She looked at him and gave him her most charming smile. "Carl, I hope you won't think I'm being too forward but there's a dance Saturday night at the new Swans Café. Why don't you meet me there about eight o'clock and we'll dance our cares away?"

Carl could hardly believe his good luck. Here he had been trying to figure out how to ask Ruby out and she had just asked him out. Oh, he did have the luck of the Irish!

Thus began the courtship of Carl O'Dell, that lucky Irishman, well half anyway, and the lovely Miss Ruby Parker.

Chapter Thirty

1908

1908 turned out to be a very prosperous year for Jane. The produce business had its highest yields ever and the boarding house continued to turn a good profit as well. In September Jane paid the remainder of her note to Charles Lungreen and became the sole owner of the boarding house as well as her produce business. She felt elated with the success she had achieved, and her life seemed almost perfect. Jane, being a wise woman, knew life was never perfect and the euphoria she was enjoying would not last forever.

Letters from Sam arrived about every other month. He seemed to have found his niche in Colorado as foreman on a large ranch near the eastern slopes of the mountains. He mentioned a particular young lady in a couple of letters but did not elaborate on the extent of their relationship. Jane longed to see Sam but accepted the fact that it could be many years before he returned even to see his family. The painful memories he left behind might be too much to come back to.

Opal was with child again, due in late summer. At times Jane looked in her dressing table mirror and wondered if she looked old enough to soon have four grandchildren. Well, it didn't matter much she did, and she loved them dearly.

Ruby and Carl continued their courtship and Jane wondered how much longer it would be until he popped the marriage question. Carl was a bit slow at getting around to some things. It was likely for the best she thought. They were still young, and Ruby continued to insist she would never leave her mother. This often puzzled as well as worried Jane. She hoped if Ruby and Carl did marry, he would be an understanding husband.

Jane and Les still went out occasion. He didn't come to dinner on Tuesday nights quite as often as he had in the past, nor did he take her out every month on his one Saturday night off. She did not question his lack of attention, as she knew one day he would appear and say his itchy feet were acting up again, so he'd be moving on. She would miss him though. He had brought a pleasant interlude into her life.

ON THE TWENTIETH OF SEPTEMBER, BLACKIE DID NOT COME to work. No one came to tell Jane why Blackie hadn't come to work. The next day Blackie didn't come to work again. Jane knew something was terribly wrong. She walked to the lumberyard after lunch and told Charles what had happened.

"I'll ride out to see what the matter is," he volunteered and immediately rose to go hitch up his buggy.

"I'll go with you."

Charles paused. "I think it best I drop you at home. You never know what might have happened out there."

"Has there been some sort of trouble?"

Charles wiped the sweat from his face with a clean white handkerchief. "I've heard some rumors that some of the folks in town don't like the blacks coming to town on Saturday to shop. They seem to think they should come when there aren't so many white ladies and children in town."

"Oh, for Heaven's sakes, they don't bother anybody while they shop. In fact, I've seen them go out of their way to stay out of the white folks' way," Jane said in disgust.

Charles returned in about an hour with a sad look. "Jane, Blackie died two nights ago. Died in his sleep they said. He had complained of an aching in his chest after supper and went to bed a bit early. Died sometime during the night."

Jane felt shocked. "He was such a stout man and avid worker; why didn't they let me know? When is the funeral? I certainly want to attend."

Charles looked at Jane and simply said, "Jane, that's not their way. They buried him yesterday."

"You mean to tell me I wasn't welcome at his funeral?"

"No, no, that's not it, they just don't think it proper for a white lady to attend a colored man's funeral, that's all, Jane," Charles put his arm around Jane in a fatherly manner while he explained, knowing Jane was hurt and felt she had been snubbed by Blackie's family.

At last, she spoke, "I see, well, I don't understand but if that is their way then that's that."

"I took the liberty of telling Junior you would need someone to take his daddy's place so for him to be here first thing tomorrow and he said he would."

"Yes, I've got to have help, but I can tell you this much, Junior don't know half what his daddy knew about gardening and the orchard, but I guess we'll make do."

Just at daybreak Jane heard a knock on the back door. If it had been Blackie, he would have then opened the door and come in for breakfast, but no one opened the door.

Jane opened the door to find Junior standing on the back porch.

"Good morning, Junior," she greeted the man who looked like a younger version of his father. "Sorry to hear about your daddy's passing. He was a fine man. He worked hard every day and never gave me one minute of trouble. That's what I expect of you," Jane stated plainly so he would know exactly what she expected.

Junior looked at Jane and nodded politely.

Junior arrived every morning, except Sunday, and worked until dark. It was true, he did not know as much about gardening and the orchard as his father, but he was willing to learn and listened closely to everything Jane told him. They got on fine.

Chapter Thirty-One

1909

Jane heard Jim calling her name and met him in the dining room doorway. His normally tan face looked strangely pale and his hands were shaking as he extended a letter toward her. He looked at her with an expression of sorrow and disbelief. Jane knew something terrible had happened before she even reached for his out-stretched, quivering hand to accept the envelope.

"Sit down, Jim," she told him and pulled out a chair. Without further words she disappeared into the kitchen and quickly returned with two cups of steaming coffee. She picked up the letter from where it lay on the table.

"I tried to read it, but I just couldn't finish it," Jim said, and Jane could hear the quiver in his voice

She pulled out the folded sheets of paper and instantly recognized Seth's bold handwriting.

March 24, 1909

Dear Papa,

It is with indeed a heavy heart that I write this letter. Sunday before last we lost our beloved Kathryn in a tragic accident. The girls and I are so grieved that it has taken me all these days to collect my thoughts enough to write to you about our terrible loss. After Sunday services the congregation often carries picnic lunches to one of the members' farm for a picnic and afternoon of yard games. He has a big grassy field near a creek where we play horseshoes, croquet, and other games. There is plenty of space for the youngsters to run and play, as youngsters will do. He always brings his wagon empty and often most of the women and children pile into the back of the wagon to ride to the farm. There is one rather steep stretch of road just before we reach the grassy field. We had experienced several days of hard rains earlier in the week and the road had become rougher than normal. About halfway down the hill one of the wagon wheels struck a large rock throwing the wagon off-kilter and it overturned. Our dear Kathryn was thrown into a pile of rocks by the embankment and her head struck one of the larger rocks. She was already gone by the time I reached her. Several others were injured but we lost our dearest wife and mother.

As Jane paused to clear her quivering voice and blink away the tears that threatened to fill her eyes, she glanced up at Jim. His head was slightly bowed; tears rolled down his weathered cheeks and dripped onto his shirtfront. She reached out and took his hand in hers and gently squeezed his work-roughened hand.

He did not look up but whispered, "Go on."

I have come to believe I cannot continue in the army and give the girls the home and care they so desperately need. I have resigned my position and we will arrive by train in another week or so. They cry every day from missing their mother. I hope I have made the right decision.

Your Loving Son,

Seth

Jane gently folded the pages and slipped them back into the envelope.

She and Jim sat in companionable silence for several minutes, each lost in their own thoughts of the losses they had each endured.

Jim lifted his head and looked at Jane with tears still filling his eyes. "We know, don't we, Jane?"

"Yes, we know," she managed to answer despite the lump in her throat.

SETH AND THE GIRLS ARRIVED EIGHT DAYS LATER ON THE mid-day train. They walked to the boarding house where Ruby and Jane greeted them with open arms. Seth embraced Jane as the old friend she had become. She noticed how gaunt he looked with dark circles under his eyes marking his grief and lack of sleep. Then he stepped back and stated in a poignant tone, "You and Papa know the almost unbearable pain I'm feeling."

Jane simply nodded. "Yes, when you're ready to talk about it I'm here to listen."

The girls ate little and talked less during the meal, but Jane could tell they felt at ease with her and Ruby. Before long Kate was talking quietly with Ruby and little Bea inched closer to Jane when they sat in the parlor after the meal.

Junior hitched up the team to the buggy and drove them to the ranch.

DURING THE MONTHS THAT FOLLOWED THEIR RETURN THEY spent many evenings at the boarding house and Jane often went to the ranch to share a meal. Eventually Seth did talk about Kathryn. It was evident to Jane that he had truly loved Kathryn. He talked about being drawn to her because of her gentle nature. She would see to others' needs and comforts above her own. They had indeed shared a loving and devoted marriage.

Jane was glad Seth had found someone of Kathryn's character. She thought back to her own two marriages and remembered how blessed she had been to have known two men of such high quality. Now she and Seth shared a new bond, a new understanding of the other because of their past experiences.

Chapter Thirty-Two

1910

In the spring Jane noticed Les displaying a renewed interest in her. She vaguely wondered if his other lady friend, whom she was quite certain he had, might have ended their relationship. She would never ask Les such a personal question but did ponder about his actions toward her. Or was it because Seth had been displaying a renewed interest in her too?

Jane genuinely liked Les but was not sure her liking would ever turn to love. Lately Les had been especially attentive to her when he and Seth happened to come to dinner on the same evening.

One evening, only Les came for dinner. Afterwards they moved to the parlor to enjoy their coffee and dessert. They sat side by side on the settee. Les casually had his arm lying along the back of the sofa gently touching Jane on her shoulder, as they talked.

Seth was riding home from some late errands and decided to drop by for a visit with Jane. As he reined in his horse at the boarding house, he could plainly see the two through the large front window. He dismounted but stood beside his horse watching Jane and Les laughing and talking. Seth could see Les had his arm around Jane's shoulder. Then he leaned close as though he was whispering something in her ear. Jane laughed and when she turned to look at Les he moved in for a kiss on her lips that seemed to linger much too long, or so Seth thought.

Seth felt a stab of jealously like he had never experienced! He took several long strides toward the house, then came to an abrupt halt. What right did he have to interfere in Jane's life? he asked himself. He knew Jane and Les had been keeping company for quite some time. Seth did an about face, as though he were still in the army, and retraced his steps to his horse, mounted, and rode home thinking of ways he could let Jane know he wanted to court her. He had lost her once, but he didn't intend to lose her again. He resolved the best place to start might be by asking her out. If she accepted, he knew he had a chance, but if she refused him—he didn't want to even consider that as a possibility.

The next week Seth dropped by on Wednesday and invited Jane to accompany him to a dance on Saturday night. Much to his relief she accepted.

Jane was thrilled that Seth had finally made a move to show he was, or hopefully was, interested in her again. She could hardly wait for Saturday night to arrive. Jane felt a little giddy, like a schoolgirl, while she dressed making sure everything was done to perfection.

"Mama, you sure have been smiling a lot lately," Ruby observed a few days after Seth had asked her out. "What's happened to make you so cheerful?" Ruby teased.

"I thought I was always cheerful," Jane answered.

"Most of the time you are but, this is different somehow."

Jane smiled. "It may be because Seth asked me to the street dance Saturday night," Jane revealed with a slight blush.

"Oh! Mama, that's wonderful. I just got in some new stock. Come to the shop tomorrow and we'll pick out a fabulous new outfit that will knock Seth's socks off!"

Ruby picked out a special dress that looked fabulous on Jane. It was emerald-green with a V-neck, fitted bodice, and full skirt that would flow with her movements on the dance floor. The V-neck showed just enough cleavage to tantalize but not be vulgar. The emerald green enhanced the color of Jane's lovely hair and eyes.

When Jane answered Seth's knock, she almost gasp when she saw the fine-looking man standing on her front porch. He smiled at her and the small lines around his eyes seemed to enhance his striking good looks. He had a fresh haircut, new blue western shirt, black pants, and an intricately carved silver belt buckle that glistened in the light. He was the personification of a successful rancher, which he had become.

The two just stood for a few seconds staring at one another. Seth extended his arm and they walked arm and arm to his buggy.

They arrived early and danced until the band quit playing. They laughed and talked as they danced. During the slow dances Seth held Jane close. She felt the familiar strength of his arms and savored his fresh scent. She remembered the day he left for the army and, as he held her, she breathed in that same fresh odor. She had never forgotten that special aroma that belonged only to Seth.

He drove her home in the buggy and walked her to the door like any proper gentleman.

"Thank you, Seth, for the lovely evening," she said with eyes twinkling in the moonlight. "I don't know when I have ever danced so much."

"Me either, I had a sergeant that used to say he was going to dance holes in his shoes. I think maybe I did that tonight," he laughed showing the dimple in his cheek that Jane always thought made him look even more eye-catching.

They stood for several seconds just looking into one another's eyes. Seth took her in his arms and kissed her the way he had kissed her years ago. Jane had never forgotten that first intimate kiss they shared in the yard in the middle of the day. It made her blush then but now it made her want him to kiss her more. It made her have those womanly feelings she tried to keep hidden away but with Seth it was becoming more and more impossible.

ONE SATURDAY NIGHT, WHEN LES AND JANE RETURNED from enjoying a particularly humorous evening's entertainment at the Opera House, when Les kissed her good night at the door he prolonged the kiss and then pulled Jane snug against his firm body. She was especially aware of his obvious need and gently pushed him away.

Les groaned as he released her, "Jane, do you know how much you stir my blood? At night I dream about what it would be like to hold you the way I want to and make love the whole damn night."

His admission did not shock Jane. She knew about men's needs and women's too, for that matter. She also knew her own strong feelings on the subject and wasn't about to change for him or any man.

"Les, you know I do enjoy your company and care about you, but I won't welcome you or any man in my bed without the benefit of marriage. I live in a very public place and would never do anything to tarnish my reputation. Nor will I do anything to have my daughters think less of me or embarrass them in any manner."

Les smiled at her. "I know, Jane, but it don't hurt to wish."

Jane smiled back at him. "I know you will respect what I've just told you, Les, and I have my doubts you're the marrying kind."

Les looked out across the moonlit yard to the garden and orchard beyond. "Oh, I don't know, Jane. I guess a man can change but I ain't promisin' nothing at this point."

"That's fair enough," she answered and went into the house without further discussion.

Deep in her heart she knew her old feelings for Seth were returning. The way he had kissed her recently indicated his feelings were growing deeper, but he had not asked her to see him exclusively. After all, she had rejected him once so he may be even more reluctant to become too involved with her again.

Some nights she would lie awake wondering if Seth disregarded her and found someone else, could she find contentment with Les if he were willing to settle down, put down his gun, and take charge of the produce business? That particular answer escaped her.

One evening Seth came to dinner on an evening when Les was working. He and Jane moved to the front porch with their coffee at the end of the meal. As they sat on the porch swing watching the day pass to night, Seth finally broke their comfortable silence. He turned to her and smiled showing the dimple in his cheek. "Jane, do you realize how many years ago it's been since we used to sit on your front porch in Erath County watching the sun set and just enjoying one another's company?"

Jane gave a small laugh, "Goodness me, it's been twelve years. Where, oh where has all of that time gone?" she asked as she looked at Seth. He was even more handsome now than when they had first met, although now there were a few strands of gray hair showing at his temples.

Seth stretched his long legs and breathed deeply. "It seems like a lifetime ago. In a way it has been. Look at where we've both been and where we've ended up, back on the front porch watching the sun set," he said with a chuckle and look of contentment.

"Yes," Jane answered thoughtfully. "Back then we were definitely set on different paths and they both turned out good for each of us. You met Kathryn and have a lovely stepdaughter, and little Bea is adorable. With lots of hard work, the children made my dream, and theirs, come to pass. We have a good business and a lovely home although we share it with others. It's been a good life, but I do miss my Sam. What a pity he ever got mixed up with that spoiled Susanna Stone and her family. Sometimes I wonder if I will ever see him again," Jane said with a reflective expression.

"Oh, I'm sure you will. Now we have trains to take us most

anywhere in the country and automobiles are getting more popular every day. Who knows, you might just drive up to Colorado one of these days." They both laughed at the absurdity of such an idea.

Seth laid his arm across the back of the swing behind Jane and lightly touched her other shoulder.

They continued to swing and after a few minutes Seth once again broke the silence. "You know, Jane, when I left here to go to Fort Clark, I almost got off that train several times and came back. I just wasn't sure then I could be a rancher or farmer and your words kept running through my mind about me resenting you if I stayed against my will. I suppose that was the longest trip I ever made," he finished in a low voice and leaned over and kissed Jane on the cheek.

Jane savored the touch of Seth's lips on her cheek. It wasn't a passionate kiss but one of a lasting and trusting friendship full of reassurance. She cleared her throat, "I must admit I was tempted more than once to write and tell you I would come be your wife, but things here just kept working out and I was so afraid of losing another husband I just couldn't bring myself to do it. I guess that just wasn't meant to be our time," she finished softly.

Jane turned to him and leaned forward. Seth hesitated for only an instant and then he pulled her close and kissed her on her yielding lips with the ardor of a man with a purpose. For Jane, the kiss stirred those old feelings. From the way Seth kissed her she felt certain he was feeling much the same.

LES CAME TO SUPPER ON TUESDAY NIGHT AND ASKED JANE out for Saturday night to go to a stage show.

"I'm sorry, Les, I've already made plans for Saturday night," she answered, not wanting to mention her plans were with Seth. This was the second time he had asked her out recently and she had turned him down.

Les sat quietly for several minutes. "Are you seeing Seth again?"

"Yes, we have already made plans to attend the stage show," she answered gently, hoping to not hurt his feelings.

"I see, well maybe some other time," he said a bit tersely. He finished his coffee but did not linger to talk as usual.

Jane felt sorry that his feelings were hurt, but she knew her feelings for Seth were growing stronger and stronger. She wanted to let Les down easy. Jane knew she could never care for him the way she cared for Seth. She had come to realize that, even if Seth turned away from her, she could never settle for second best. As much as she liked Les and enjoyed his company, most of the time, she knew she would never develop deep feelings for him the way she had for Seth. She was willing to take her chances that this time things would work out between them.

A few days later, Les appeared at the boarding house one afternoon after lunch. Jane was surprised to see him that time of the day, as she knew he was on duty.

"Les where is your badge?" she asked when she noticed he didn't have it pinned to his shirt.

"That's what I come to tell you. I turned it in this mornin'."

Jane looked at him in shock. "Why in the world did you do that? I thought you liked working for Marshal Mills and liked it here!"

"Marshal Mills is a fine man to work for. I have no quarrel with him or this town. I've just been thinking it's time for me to be moving on."

Jane just stood staring at him with her jaw slightly agape at his unexpected announcement. She was totally taken aback by the suddenness of his leaving. "I, I, don't know what to say. You have certainly taken me by surprise. Are you sure nothing happened you're not telling me about?" she questioned, still amazed at his hasty decision.

Les had spent a considerable amount of time sizing up the situation between him and Jane. He was enough of a poker player to know when he had a winning hand or a losing hand and this had turned out to be the losing hand. It was time to get out of the game.

"Jane, I know we've been seeing one another on a regular basis but I told you from the start how I get itchy feet."

"Yes, that's true but . . ."

Les reached out, took Jane's hand, and placed it on his chest near his heart in a tender manner. "Ever since Seth came back here, I could see it almost from the start that he's the one you want, not me," he said gently.

"Oh, Les, now how would you know such a thing?"

"All I had to do was watch you two and that is part of my business, to watch how people act. Each of you looking at the other in that special way when you thought the other one wasn't looking. Damn, Jane, it was plain as day after a while when Seth quit grievin' for his wife that he was in love with you, and I believe you're in love with him." Les gave a short laugh, "Now ain't it funny what others see and figure out before the two people involved seem to know what's going on."

Jane gave Les a tender hug. "I'll miss you. You brought something back in my life that I thought was gone forever."

Les looked a bit taken aback by her statement. "Just what did I bring back into your life?"

"Hope."

"I'm glad we met again. You are one special lady. At times I have wished I were the one you fell in love with." They hugged once more and then he was gone. She hadn't even asked him where he was headed. Jane smiled to herself he probably didn't know anyway.

Chapter Thirty-Three

Ruby was humming as she put the finishing touches on the parlor decorations for her twentieth birthday celebration. Tonight, they were having a grand party, by Stamford standards, and she and Carl O'Dell would announce their engagement.

Ruby had met Carl a little over two years ago when he came to her shop pretending to buy a gift for his girlfriend. Ruby had liked Carl from the start. On her nineteenth birthday Carl had brought the two gift-wrapped boxes of jewelry he had bought for his supposed girlfriend and confessed to Ruby he had made it up so he would have an excuse to come to the shop to see her. He said he wanted to ask her out on a date but was afraid she might turn him down until she got to know him better. Ruby laughed about what he had done. She told him she was fond of him from the first day they met and thought he had exquisite taste in jewelry.

Carl was witty and a hard worker. He wanted to be a farmer, which was fine with Ruby, as long as they lived at the boarding house with her mother. Carl seemed to think that a bit strange at first and still didn't fully understand Ruby's need to stay with her mother. Since he was an easy-going fellow, he saw no need to press the issue and felt certain she would change her mind in time.

Ruby heard heavy footsteps on the front porch and glanced out the window of the front door.

"Mama," she called. "Marshal Mills and one his deputies are here. He must have come to pick up the pies for the Baptist Men's Meeting."

Jane came into the parlor wiping her hands on her apron, just as the marshal knocked. "He's not supposed to get the pies until tomorrow," Jane said a bit perplexed.

She opened the door and invited the men inside.

"Marshal, you're a day early for the pies," Jane told him as he and the deputy removed their hats.

"Oh, yes, Ma'am, I'm not here for the pies today."

Jane gave him a questioning look.

"Mrs. Parker, I got a telegram from a Sheriff Tully down in Erath County where you folks used to live, and he wanted me to warn you that a man you helped capture, Jackson Polk, has escaped from the state pen."

Jane stood transfixed with shock. Before she could collect her wits to ask questions Ruby chimed in.

"Oh, don't worry about my mama taking care of us if he dares to come around here. She's the bravest person in the world," Ruby bragged. "I was only seven when it happened, but I know all about it. Mama held him and his partner off at gun point once and she'll do it again," Ruby informed the men without hesitation. Before Jane could say anything, Ruby continued telling the marshal and deputy all about the men breaking in during the night, and Jane sending Sam to fetch the neighbor, and on and on. Jane stood listening to Ruby's very accurate account of the incident that had taken place in Erath County. How did Ruby know all of this? she wondered. The marshal would nod his head from time to time but never interrupted Ruby's account of what had happened.

"Thank you, Ruby, for filling us in on the details of what happened," Marshal Mills said. "I think it's unlikely Polk will show up here but stay alert. If anybody comes along that you feel uneasy about get in touch with me or one of the deputies as soon as you can," he told them.

As he looked around the room he said, "Mrs. Parker, I know your property is just on the outskirts of the city limits, and I don't know how much it would cost you to have a telephone line run and a telephone put in, but it might be worth checking into. That way, if anything happens that you need help, you could get in touch with us lots faster."

"I've been thinking about putting in a telephone, more for the guests' convenience, but just hadn't gotten around to finding out about the cost. I'll go this very afternoon and talk to Mr. Stanley at the telephone company."

"Good, I think that would be real helpful and, like I said, if you see anyone you think might be this man you let me know. You know people change over twelve or thirteen years and with a different hair cut or change in facial hair he might look a lot different than when you last saw him," the marshal advised.

That very thought had been running through Jane's mind. She could clearly picture the way Jackson Polk looked years ago, but as the marshal said she might not recognize him right away now.

"Thank you for coming by, Marshal; I'll see about the telephone today," Jane assured him.

As the two men walked away Jane turned to Ruby. "How did you know all of that, did Opal tell you?"

"No, Mama, I was just pretending to be asleep. Somehow, I knew I didn't need to be bothering you while you were holding that gun on the one behind the door, so I just pretended to be asleep. I never was afraid because you were right there beside me with the gun. Oh, Mama, you are brave; I'm still not afraid as long as I'm here with you,"

Ruby confessed and gave her mother a loving hug. It was reassuring to Ruby to know her mother was still her protector even if she was a grown woman now.

That night, when Jane was getting ready for bed, she opened the drawer in the table beside her bed. There lay the same loaded pistol that had perhaps saved them many years ago. She gently picked it up and laid it on the top of the table. She lay in the darkness for a long while, thinking about that single incident that had set their lives on such a different course than she could have ever imagined. The reward money along with the money from her uncle and aunt had paved the way to all they had now: the huge vegetable garden, the orchards, and this fine house that not only provided shelter but also helped make them a very comfortable living. It could have all turned out so tragic in an instant but, thank God, it had not. At last Jane drifted to sleep, not worried, just vigilant.

Ruby closed the door to her room and prepared for bed. She sat on the side of the bed thinking about the night of the incident when she was only seven. As she had told her mother she had not been afraid then because her mother was there to protect her. Being a child, of course, she didn't realize how dreadful that night might have turned out. Ruby fluffed her pillow and lay down. She closed her eyes, but they flew open when she heard a slight noise outside her door. She lay very still listening, but she heard nothing else. Ruby turned on her side and then on the other side. She would stare at the closed door wondering if it might burst open and that awful man would be standing there. Then it occurred to her that she did not know what that man looked like. Her eyes had been closed when they led him out. How would she know who he was if he did come around? Ruby slipped out of bed and, as quietly as possible, scooted her dressing table in front of the door. Then she prayed the house would not catch on fire. At last, she drifted into a restless sleep. She had incoherent dreams about faces, and faces, and more faces, but they were in shadows and she could not clearly see any of their features.

When Ruby awoke, she was glad to see the first rays of morning light seeping in around the windows.

Chapter Thirty-Four

JUNE 1911

"Mama, don't you think we could take the train to Abilene and shop for material for new bedspreads and curtains? These are really starting to look faded." Ruby asked her Mother as they finished breakfast.

Jane put down her napkin and took the last sip of her coffee. "Yes, we do need to make new bedspreads and curtains and soon, before you get busy making dresses for your wedding," Jane agreed.

"I could look at material for my dress and for the two bride-maids and flower girl too." Opal and Kate were to be her attendants and Bea the flower girl. "I saw in a magazine that some city weddings have six to ten attendants, can you imagine?"

"Sounds silly to me," Jane answered. "Why would you want so many people in a wedding? It's supposed to be about the couple anyway," Jane went on.

"Well, Mama, I do want to share this day with those I love most. I'm just sorry Sam won't be here to walk me down the aisle and give me away," Ruby said with a tinge of sadness.

"Me too, honey, I do miss Sam but no telling when we'll ever see him again. He's already been gone five years. I'm glad he's happy working on the ranch in Colorado. In his last letter he said Uncle Jim would be proud to see how good of a cowboy he's turned out to be," Jane smiled.

"Did I tell you what I heard while in town yesterday afternoon?" Ruby asked, as her mind drifted to a different subject.

Jane was accustomed to Ruby's sudden change of subjects.

"No, what did you hear?" Jane asked, knowing how Ruby liked to keep up with the latest gossip.

"Well, it seems Max has gotten that Lilly Mae Crown in a family way. When her papa told Max that he had to marry her, Max said he wasn't going to, so Lilly Mae and her papa went to the lumberyard to talk to Mr. Lungreen. Apparently, there was a big row and her papa threatened to shoot Max. Mr. Lungreen said if he missed, he would shoot Max but not kill him, as he was most certainly going to marry the girl. Eventually, Max agreed, but isn't that embarrassing to have the entire town know what you've done?" Ruby finished with a shake of her head.

"Yes, that is embarrassing, especially for the poor girl. She must care a lot for Max to have slept with him without being married," Jane sympathized.

"Can we go to Abilene tomorrow?" Ruby asked, bringing Jane back to their previous concerns.

"Yes, I think that would work out. I'll see if Opal and the kids can come over to keep an eye on things while we're gone."

"I sure hope Opal don't get pregnant again before the wedding. The style of dresses I picked for the bride-maids won't look very flattering on someone with a rounded belly," Ruby said as she left the table.

The next morning the two women caught the 8:15 a.m. train to Abilene. They had decided to spend the night in order to get all of their shopping done.

Opal assured them everything would be fine until they got back on the 4:00 p.m. train the next afternoon.

When the 4:00 p.m. train arrived with no Jane and Ruby on board, Opal began to worry. Aidan soon arrived and he too was concerned but didn't want to let Opal know as he could tell she was getting more upset by the minute.

Seth rode up about five o'clock and said he had just come from the telegraph office. If they had sent a wire as to why they weren't on the train, surely the telegraph man would have given it to him to deliver.

The three sat discussing the possibilities and Seth finally said he would catch the morning train to Abilene to find out what had happened. Opal felt relieved when he volunteered to make the trip.

"Why don't you folks go on home with the children and if they show up somehow or I hear anything I'll call you. I'll stay here until about 9:00 p.m. in case someone comes wanting a room," Seth volunteered.

"Oh, Seth, you are a dear," Opal said appreciatively. "The only empty room is number eight, but it's ready if someone comes," she told him.

As they stood to leave, Seth looked up the road toward town, "Looks like somebody coming now in one of those new automobiles. There seem to be more of those motor cars every week," he commented.

As the car approached it was going at what looked to be a rather fast speed, weaving just a bit from side to side. The sound of laughter could be heard above the sound of the engine as it careened off the road and came bounding into the yard. The three adults stood at the top of the steps taking in the curious sight of the oncoming auto. They were all sure it was only going to stop when it hit the front steps. Opal grabbed her children and hurriedly moved back against the wall. At the last second it did a sharp turn and came to a screeching, abrupt halt at the bottom of the steps. The three adults were staring in stunned silence as Jane and Ruby greeted them with exaggerated waves and hoots of laughter.

At last, Seth found his tongue. "What in the name of Heaven are you two doing with that automobile?" Before they could answer, he went on. "Don't tell me you two drove that thing all the way from Abilene?" he asked in disbelief.

"Indeed, we did!" Jane answered from the driver's seat. "Ruby drove part way and I drove the rest. We were a little rough at first but, well, we made it!" Jane laughed.

Seth looked at Jane and saw the sheer delight that shown on her face and the excitement in her pretty eyes. He could hear the pride in her voice and realized again what a remarkable woman Jane Parker really was.

"Mama, I can't believe you let Ruby talk you into buying this thing!" Opal sounded incredulous as she gestured toward the shiny new automobile.

Ruby laughed, "You are mistaken, dear sister, this was Mama's idea, not mine," she told Opal as she climbed out of the car.

"Well, whoever's idea it was, I think it's great and just glad you both made it home safe," Aidan added. "I wouldn't mind having one for myself."

Opal gave him an inquisitive look. "Why, you could only drive it mostly around town. The country roads are hardly more than cow trails."

"Times are changing. It won't be long before even the country roads will be drivable," Aidan answered in his practical manner.

"Want me to drive you home, sister?" Ruby offered with an impish little grin, knowing Opal would refuse.

"Not on your life," Opal tartly replied.

After Opal and family departed, Jane and Seth sat on the porch swing enjoying a glass of lemonade as a full moon rose over the eastern horizon. The moonlight glistened off the contours of the shiny new car.

Seth asked the question he had wanted to ask ever since Jane and Ruby's return. "Jane, why did you buy an automobile? Have you been thinking about it or was it just a spur of the moment thing?" Seth really couldn't imagine Jane doing much of anything on the spur of the moment.

"I've been thinking about it for a while. I figured that with an automobile we could carry part of our extra produce to Avoca or even the fifteen miles to Lueders to sell. In that automobile we can go there and back so fast it almost makes my head swim to think about it," Jane told him with a laugh.

Seth turned to Jane. "Jane, you never cease to amaze me and at times you make my head swim," he said tenderly. "I was remembering the night we first met and how brave I thought you were to hold off those two men and send Sam for help. I knew you had to be scared but you never flinched. Through all these years I've known you, time and again you take the lead and never falter. That's a mighty fine quality, Jane Parker," he said and took her hand in his and brought it to his lips for a gentle kiss.

Jane was rather stunned by Seth's unexpected speech but so pleased to know he seemed to admire her. She knew that her feelings for Seth had fully been rekindled over the past several months. "Thank you, Seth," she managed to whisper and wished he would not stop at just kissing her hand.

"Jane, I've been thinking that maybe it's not too late for you and me to try again at love," he said, as he continued to hold her hand and slipped his other hand and arm across the back of the swing.

"Is that right? Well, as a matter of fact I've been thinking along those same lines myself lately," Jane confessed, pleased to know they were both thinking the same way.

"Indeed!" was all Seth said as he continued to study Jane's profile. "I'm mighty glad to hear that, Jane. In fact, I'm so glad to hear you say that that I would like to ask you once again to become my wife. We can court for a spell or just go ahead and get married, whichever you'd rather," he finished in a rush, as though he was afraid the words might get lost before he finished saying them.

Jane sat quietly as though considering what Seth had just purposed.

Through the open window came Ruby's unmistakable voice, "Mama, for Heaven's sakes, say 'Yes!"

Jane and Seth looked at each other in surprise but couldn't suppress their laughter.

"Yes, Seth, Yes, and not because Ruby told me to say yes," Jane told him with apparent happiness reflected in her eyes and smile.

The front door burst open and Ruby rushed out the door grabbing them both in a big hug and kissing their cheeks. "That's wonderful. I just knew you two would get together sometime. Now I'm going to my room to listen to the Victrola and you two can enjoy the privacy of the porch," she said as she opened the door to re-enter the house. Ruby stopped and looked at them again. "This doesn't change a thing. Carl and I are still living here. I'm not leaving you, Mama." With that Ruby disappeared into the house and a few seconds later they heard the music from her Victrola.

Seth and Jane instantly scooted toward one another. He took her in his strong arms; they clung to one another, each knowing they would not let go this time. At last, they were ready to loosen the restraints on the guarded feelings they had each held inside for so long. Their lips met and the two shared a long, passionate kiss like a man and woman in love.

On the next Sunday afternoon, under a clear blue sky, Jane and Seth stood on the front porch of *The Parker House* and exchanged their wedding vows in front of God and a host of relatives and friends.

They gazed into one another's eyes and shared a secret smile. They had each traveled a long journey since sitting on Jane's porch in Erath County, watching the sunsets but at last, they were together where they now belonged.

Epilogue

JUNE 1915

Ruby sat in the shade of the big front porch slowly swinging as she fanned herself. She felt hot and uncomfortable. It was hot no matter where she sat. She slowly moved her hand over her rounded stomach trying to calm the kicking child within.

"There you are," Jane said as she joined Ruby outside where it seemed a bit cooler.

"I hope Aiden's right about my due date. Only three more weeks," she said with a sigh.

"Me too, honey. The last couple of months seem to drag on forever," Jane sympathized, remembering her own pregnancies. Jane was thankful Ruby had stayed healthy through this pregnancy and was almost ready to give birth. Her miscarriage two years earlier had devastated Ruby and Carl. This time they had been on edge for several months.

"Have you and Carl made a decision about the names for a girl or boy?"

Ruby laughed. "You know how hard it is for Carl to make up his mind about most anything. I was beginning to think he would never settle on the wallpaper for the baby's room."

Jane snickered. "Tell him if he hasn't made a decision by the time the baby's born that Seth and I will name the baby."

Ruby and Jane both hooted at that suggestion.

Ruby glanced toward the street as a dark green farm truck came to a stop.

"Wonder why Seth's coming home so early?"

"I guess we'll soon find out," Jane answered.

Seth smiled at his lovely wife. Jane was still an attractive woman, even with a few strands of gray running through her auburn hair. She hardly looked a day older than when they first met. As he climbed the steps, he removed his hat and swiped at the sweat on his brow with the back of his sleeve. "It's getting mighty hot this afternoon."

Jane stood and started toward the front door. "I'll get you a cold glass of tea," she smiled at her husband. Seth's hair was streaked with silver. Jane thought it gave him a distinguished look.

Seth followed Jane inside. Ruby could hear the low rumble of their voices but couldn't understand what they were saying. She was tempted to slide across the swing, so she'd be nearer the open window. Then she might be able to hear what they were talking about. Before she could move Jane and Seth came back outside.

"I'll go by and invite Opal and Aiden to dinner tonight," he said as he started down the steps.

"Why would you invite them tonight?" Ruby asked, her curiosity on high alert.

Jane and Seth exchanged an amused look and chuckled. "You'll have to wait until tonight, Ruby," Seth answered as he headed toward his truck.

After Seth drove away Ruby turned to Jane. "Mama, you could tell me or at least give me a hint," Ruby gave her mama that imploring look and tried to sound persuasive.

Jane laughed more and shook her head in the negative. "This time you'll have to wait with the others. I was a bit surprised to not find you with your ear stuck to the window," Jane continued, amused. She was all too familiar with the lengths Ruby would go to so she wouldn't miss out on a chance to know everything first.

"Do you feel like helping me snap some beans?" Jane asked as she went inside to get the beans. She soon returned with the bowls heaping with fresh beans from the garden.

The faint whistle of an incoming train could be heard in the distance. "Sounds like the four o'clock train's right on time," Jane commented.

"There may be some unhappy folks we only have one room left."

They continued to swing slowly as they snapped the beans.

Ruby glanced toward the road. "Looks like a man coming first," Ruby remarked.

"I'll show him the room," Jane said as she rose to greet the visitor.

"Mama! That's not a visitor," Ruby exclaimed. "It's Sam!" she almost shouted.

Jane took a good look at the approaching man. He looked a bit older, more mature but it was her Sam. She ran down the steps and across the yard with her arms outstretched. "Sam, Sam!" she shouted with pure joy bubbling in her voice.

The tall young man stopped and looked at the woman running toward him. He threw his western hat in the air and returned her shout. "Mama, Mama! give me a hug," he grinned, and his blue eyes sparkled as they embraced. He lifted his mother off the ground and swung her in a circle.

Jane kissed him several times and he continued to hold her close. Tears of surprise and delight filled Jane's eyes. "Why didn't you let us know you were coming?"

"I wanted to surprise you," he grinned as they walked toward the porch.

Sam stopped when he saw Ruby standing at the top of the steps. He let out a low whistle. "Look at you, little sister," he grinned. "I'm not going to try to lift you and swing you around," he teased and rubbed his back as though it already hurt.

"That's just fine, but you better get up here and give me a hug," Ruby demanded.

SAM AND JANE TALKED AS THEY WALKED THROUGH THE spring garden and orchard.

"I can hardly believe all of the places you've been. Nearly every letter came from a different place," Jane exclaimed.

Sam grinned. "Once I started traveling, I wanted to see more and more of this great country. Mama, someday you and Seth need to travel out west. You won't believe how tall the mountains are, at times they seem to get lost in the clouds. The canyons are such vivid colors and go on forever and the rivers run swift. The trails are so rough it makes me wonder how people ever reached California." Sam's expression told Jane how much he had loved his life of adventure.

Then he walked slowly through the house taking in the changes since he had left nine years ago. He stopped outside Ruby and Carl's room. Hanging on the wall was a framed newspaper article describing the attempted arrest of Jackson Polk and another escaped convict. Both men had been shot to death when they attempted to steal the sheriff's car. *Strange,* he thought, *his partner, Lewis Boston, back in east Texas was shot and killed while trying to run from the law.*

The family gathered for the evening meal. There were squeals of surprise at seeing Sam, hugs and hoots of laughter as stories were told, and Jane felt as though her heart would burst with joy. She looked at Seth as he leaned forward to give Jane a loving kiss on her lips.

"It sure feels right to have them all here," he said softly.

"Oh, yes, it does," she agreed.

After a while Seth stood. He tapped the side of his glass with the back of his spoon to get everyone's attention. "Kate and Bea, would you take the children outside so we can have one of those boring adult conversations?"

The adults laughed as the girls and Opal and Aiden's children almost ran out of the room.

Seth looked around the table and ended by smiling at Jane. "Jane and I have been discussing selling the ranch."

"You could have told me that, Mama," Ruby complained.

Her remark caused more snickers.

Carl gave Ruby a sympathetic look and kissed her cheek. "Honey, you don't have to know everything first."

Seth cleared his throat and continued. "We will sign the final papers next Monday."

"Goodness, that is a surprise," Opal commented.

"It sure is," Aiden agreed. "What will you do with all of your spare time?"

"I had planned to take over the gardening business but now that Sam's back I'm sure I can find plenty to do, like run for mayor," Seth finished with a big grin.

There was instant chatter about Seth's big plans.

Sam stood and everyone looked in Seth's direction as Sam lifted his glass. "Congratulations, Seth. I'm sure you'll handle the garden business just fine and make a distinguished mayor."

"But Sam, aren't you going to take over the produce business again?" Ruby asked, puzzled.

Sam slowly shook his head from side to side. "No, I'm just here for a visit. I'm joining the military and aim to train as a pilot in a few years. Airplanes are the way of the future," he stated, showing his excitement. "I want in from the beginning," he finished, as he looked at the shocked faces staring back at him.

Finally, Jane managed to squeak, "Sam, that's so dangerous!"

Sam looked at the worried look on his mother's sweet face. The lines in her forehead seemed more prominent. He had seen that look for years. The first time he remembered seeing that look was the night the outlaws broke into their house. He saw it again when she found out about him and Billy cutting off the rattlesnake rattles and later when Opal fell in the muddy, flooding river and countless times since. He hated to be the one to worry his mother, but he had to find his own way through life. Sam walked slowly to his mother's side, leaned down, and kissed her tenderly on her cheek. "I'm sorry, Mama, but I have to go."

Jane realized she loved Sam enough that she would never try to hold him back. She must accept that Sam would never be happy here running the produce business. Like other mothers, she would pray for his safety and that he would return as often as he could to see her and the family.

Afterword

Chapter One was based on a true incident that happened to my maternal grandmother when she was seven years old. She lived with us most of my younger years and told many stories of her young life.

Judy McGonagill

The River Rider

THE HEART OF TEXAS, BOOK TWO

Luke felt the lash of the horsewhip across his back. It bit into his flesh that was only covered with a thin shirt. He bit back a wince.

"You should have had this barn clean by now," he heard his brother-in-law, John Martin, snarl as he drew back the whip to deliver another lash.

Fourteen-year-old Luke knew this would be the last lashing he would ever take from John Martin or any man. He was taller than John now and lots stronger from the endless days of grueling, hard work he was forced to endure for his vile, deplorable brother-in-law.

Anger and hatred seethed within his soul, threatening to overflow and choke him as memories of the lustful glances John gave young Rachel when he thought no one was looking. Luke grabbed the pitchfork leaning against a stall, whirled and let out a roar, charging John like a raging bull, intent on impelling him against the wall of the old bam. Then he would watch with pleasure while John Martin's life ebbed away, and his soul stepped into everlasting Hell.

John lunged sideways to avoid the strike, but not before Luke adjusted his aim, plunging the fork's prongs into John's upper thigh.

The man hit the dirt, yelling in agony as Luke yanked the pitchfork free and raised it to deliver the final blow.

Dislike had turned to distrust and then to hate. The loathing he felt for John had been building for two long years. Every lustful glance at his sisters, each lash of his whip, kick of his boot, or curse shown bright in his mind's eye. Now it would be ended. Luke fully intended to kill John. "No! Please, No!" John yelled. "Please boy don't do it, don't kill me!" Blood gushed around John's hand clamped around his thigh, to pool in the dirt. But Luke could only see John eyeing little Naomi with that same lustful leer.

John knew he had worked the boy relentlessly because he could. He also knew he had taken advantage of Luke and his sisters because they were at his mercy. Now he was likely about to pay the ultimate price for what he had done.

If the law ever caught him for this, he would never be tried for murder. Too many people had witnessed John's abuse over the years. All he would have to do was plead self-defense.

The bastard slithered backward, like the snake he was. "I, I'll never strike you again, I promise!" Luke trailed him, ready to strike the final blow. "Luke, Luke, think of your sister. What will poor Ruth do with two babies and no husband? Surely you don't want to make her a widow with two babies to provide for." The man's back hit the barn wall.

"I'll do anything you say, give you anything you want," John pleaded in a quaking voice.

Luke still held the pitchfork firmly, ready to thrust the final blow at any moment. When he heard John's last plea he paused. Perhaps there was another way to rid himself and Naomi of the loathsome man. "Give me three of your best horses, provisions for a week, and five hundred dollars." Luke had thought of asking for John's fine new automobile but knew it would be too easy for John to find them. Besides, with horses they could cut through the countryside making it much harder for him to send someone after them if he were so foolish.

"I'll take Naomi with me, and you can burn in Hell!" Luke snarled. "If you ever cross my path again there will be no bargaining for your life. If I ever hear of you mistreating Ruth or those children, you will be shown no mercy. You will be begging me to use this pitchfork to end your sorry life before I'm through with you," Luke vowed as he glared at the piteous man lying in the dirt at his feet, now at his mercy. "It's yours, it's yours," John breathed a deep sigh of relief realizing his life had been spared. For an instant he had no doubt his life hung in great peril. "Please, help me to the house," he begged as he reached out toward Luke.

About the Author

Judy McGonagill is a native Texan and loves the rich history of the Lone Star State. Judy grew up in a small town where church and school was the focus of the community. Her maternal grandmother lived with her family and often told stories of her younger life. Judy found her stories fascinating and they strongly influenced her interest in history and telling stories. She has been married to her beloved husband for many years and they have two adult sons. She is a retired teacher with an interest in history and enjoys writing historical novels.

www.ingramcontent.com/pod-product-compliance
Lightning Source LLC
Chambersburg PA
CBHW020545020726
47494CB00006B/1922
* 9 7 8 1 6 4 4 5 7 3 0 9 9 *